I0682549

For the Love of Grace

THE CALLAGHANS & MCFADDENS: BOOK 2

Kimberly Rae Jordan

THREE**STRAND**
P R E S S

A CORD OF THREE STRANDS IS NOT EASILY BROKEN.

Kimberly Rae Jordan
PO Box 40083 Lagimodiere PO
Winnipeg, Mb R2C 4P3
Canada
www.kimberlyraejordan.com

Publisher's Note: This is a work of fiction. Names, characters, places, and incidents are a product of the author's imagination. Locales and public names are sometimes used for atmospheric purposes. Any resemblance to actual people, living or dead, or to businesses, companies, events, institutions, or locales is completely coincidental.

Book Layout © 2014 BookDesignTemplates.com

For the Love of Grace/ Kimberly Rae Jordan. -- 1st ed.
978-1-988409-19-1

There is no fear in love;

but perfect love casts out fear.

1st John 4:18

GRACE ANDERSON STARED straight ahead at the white wall of the small hospital room. Until that morning, she had been convinced—totally convinced—that she would not be in this place again, watching as death took someone else she loved. She gripped her hands tightly around her phone and bit her lip. How was it that she had to make this decision? She had just turned eighteen—barely a legal adult—and now she was faced with making a life or death decision for the one person she loved above all others.

Where was God in all of this? Why was He taking away all her family from her? The people she'd loved with all her heart were now gone. One by one. First her parents and now the only grandparent she'd ever known. She just didn't get it. She just couldn't figure out why God would do this. It was like her love was a curse.

Swallowing past the lump in her throat, Grace pulled her chair closer to the bed and took her grandmother's hand. She looked down at their clasped hands through blurred vision. Though her grandmother's grasp felt fragile, Grace knew how strong it was. Whether she'd been kneading bread, stirring a batch of Grace's favorite stew, pulling weeds in her garden or knitting a scarf, her hands had been steady and strong.

Not anymore.

"Grace?"

She turned toward the sound of the soft voice and saw Emily Callaghan standing just inside the doorway of the hospital room, a look of concern on her face. Without waiting for an invitation, the older woman crossed the room to where Grace sat and bent to give her a hug. Grace held herself stiff for a moment then sank into Emily's embrace.

Since her grandmother's cancer diagnosis three months earlier, Emily—her best friend, Makayla's mom—had been there as a support for both of them. She'd gone with them to appointments, made meals and had been there for Grace as a shoulder to cry on more than once. But what she'd done more than anything was to assure her grandmother that they—the Callaghan-McFadden family—would take care of Grace. Emily and Steve had stepped in to help her grandmother prepare her legal affairs to make sure Grace's future was secure.

And now, as she prepared to make the most difficult decision of her life, Emily was once again by her side. Still holding her grandmother's hand, she reached for Emily's, praying as she did that the love she now had for Emily and her family wouldn't cost them their lives. Maybe if she held part of herself back—if she didn't let herself love them the way she had loved her family, if she didn't let them become that important to her—maybe then they would be safe.

As the last person to claim every part of her heart slipped away to heaven, Grace grieved the loss of her grandmother along with the dream she'd had of one day having a loving husband and children. She just couldn't take the chance of loving someone so completely again.

Whatever God's plan was for her life, it had better not include any more loss.

Her heart couldn't handle it.

"I THINK WE SHOULD get married."

Grace looked up from her phone to stare across the restaurant table at Franklin Moore. "What?"

"I know we haven't really talked about it," he said with a shrug. "I think it would be a good idea."

Saying they hadn't talked about it was an understatement. When Franklin had first asked her out after they'd met at a church function, she'd let him know that she wasn't in the market for a relationship. He'd told her that he wasn't either, but there were times he needed a date, and he thought they looked good together. So they'd kind of fell into being a couple, and now it looked like it was going to be the same with getting married.

"You don't love me, Franklin," Grace reminded him. She set her phone down on the table and gave him her full attention.

"You don't love me, either," Franklin responded. He had also put his phone down, so he clearly felt this was important. "But I still think it could work."

Grace wondered why she wasn't shooting down the idea right off the bat. Most likely because she was getting tired of people asking when they were going to get married since they'd been dating for a couple of years already. "I don't want children."

"I don't either." Franklin pushed his empty plate toward the middle of the table and leaned forward on his arms. "I think we get along pretty good. I'm not interested in a love match. My parents say they love each other, but it has constantly been one fight after another. You've seen them together." Franklin grimaced, his handsome features twisting. "I prefer what we have."

Grace shuddered as she recalled the two meetings she'd had with his parents. It had been horribly uncomfortable to be around the squabbling couple. Thankfully, they spent most their time in places other than Winnipeg, so Grace had only met them twice in the two years she and Franklin been dating. They had been a shocking contrast to the loving marriage she'd seen from Steve and Emily Callaghan. Maybe a marriage to Franklin would fall somewhere in the middle. They wouldn't have the loving, close relationship like Steve and Emily's, but they also wouldn't fight like Franklin's parents.

"Can I get you anything else?"

Grace glanced up at the blonde waitress standing beside their table. "Nothing for me thanks."

"What would you recommend for dessert, sweetheart?" Franklin asked with a wink.

Grace wondered if that would change once they were married, but somehow she doubted it. Thankfully, she didn't really care if he flirted with other women. If she loved him, it would be different, but since she didn't, all she did was roll her eyes at his interaction with the waitress.

Once he had placed an order for a brownie sundae, Franklin brought the conversation back to getting married. "If you agree, I'll get a ring for you. Unless you want to pick it out for yourself."

"How about I pick it out for myself?" If there was no sentiment attached to the ring, she might as well pick out something she liked.

"Sounds good. Just let me know when you've found what you like, and I'll buy it for you." He grinned. "And then we can post a picture and make it Facebook official."

Grace laughed. "Yep. Gotta make sure we get it up on all our social media."

As they went on to discuss the wedding itself, Grace mulled over what she was going to say to Makayla and Tami. They had objected to her relationship with Franklin almost from the start. Finding out she was going to marry him, they would no doubt raise even more objections. Too bad they were going to fall on deaf ears. Her deaf ears. In the five and a half years since her grandmother's death, she hadn't changed her mind about love and the risk it carried.

But later that night, in her room in the apartment she shared with Tami and Makayla, Grace had a moment where she mourned what marrying Franklin would mean. Though she'd never let her herself dwell on a future where she'd be marrying for love, in the dark of night, she let herself mourn the loss of it.

And the man who might have loved her.

Chapter One

*Y*OU'RE FIRED." Bennett McFadden didn't often have the need to say those words, and they left a bad taste in his mouth. The man in front of him opened his mouth as if to reply, but Bennett cut him off with a slash of his hand. "I want you and your crew off the premises within the hour."

"Bennett. C'mon, man." Stanley Timmons crossed his arms. "I told you that it was just some new kid, and I'll make sure he's gone. There's no need to sever our arrangement."

"There is every need," Bennett said as he brushed back the edges of his suit coat and put his hands on his hips. "You are full of excuses and placing blame everywhere but where it belongs. On you. If the kid didn't know what he was doing, then you're not training your guys like you should. That's on you. Not the kid. The guys working for you deserve a better supervisor. If you'd taken responsibility for what happened here today, we'd be having a different conversation. This isn't the first time you've done it on our sites, but I guarantee it's the last."

The man looked like he was going to blow his top, but Mitch stepped to Bennett's side and a few of their guys also moved closer. Finally, Stanley gave a curt nod then shouted over his shoulder. "Pack it up."

"We'll mail out your payment for the work done by the end of the week." As the man stalked away, Bennett turned to Mitch. "Get that kid's information because I have a feeling he's going to be losing his job. If he seems trainable, see if we can find a spot for him. I'm going to call Evan at Master Kitchens to see if they have a crew that can help us out."

Mitch nodded. Bennett wasn't sure his brother supported his decision one hundred percent, but Bennett believed in dealing with companies who treated their employees respectfully. He wasn't upset at the kid for the error. Mistakes happened to everyone. The kid had apologized profusely for making the wrong cuts for the countertop, so he hadn't deserved to get thrown under the bus. Stan hadn't had a qualified supervisor on site to make sure that the poorly trained guys he was sending out didn't make mistakes. That was definitely on him.

"We'll talk at the office later," Bennett said to Mitch. "I have to get back and meet with Ethan."

"Okay," his brother said with a nod. "I'll stop by after I make sure things are on track here."

Twenty minutes later, Bennett pulled his truck into the spot reserved for him at the C&M Builders office and put it into park. After turning the engine off, he sat for a moment, trying to calm the anger that still pulsed through him. He'd hoped the drive from the job site to the office would have been enough time to settle down, but apparently it wasn't. Not many things made him this angry, but seeing that guy treat the kid who worked for him so badly had pushed several buttons.

Normally, he wouldn't have been aware of what had transpired, but he'd happened to stop by the site since he passed it on his way to the office from where he'd been at a meeting. The first thing he'd heard as he'd stepped into the building had been a voice raised in anger, shouting one expletive after another. Then he'd seen the young kid cowering before Stanley as if he was afraid of being hit. That had been the last straw.

Mitch had arrived right behind Bennett, having been alerted by the site supervisor that something had happened. In another situation, Bennett would have let Mitch take care of the problem, but the anger that had taken hold of him had demanded he take action. So he had, but the anger still hadn't abated which made him wish he had time for a trip to the gym for a sparring session with a punching bag.

Finally, after letting out a long breath of air, Bennett opened the truck door, wincing at the wall of heat that greeted him. It was an exceptionally warm day for late June in a city where temperatures were still pretty moderate at that time of year. And the heat only added to his agitation because it made him feel sweaty and sticky, and he still had at least five hours to go before he could change out of the suit he wore.

Eager to get into the air-conditioned building that housed the C&M Builders' office, Bennett quickly retrieved his briefcase from the back seat of the truck and headed for the door of the large brick building. As he walked into the foyer area, his stride faltered and what remained of his anger fizzled out when he spotted the woman sitting behind the receptionist desk.

Grace Moore looked up as he approached her. He saw right away the toll that the past month had taken on her, and he was surprised that she was back at work already. With her blonde hair pulled back, the dark circles under her blue eyes were more pronounced, even with the makeup she wore, and her face bore a gauntness that he'd never seen on her before. Thankfully, it seemed the injuries she'd sustained—which had consisted of cuts and bruises—in the accident had healed. At least the visible ones.

"Good morning, Grace." Bennett set his briefcase on the desk, gripping the handle. "I didn't realize you were going to be in today."

"I don't have anything else to do." Grace shrugged as her gaze slipped from his. "I figured I might as well come to work."

Bennett frowned, understanding why the bubbliness of her personality was absent but missing it all the same. "As long as you're sure you're up to it."

"I'm sure," Grace picked up the stack of papers in front of her and tapped them against the desk. "I need something to keep me busy."

Though he didn't want her to be back to work too soon, Bennett could see how she might need time where she had something besides grief to occupy her thoughts. "I'm glad you're back." He lifted his briefcase off the desk. "We've missed you, but we'd understand if you need to take more time off."

Grace's gaze met his briefly before she nodded. "Thank you."

"I'll talk to you later." With one last glance at her, Bennett headed down the hallway.

"Good morning, Bennett."

Bennett spotted Ethan Collins, his sister's fiancé, coming out of his office. "Hey, Ethan."

The man fell into step beside Bennett as he walked toward the back of the building where his office was located. "How did your meeting go this morning?"

"Fairly well." Bennett stepped into his office and set his case down beside his desk.

Ethan followed him into the room and went to stand behind one of the chairs in front of Bennett's desk, his hands gripping the back of it. "Sorry I couldn't take that meeting."

Bennett shrugged out of his jacket and hung it up. As he rolled up his sleeves, he glanced over at Ethan. "Don't worry about it. That's why it works well to have both of us available to do things like this. Besides, it was more just an information session so we can prepare the bid next month." Bennett dropped down on his chair and let out another long breath. "How was *your* meeting?"

Ethan sat down across from him and began to fill him in on the meeting he'd had. As the man talked, Bennett acknowledged again how fortunate they'd been the day Ethan had sent his application to C&M Builders. And not only for the company's sake. Just a week ago, Ethan had proposed to Makayla and—no surprise—she'd said yes. Given the rough month they'd been through with Grace, it had been welcome news.

"Did you know that Grace planned to be in today?" Bennett asked after Ethan had finished the report of his own meeting.

Ethan shook his head, his mouth tightening. "Makayla said Grace called her on the way to work to let her know she was going to be in."

Bennett wasn't sure how he felt about it. Of course, Grace was a grown woman and could make her own decisions. No one else could really determine for her whether it was time for her to return to work or not. "I just don't want her to overdo things."

"I know Makayla is worried about her as well," Ethan said as he leaned forward, bracing his elbows on his knees.

Bennett wasn't surprised to hear that. Makayla and Grace had been friends since high school, so it was only natural that Makayla, along with their other friend, Tami, were concerned about Grace since her husband had passed away from his injuries after the two of them had been in a horrible car accident.

"By the way," Bennett began, eager to get the image of Franklin's broken body out of his mind. "We need to cut a final payment cheque for Stanley Timmons."

Ethan's eyebrows rose. "We do?"

Bennett nodded, glad that the other topics of conversation had given him the time to be able to recount what had happened without the anger. Even without the anger driving him, he knew that he'd made the right decision. When it came to vulnerable people—angry or not—Bennett would always step in to protect them.

GRACE MOORE WAS HAPPY that there was plenty of stuff to keep her busy on her first morning back. She hadn't been sure how returning to work would be after almost a month away, but for the most part, people had just let her do her thing. That had included a lot of catching up on work that had fallen by the wayside in her absence, things like filing and shredding. The only downside to work was that while it kept her hands busy, her thoughts were still free to wander. And that was the last thing she wanted.

It had been her desire to escape being alone with her thoughts that had propelled her back to work. The days following Franklin's death had passed in a blur of busy activity since she'd had to tackle all the details pertaining to his death and funeral. Then there had been legalities to deal with, but now, a month later, things had begun to die down enough that she could breathe and think. And she didn't want that.

Maybe if she'd had kids to occupy her, it might be different, but they'd had none, and Grace was grateful for that. Though people might think she would be a pro at grieving by now, in truth, she barely knew how to deal with her own grief for Franklin. She couldn't imagine what she would have done with grieving children.

"Do you want to go out for lunch?"

Looking up from the papers she was preparing to file, Grace saw Makayla standing beside her desk. She tried to ignore the concern on her friend's face as she said, "I'm not really very hungry."

That was the absolute truth. Her appetite had been next to nil for the past few weeks, and the occasional bouts of nausea hadn't helped the matter much.

Makayla's brows drew together as she frowned. "Are you sure? Can I bring you something?"

"Where are you going?"

"Just to Tims."

"Maybe bring me some soup?" Grace suggested, hoping it would help to ease the concerned look on her friend's face. Though she wasn't really hungry, the thought of a bowl of soup from Tim Hortons held more appeal that anything else would have.

"I can do that," Makayla replied, a smile replacing the frown. "We'll be back soon."

Ethan appeared from the hallway and smiled at Grace. "Are you coming with us?"

"No, but Makayla offered to bring me something back."

Ethan exchanged glances with Makayla, and for a moment, his smile dimmed, but then it quickly returned. "That's good. We won't be gone too long."

"Don't rush on my account," Grace said. "I'm not starving."

She watched them as they headed for the door, her heart aching when Ethan flashed Makayla an affectionate smile as he reached out to take her hand. She and Franklin hadn't had that type of easy affection, the PDAs. Though things had been changing for the better between them since the beginning of the year, the potential of what they could have had was now lost. Would they have ever gotten to the point where they shared something like what Makayla and Ethan had?

Emotion tightened her chest once again, and Grace took a deep breath to try to ease the pain. The last thing she wanted was to break down as she sat behind her desk. Resolutely, she turned her attention back to the stack of paper in front of her. Normally she'd work through it quickly, but she needed this to last longer than usual. She didn't want to run out of work.

When Ethan and Makayla got back a little while later, she followed them into the small lunchroom. There was a monitor in the room that was connected to a security camera in the foyer so she'd be able to see if anyone entered the building while she was away from the front desk. Though she would have liked to take her food back to her desk, she resisted the urge. Sinking down onto a chair at the table, she watched as Ethan and Makayla unpacked the food they'd brought.

"I can smell the food all the way in my office," Bennett said as he walked in. He came to the table and peered over Makayla's shoulder. "I hope you got it right this time."

Makayla elbowed him, causing him to straighten and rub his side. "I always get it right. It's not my fault that you change your mind after I leave to pick it up. You keep complaining, and you'll be picking it up next time."

"That will never happen." Bennett moved to sit next to Grace. "I don't think you'd trust me to get yours right."

Grace felt a smile tugging at the corners of her lips. She'd always envied the relationships the Callaghan and McFadden siblings had with each other. She was most familiar with Bennett and Makayla's relationship because she was best friends with Makayla and also because the three of them worked together. As an only child, Grace had never known what it was like to have a sibling to squabble or to hang out with. It had always been just her.

"Eat up, Gracie," Makayla said as she set a container of soup and a roll in front of her. "I got you the cream of broccoli and cheddar. I know it's your favorite."

Gracie took the spoon Makayla handed her then pulled off the lid of the container, inhaling the smell of the soup. Surprisingly, her stomach rumbled a bit with hunger. She waited until everyone had taken their seats and Bennett had said grace before she dipped her spoon into the bowl. After a couple of spoonfuls, she tore off a piece of the roll and popped it in her mouth.

Conversation swirled around her as she slowly ate her soup. It was a step toward normal, but yet normal—whatever that might be—still seemed so far out of reach. It was likely she'd never get back to that normal. It would be a new normal. Just one of the many she'd experienced in her life. Unfortunately, her new normal never seemed to last long. The longest stretch of *normal* had been the time between her grandmother's death and marrying Franklin.

Now she was having to adjust all over again. But this would be for the very last time. She resolved once again—as she had following her grandmother's death—to not allow anyone into her life who, if they were taken away, would require such a dramatic change that she'd have to find a new normal once again. Normal from now on was going to be her, on her own, with just the friendships she already had in her life.

"How was your soup?" Makayla asked.

Gracie glanced over at Makayla's expectant expression. Unfortunately, though she'd managed to eat it all, she hadn't really registered the taste. "It was good. Thank you."

"You managed to get mine right, sis" Bennett said as he sat back in his chair. "So thanks for that."

"That sarcasm is making me wonder if maybe next time, your order will be mysteriously missing when we get back."

Bennett chuckled. "Then I'll be sharing yours."

Makayla tossed a scrunched-up napkin at Bennett. "The only person I share food with these days is Ethan."

Grace was glad for the normality of their banter. At least they were comfortable enough around her to be joking together. She was a bit tired of people treating her like spun glass because of what had happened. She had enough sad moments when she was alone, she didn't need more of them when she'd worked up the courage to leave the condo and face the world. Of course, she did have moments when she wanted to scream at the world. How dare life go on around her as if nothing had happened when her world had completely imploded?

Most days her emotions were all over the place. She hoped that coming back to work and having a schedule would help with that. Nothing could change her situation, and she couldn't forget about it, but coming to a place where Franklin hadn't been present on a regular basis would hopefully help her be able to put aside her grief. Even for just a bit.

Once their lunch had been cleared up, Grace left them to return to the front desk. She hadn't been there too long when the front door opened and two teenage girls walked in followed by Steve Callaghan.

"Grace!" Danica Callaghan ran around the end of the desk to where Grace sat. She got to her feet in time to be engulfed in the teen's arms. "I didn't know you were here today. I'm so happy to see you!"

"I'm happy to see you too, sweetie. How have you been?"

She listened as both girls recounted what they'd been up to. They were both off school for a teacher in-service day and had come in to help with office work, unaware that Grace had returned to work. Grace accepted a hug from Steve before he headed down the hallway toward the offices. She helped get the girls settled in with a couple of small tasks, grateful for the distraction of their conversation. Thankfully, they were happy to chat about the things going on in their lives. The guys they thought were cute. The makeup they wanted to buy.

It was all so normal.

Grace took a deep breath and slowly let it out, relief flooding her.

Chapter Two

*B*ennett had been glad to see Grace sitting at the table when he'd walked into the lunchroom. Though she hadn't joined in their banter like she might have previously, just the fact that she had been there with them at all was a good thing. He wondered if she'd ever be the person she'd been prior to Franklin's death.

Though she seemed to have recovered from the previous losses in her life—her entire family—Bennett wondered if she would recover from this one. Grace had definitely suffered more than her share of loss in her life. He didn't know another person who had lost so much in their life.

Bennett settled into the chair at his desk and stared blankly at his monitor. He wished there was more he could do for Grace, but he had a feeling that she would brush aside any of his attempts. She hadn't even let him do things for her before all of this. Through Makayla, they had become friends as teenagers, and it had seemed—briefly—that there was a possibility for more, but when her grandmother had gotten sick, Grace had pulled back without explanation.

"Can I talk to you?" Makayla dropped into the chair across from him.

"Uh. Sure. Have a seat," Bennett said with an arch of a brow.

"I'd like to offer to have Grace move back into the apartment with Tami and me."

Bennett frowned as he considered Makayla's idea. "Do you think she'd be interested in doing that?"

"I'm not sure," Makayla said with a shrug. "But I figured I would offer."

"You don't need my permission," Bennett reminded her. "That would be up to you and Tami."

"I know, but I just thought I'd run the idea past you before I talked to her." Makayla shifted on her seat. "I would like to have her closer to us. She doesn't have anyone else now."

Bennett nodded. They had essentially been Grace's family since her grandmother had passed away. She'd been like another sister…well, to his siblings anyway. Bennett had never viewed her that way.

"It might be too soon," Bennett cautioned. "It's only been a month."

He still hadn't been able to forget the horrible, sick feeling in his stomach when his mom had called him with the news that Franklin and Grace had been in an accident. The large truck that had unexpectedly accelerated through the intersection had hit the passenger side of Franklin's car. Grace had been the one driving, so Franklin had borne the brunt of the impact and had never regained consciousness. Over the next few days, Grace had remained at his side, waiting and praying. Bennett had gone up to the hospital several times, as a friend to Grace but also because of the friendship he'd been forging with Franklin. He and his family had stood by her as Franklin's body had deteriorated. And then it had all ended one Saturday afternoon.

Everything had changed for Grace. For all of them. Though they'd had a rough start with Franklin, thanks to much prayer and Ethan's persistence, the man had undergone a metamorphosis. But his death had put a stop to that journey. And that experience had hammered home the importance of never giving up on someone. Of persisting in prayer even if it seemed hopeless that change would ever happen.

"I won't pressure her," Makayla said. "I just want to present her with the opportunity to move closer to her support system. The fact that she's come back to work says that maybe she might be ready to consider something like this."

Bennett hoped that Makayla was right. He found that he liked the idea of having Grace close once again. As a big brother to Makayla, he'd always felt protective of her—when he wasn't wishing her away because she was annoying him. That protective nature had extended to Makayla's friends, especially Grace. Though she had pushed him away for whatever reason, he hadn't lost the urge to protect her, just as he did his sisters and Tami.

"Let me know what she says."

He'd expected Makayla to leave once they'd finished talking about that subject, but it was clear that his sister had something else on her mind.

"I'm having a hard time planning the wedding," Makayla finally said, a miserable look on her face. "I used to plan it out all the time when I was younger, but I'm finding it challenging now that I have to do it for real."

"Is it because of what happened to Franklin?" Bennett asked since that seemed to be the most logical explanation.

"Probably." Makayla's shoulders slumped. "Part of me feels guilty for being so happy and excited about marrying Ethan."

"I don't think Grace would want you to feel that way."

"Maybe not." Makayla shrugged. "But that still doesn't stop me from feeling that way. I haven't even had the chance to ask her if she's willing to be my matron of honor. Or maid of honor. I'm not even sure what to call the role for her."

Bennett felt for his sister. She tended to take on the emotions of those around her, so the pain Grace was going through was no doubt weighing heavily on her. "I don't think Grace would want you to put your life on hold because of her situation. Besides, if all of this has taught us anything, it's that life is short. Don't put things off. Plan your wedding and enjoy yourself. The important thing is that you and Ethan get hitched."

"You're right." Makayla straightened in her seat. "Thank you."

"Just don't make me wear a tuxedo."

She grinned. "I think you're safe there. Ethan wouldn't agree to that either."

"Glad to hear it," Bennett said, smiling in response.

Makayla got to her feet. "Talk to you later."

Bennett hoped that Makayla would be able to set aside the unnecessary guilt she was carrying so that she could plan the wedding she wanted and deserved to have.

Once Makayla had left, Bennett turned his attention back to the work waiting for him.

"SO HOW IS GRACE doing?"

Bennett looked at the woman seated across from him. Ellie Davenport had long blonde hair that lay in a glossy curtain over her shoulders. Her light blue eyes regarded him closely as she waited for his response.

"She seems to be doing okay," Bennett said as he picked up his glass of water. He took a drink then set it down, looking around for the waitress. "She was back to work this week."

"She's back at work already?" Ellie asked. "I would have thought she'd need more time."

Bennett shrugged. "Everyone grieves in their own way. I guess Grace needs to be working."

Ellie's eyes narrowed as her brows drew together. "I hope that she isn't doing too much too soon."

Bennett felt a knot form in his stomach as he watched Ellie fiddle with her silverware. They had been dating for the last three months, and it had been going…okay. Unfortunately, he wasn't sure the relationship was going to last much longer. Ellie just hadn't seemed to fit in with his family, and lately, she had seemed to be threatened by his friendship—

if he could even call it that—with Grace, acting resentful of the time he'd spent helping to arrange Franklin's funeral.

Now it seemed that every time they were together, the conversation ended up focused on Grace. And he could tell that the news that Grace was back at work bothered Ellie. He didn't know what he could do to reassure her that she had nothing to worry about where Grace was concerned. And frankly, he didn't feel like he should have to.

"I haven't really talked to her at length about how she's doing or why she's back at work, but I would imagine that Makayla has been talking with her." Bennett didn't bother to mention that Makayla was hoping to have Grace move back into the apartment building. He had a feeling that Ellie would be very unhappy with the news that he and Grace were living under the same roof, so to speak, if Grace moved back.

Bennett really didn't think he'd given Ellie reason to be jealous of Grace. He hadn't treated Grace any differently than he had any of the other women in his life, so he had no idea why Ellie was acting the way she was. It was making him analyze his every interaction with Grace, and that was adding stress to his relationship with Ellie. He was afraid of saying the wrong thing where Grace was concerned, and it was starting to annoy him. He didn't want to be in a relationship where jealousy reared its ugly head for no apparent reason.

After seeing how Steve had treated his mom, Emily, Bennett had resolved to follow the man's example. When he was on a date with Ellie, he kept his attention on her. His phone was turned off, and he didn't take it out of his pocket at all while they were together. There was absolutely no reason why Ellie should be jealous, but if she couldn't get it under control, things were not going to work out between them.

"How was your week?" Bennett asked, hoping a change of subject would help.

Ellie stared at him for a moment before answering. "It was fine. Work was busy, as usual. How was your week?"

As he shared about his week. Bennett was careful to avoid any mention of Grace. Thankfully, it wasn't difficult since they hadn't interacted much. Unfortunately, the start of their conversation had added a tension that just didn't seem to dissipate even with the change of subject.

By the time the evening was over, Bennett knew that their relationship was over too. It made him sad, but if Ellie saw things that weren't there and then allowed that to make her jealous, he just couldn't deal with it.

He walked her to the door of her house but declined the invitation to come in for coffee. No doubt she'd read something into that too, even though he had never been comfortable going into her house when it was just the two of them. He didn't break up with her right then—even though maybe he should have—but he knew he would have to do it sooner rather than later.

GRACE STARED AT THE shower curtain. The flower pattern was not as appealing to her as it had been when Franklin had bought it several months ago. Of course, right then, nothing was all that appealing. Throwing up her guts didn't make anything appealing to her, but she'd had another crying jag which had left her doing just that. She'd always had a weak stomach, but the way she'd been throwing up lately was ridiculous.

She sighed as she leaned back against the wall. Her stomach was still rumbling enough that she wasn't confident that she could leave the bathroom without having to make a rapid return. She took small sips from the glass she'd filled with water. Her heart hurt, and her insides were in knots. She was a mess.

Would she ever feel normal again? Would the tension in her head ever ease? Would the ache in her heart fade away? Would she ever feel comfortable in her body again?

Her stomach clenched, then threatened to reject the little bit of water she'd just put into it. She took deep breaths, trying to calm the upset within her. All she wanted to do was crawl into bed and sleep for days, but that couldn't happen until her stomach calmed down.

The flowers on the shower curtain suddenly dragged up a memory of the flowers at Franklin's funeral. Tears pricked at her eyes as she swallowed hard against the lump in her throat. She couldn't believe that she still had tears left to cry. It felt as if she'd shed so many that there should be none left.

Grace reached out and grabbed a towel to wipe away the tears that spilled down her cheeks. At least her breakdown was happening in the privacy of her home and not at work. There had been a few moments when she'd thought that maybe she would have a meltdown at work, but she'd managed to hold it together. She hadn't wanted anyone telling her that maybe she was back to work too soon. She needed to leave the condo. Needed to leave the place that held the most memories of Franklin for at least a few hours each day.

After about ten minutes, Grace figured it was safe to leave the bathroom. Moving slowly, she walked into the bedroom and to the bed where she climbed under the covers, tugging them up to her chin. She'd already locked up the condo since she'd known she wasn't planning to go out after she'd gotten home from work. Sleep was the only thing she wanted. Maybe tomorrow she'd try to eat food—after she went and bought some.

THE DREAMS CAME as they did every night it seemed. Dreams of what might have been. Without fail, she woke to tears and an aching heart. How much longer would that go on?

Grace flopped over onto her back and stared up at the dark ceiling. At that moment, sadness warred with anger for uppermost position in her emotions. If only she'd stuck with her plan. If only Franklin hadn't changed. Maybe things wouldn't have ended up the way they had. At the very least, she wouldn't be hurting so badly.

She'd known the type of man Franklin was when they'd started dating. When he'd first asked her out, she hadn't been interested. But once she'd realized that he wasn't any more interested in a love-based relationship than she was, Grace had said yes. None of her friends had understood what she saw in him even though he was handsome and rich, and she hadn't bothered to try to explain it because she knew people would think she was nuts.

And maybe she was. What woman in her right mind would accept that, instead of a loving husband, she had one that flirted with other women?

She probably shouldn't even have married Franklin, but agreeing to marry him had helped her to stop thinking about what might have been. In many ways, Franklin's reasons for marrying had mirrored her own. Their pasts had both played a huge role in their willingness to embark on a marriage without loving each other. Though she hadn't wanted to admit it at the time, Grace had come to realize that she'd married a man she hadn't loved to keep her from thinking about the one she could have loved. Maybe she had been a little crazy when she'd made her decision shortly after the death of her grandmother to not love again, but she had needed to do that to keep from losing her mind.

And it had been going fine until things had changed with Franklin. Earlier in the year, he'd begun to listen to the men around him—especially Ethan—who had admonished him on the way he'd behaved around other women and how he treated her. At some point, Franklin had started to take the men's words to heart and began to change. He'd started to attend a Bible study with Bennett and Ethan along with some other men.

And as the changes had unfolded in Franklin, Grace had started to love her husband in a way she had never thought she would. And then, just like she'd feared, he was taken from her. She had known it would happen. Just known it. Which was why she hadn't wanted to love Franklin.

But she hadn't been able to stop herself from falling for Franklin when he began to change into a man who sought after God and wanted to be the husband he knew Grace deserved. The whole journey had been something Grace had never envisioned embarking on. But she had…and now she was dealing with heart-wrenching pain because of it.

When her cell phone rang, Grace debated ignoring it, but the ring tone was the one she'd assigned to Makayla. If she didn't answer, no doubt her doorbell would be ringing in short order. And right then, she'd rather talk to Makayla over the phone than in person.

She rolled to the side of the bed and picked her phone up off the nightstand. After tapping the screen to accept the call, she put it on speakerphone then set it on the pillow beside her.

"How are you doing?" Makayla asked after Grace answered the call. "For real."

"I'm surviving," Grace said as she rubbed a hand over her eyes. At least what she'd told Makayla was basically true. She *was* surviving.

"How was it being back to work? Was it too much for you?"

"Not at all. I'm glad for the distraction. It felt good to get back into the job. I needed it." And that was no word of a lie. "Getting out of the house was good for me."

"I'm glad to hear that. I didn't want you to feel pressured to come back too soon."

"No one was pressuring me," Grace assured her. "I did it for myself."

There was a beat of silence before Makayla spoke again. "I want to run something by you. Give you an option to consider when you're ready."

Grace frowned at the uncharacteristically hesitant tone of Makayla's voice. "What are you talking about?"

"I just wanted to let you know that if you wanted to, you are welcome to move back into the apartment with Tami and me. We didn't do anything to your bedroom that we can't undo."

Grace lay there for a moment considering the offer. "I'm not sure I'm interested in moving just yet. I think I read somewhere that I shouldn't make a major decision like a move while my loss is still so fresh."

"I understand that. I just wanted to give you the option if you should ever need it." Makayla paused. "I just really want you close by, so I guess this offer is kind of selfish."

Grace couldn't help but smile. It was exactly something that Makayla would want. Though Grace did like the idea of having her friends closer, she didn't think she was ready to leave the home she'd shared with Franklin just yet. Even though she left the condo for work to escape the memories, she wasn't sure that she could handle going home to a place where there were other people. She needed a break from everyone at the end of the day. That way she could grieve in whatever way she needed.

"Thank you for the offer, and I'll keep it in mind. Even if it's just for a night, I might take you up on it."

"Well, you know the address if you ever need a place to crash."

"How are the wedding plans going?" Grace asked, eager to change the subject.

There was a pause then Makayla spoke, hesitancy—again—clear in her tone. "I really haven't had too much time to work on stuff."

Grace had a sudden thought. "Are you concerned about talking to me about your wedding plans?" When Makayla didn't reply right away, Grace said, "Seriously, Makayla, don't worry about that. I want to hear about what you're planning."

"So you're still up for being my matron of honor?"

"Of course I am." Grace had always assumed she'd play that role in Makayla's wedding. Or was she just a maid of honor now since she wasn't technically married anymore? "I would be angry with you if you didn't have me in your wedding party. We all had a deal."

"Yes, we did," Makayla agreed. "We'll have to go look for dresses soon. Ethan doesn't want a long engagement."

"I agree with him," Grace said. She loved both Makayla and Ethan and was happy for them. But now she knew better than most people that life was too short to waste on planning a wedding when the most important part was their life together after the ceremony.

"I'll tell him that," Makayla said with a laugh. "He's been recruiting people to his side for an early wedding date."

"You don't want that too?" Grace asked.

"Actually, I do, but I like to see him pleading his case to everyone." Makayla laughed, and Grace smiled. It felt almost foreign to use those muscles, and yet it was a relief to know that she could still smile.

For the next little while, Grace found herself transported to a different time. A time before her world had fallen apart. She'd had many a conversation on the phone with Makayla while laying in this bed. For those few minutes, she felt normal.

When the conversation ended, she lay there, waiting for Franklin to come into the room and ask what they'd been talking about. Then she remembered that couldn't happen, and her stomach clenched. Clutching the phone in her hand, Grace curled onto her side and let the hot tears slip down her cheeks.

$\mathcal{T}$HE OPENING OF THE FRONT DOOR drew Grace's attention from the email she was composing. Bennett walked in, brief-case in hand, his dark brown hair ruffled from the windy day. He wore a dark gray suit with a paisley tie in shades of greens and blues, and he looked every bit his role of CEO of the company. His gaze met hers as he approached the desk with a smile.

"Good morning, Grace," he said as he ran a hand through his hair, returning it to its normal style. "How are you doing today?"

"I'm doing pretty good." There was no way she was going to go into detail about her emotional state with Bennett McFadden. The man had a tendency to try to fix things. She did *not* need that in her life right now. And for the most part, what she had said was true. She was doing as well as could be expected considering her circumstances. Once upon a time, she might have divulged more information to Bennett, but not now.

"I'm glad to hear it." While his words might have sounded like he accepted her response, his expression said otherwise. "I'm going to be on a video call for the next little while. Can you send my calls to my voicemail or take a message, please?"

"Will do," Grace said with a nod, grateful that he wasn't going to press for more details.

With one last smile, Bennett headed down the hallway to his office. Grace watched him go, then turned her attention back to her monitor. Her stomach suddenly clenched, and for a moment, she wondered if she was going to have to make a rapid dash to the bathroom. This was the first time the nausea had hit her without it being related to a crying jag.

She blew out a few breaths, trying to keep the swell of nausea from overwhelming her. The last thing she wanted was to be sick there at the office.

"Are you okay, Gracie?" Makayla's voice broke through her thoughts.

Grace looked up to find Makayla standing across the desk from her. Fighting the nausea, she continued to inhale and exhale.

"Gracie?" Makayla walked around the desk and came to her side, resting her hand on Grace's shoulder as she dropped down on her knees beside her. "What's going on?"

"Not sure. I feel like I'm going to be sick." Gracie swallowed and picked up her water bottle to take a small sip.

"Has this happened before?" Makayla asked, her eyes wide. "You're really pale."

"I've been sick before, but usually it's when I get upset. After I've been crying."

Makayla looked around. "Did something upset you?"

Gracie shook her head. "It just kind of crept up on me." She pressed a hand to her stomach. "I think I just need to go to the bathroom for a few minutes."

Her friend straightened and helped Grace to her feet. "Can I get you something to drink? Ginger ale? Some tea?"

"I think I'll be okay." Grace picked up her water bottle. "I'll be back in a couple of minutes."

Makayla let her go, and Grace was relieved to reach the bathroom, locking the door behind her. Just in time, she reached the toilet and emptied her stomach. Once there was nothing left to throw up, Grace leaned back against the wall. She closed her eyes and let out a long breath. After taking a sip of water, she swished it in her mouth and spat it out.

She waited for several minutes, wondering if she dared leave the bathroom. It seemed strange how the nausea came on so suddenly. And apparently, it was leaving the same way. When her stomach seemed to have settled, Grace washed her hands and left the bathroom.

Makayla was seated in her chair, looking at her phone. She lifted her head as Grace approached.

"Feeling better?" she asked as she got to her feet.

Grace nodded. "I think it's passed. I'm still not sure what brought it on."

Makayla stared at her for a long moment. "I know this is probably not what you want to hear, but is it possible that you're pregnant?"

Grace automatically shook her head. She didn't want to consider that. Didn't even want to think along those lines. "I think it's just my emotions. Usually it's happened when I've been upset and crying. I've just been trying to not have any sort of emotional moments here at work. Maybe that was just my body's way of forcing them out of me anyway."

Makayla looked skeptical, but she didn't push her suggestion. "If you need to go home, feel free. You don't need to hang around here if you're not feeling well."

"I think I'll be okay." The nausea had faded away, though she still felt a bit blah, but she figured she could stick it out for the rest of the day. Grace really didn't want to go home and have to be alone with her thoughts.

"Okay. Well, if that changes, let me know."

Once Makayla had left her alone, Grace took a few more sips of water and tried to focus on her work. When the main phone line rang a few minutes later, Grace was grateful for the distraction.

"Good afternoon. C&M Builders. How may I direct your call?"

"I need to speak with Bennett." The woman's voice was demanding. "He's not answering his cell phone."

"I'm sorry, but he's in a meeting at the moment. He asked me to take a message, or I can connect you to his voicemail."

There was a pause then the woman said, "Connect me to his voicemail, please. Also, tell him Ellie called, in case he doesn't check his messages right away."

"I will pass the message on to him when he's finished with his meeting."

"Thank you."

Before Grace could respond, the line went dead. She stared at the receiver for a moment then hung it up with a shrug. Ellie's attitude had always been a bit abrupt. Grace had no idea why, since she'd only ever been nice to the woman. But somehow, from the first time they'd met, Ellie had decided to be abrupt and distant. They'd never developed any sort of friendship. At times, Grace had wondered if the woman saw her as just an employee even though it was fairly obvious she was close to the McFadden family.

Thankfully, that little interruption had allowed her stomach to settle completely, so she was able to focus on her work.

"Hi, Grace. Were there any messages for me?"

Grace glanced up at Bennett, noticing that he'd abandoned his suit coat and rolled up his sleeves, which seemed to be his default outfit when he was in the office. "Yes. Ellie called when you didn't answer your cell." Bennett's brow furrowed. "I think she left a message on your voicemail, but she also wanted me to tell you she called in case you didn't check your messages right away."

When Bennett sighed with a frown, Grace wondered if there was trouble in paradise. "Was that the only message?"

"Yes. There were a couple of other calls, but they were happy to talk to your voicemail."

If she'd continued the close friendship they'd shared in high school, Grace might have felt comfortable asking Bennett what was up with him and Ellie. Although, quite possibly, if she'd allowed that friendship to continue, there would be no Ellie.

Grace immediately tried to shut down those thoughts. She'd made her decision in the past based on what she felt were very valid reasons. Those reasons were even more valid today.

"Okay. Thank you," Bennett said before heading back to his office.

Whatever problems Bennett may or may not be having with Ellie had nothing to do with her. If he needed any advice regarding that situation, he had Makayla and Tami to help him out.

If she sometimes missed the friendship she'd shared with Bennett in their teen years, Grace figured losing that closeness was it was a small price to pay to keep him safe.

BENNETT ROLLED HIS SLEEVES back down then reached for his coat. The building was quiet as he left his office. He knew he was the last one there since Ethan had popped his head in earlier to tell him that he and Makayla were leaving. It wasn't that work had necessarily kept him late, but he'd told himself he wasn't going to deal with the Ellie situation while he was at the office. That was his private life, and it had no place at work. So he'd stayed late...

He wasn't happy that she'd phoned the office. And even less happy that Grace had had to deal with her. No doubt Ellie hadn't been very pleasant to her.

Bennett sighed as he climbed into the cab of his truck. He'd barely turned the key in the ignition when his phone rang. It didn't surprise him to see Ellie's name pop up on the screen. He waited for the Bluetooth to pick it up then said hello as he backed out of his spot.

"Why didn't you call me back?" Ellie asked, her voice soft. Bennett knew she was trying not to appear riled by the fact that he hadn't. "Did she...did you not get my message?"

"I did," Bennett said as he watched the traffic on the road in front of the office. "I had work that needed my attention. I thought we'd said everything we needed to say last night."

"Bennett, please." Ellie's voice was still soft. "I think we need to talk some more."

He accelerated out onto the road when he saw a break in the traffic. "Let me just ask you one question."

"What's that?"

"When you called the office and Grace answered, did you ask her how she was doing?" The pause told Bennett everything he needed to know. Ellie had been a bit standoff-ish with his family overall, but he'd figured that in time she'd warm up to them. Unfortunately, she'd been outright rude to Grace at times, and he couldn't figure out her reasons for doing that. "Grace has been part of our family since she and Makayla were in high school. I'm not sure why you've decided that she wasn't worthy of your consideration. My family has always been about inclusion, not exclusion. Unfortunately, you're not showing that type of spirit."

"I can be that way, Bennett," Ellie pleaded.

"You don't seem to understand, Ellie. I need this to be something that comes naturally to the woman I'm with. Our family always has room for more. You didn't need to shove someone aside in order to make room for yourself. That's not how it works for us. It would never work because Makayla wouldn't choose you over Grace. So since you decided to keep Grace at arm's length, by default, you've placed the majority of my family at arm's length as well because they all love Grace. It would just never work."

"Well." The one word held a hard edge. "it seems to be a fine coincidence that you're breaking up with me just when Grace is available."

"If Franklin's death has done anything, it's revealed your true nature to me. If you'd embraced Grace and even made an effort to support her, we wouldn't be having this conversation." Bennett guided the truck through traffic, eager to get home. He was so done with this day.

"I think you're blind, Bennett," Ellie said, not even trying to take a soft approach with him any longer. "Or you're lying to yourself."

The line went dead, and Bennett let out a long sigh. Though there might have been a time when Ellie's assumption had been correct, that time was long gone. He didn't appreciate having Ellie put those thoughts back in his head. Franklin's death didn't mean that he had another chance with Grace. She had made it clear over the years that she wasn't interested in that type of relationship with him, so her husband's death didn't change anything.

However, that didn't mean that he wanted to be with someone who wouldn't even give Grace the courtesy of their sympathy.

Bennett climbed the stairs to his apartment, hearing voices drifting down from above him. He recognized Makayla's voice, but it was her words that stopped him in his tracks.

"I asked her if she was pregnant," Makayla said.

"And what did she say?" Ethan asked.

"She said she wasn't. She thinks it's just her grief that's making her feel sick."

Bennett gripped the railing, the thought of Grace being pregnant caused him to immediately think about how he could help her. He hadn't even considered that pregnancy might be a possibility. If what Makayla was saying was true, the future was going to significantly change for Grace. She was going to need the support of his family more than ever, and he'd be happy to offer his support as well.

In whatever form that might take.

Chapter Four

*G*RACE STARED DOWN at the white stick sitting on the bathroom vanity. After a couple more out-of-the-blue episodes of throwing up, she'd decided the quickest way to rule out pregnancy was to take an actual test. So there she was, waiting for the test result and hoping with all her heart that it was negative because she just wasn't sure she could handle it if she was pregnant.

Surely God wouldn't expect that of her.

Her stomach clenched at the thought, and Grace reached out to flip the test over face down. There was no need to wait for the result. It was negative. She didn't need the test to tell her that.

She walked from the bathroom into the master bedroom then headed out to the kitchen. After throwing up earlier, she now found herself hungry. Hopefully, there was some appetizing food in the fridge or cupboards. She hadn't been great at keeping groceries in the house since Franklin's death. In fact, if it weren't for Makayla showing up with bags of food once a week, she'd probably not eat much at all.

Thankfully, the bread she found was fresh, and the chunky peanut butter was brand new. She put two slices of bread in the toaster, then spread peanut butter on them while they were still hot. Hot toast with peanut butter had always been a favorite, but it tasted especially good that night. So good, in fact, that she made two more slices. She also drank a glass of warm milk in hopes that it would help her sleep.

When she returned to the bathroom to get ready for bed, Grace stared at the test then slid it against the back of the vanity without turning it over.

Still negative.

She took off her makeup then brushed her teeth. With one last look at the test, she flicked off the light and headed for bed. Two more days and it was the weekend. Of course, she could probably call in sick the next day, and no one would give her any hassles. But she wasn't going to. She wanted life to get back to normal. Well, as normal as things could be anymore.

And that was why the test was negative.

The nightmare came not long after she'd fallen asleep. Grace woke, drenched in sweat, her heart pounding. She gasped for breath between her sobs. The sounds of crunching metal echoed in her ears. The smell of burning rubber and gasoline seared her nostrils. It was so thick in the air she could taste it. The heat of the fire licked at her skin.

And then she began to scream.

For far too long she felt like she was right back there, dealing with the aftermath of the accident that had ripped her world apart. The guilt she felt pressed down on her even though she knew the accident wasn't her fault. Franklin had asked her to drive because he'd had a headache. The driver of the truck had been in the wrong when he'd gone through the intersection. It hadn't been her fault. But she'd lived, and Franklin had died.

She fought to free herself from the bed, kicking at the sheets that were wrapped around her legs. Finally, she jerked free from them and slid onto the floor on her hands and knees. Her stomach heaved, but nothing came up.

When she finally stopped shaking, Grace pushed herself back to sit against the side of the bed. She tipped her head back, lifting her hands to press them to her damp heated cheeks. Maybe Makayla was right. Maybe it was time to see about getting some counseling. Get some professional help. Would that help her to never have the nightmares again?

Fresh tears rolled as the heartache began to bleed over the shock. She didn't want to have to deal with this. She didn't want to have to wake up to the knowledge once again that her heart had been ripped out of her chest. Why did God think she was strong enough to handle heartache and loss upon heartache and loss?

She couldn't keep doing this.

She just wasn't strong enough.

She wanted her family.

She wanted her husband.

This was not the life she wanted. Not the one she had dreamed of having as a young girl. After losing her parents, she'd managed to keep her dreams alive, but when her grandmother had died, she just couldn't do it anymore. And then—even though she hadn't planned to—she'd let her walls down, let Franklin in, only to have it all taken away again.

She just couldn't do it again.

Pushing up to her feet, Grace went into the bathroom and got a drink. She saw the test, but there was no way she could deal with the possibility of being pregnant right then. No way did she want it to be positive because it would just be one more thing that could be taken away from her.

After a few hours of, thankfully, uninterrupted sleep, Grace called Makayla to let her know that she wasn't up to going into work that day. Though her friend probed for details, Grace managed to brush her concerns aside. Her next step was to try to find a counselor to help her get past the nightmares.

"NO GRACE TODAY?" Bennett asked Makayla when he spotted her behind the reception desk. He'd been in the office since seven and had only now popped out to refill his coffee. It was almost ten, and usually Grace was in by nine. Since Franklin's death, Makayla had been the one to take up most the slack at the front desk in Grace's absence.

Makayla sat back in her chair, her brows drawn together. "She phoned early this morning to say that she had stuff she needed to do today and wouldn't be in."

"Is she okay?"

"Who knows for sure," Makayla said with a shrug, then she sighed. "She's just not opening up the way she used to. I suggested she go to a counselor, but she said she didn't need to."

"Maybe it's too soon?" Bennett had no idea how counseling worked. He wondered if maybe his mom could help Grace. She'd also lost her husband and been left a widow at a young age. More than any of the rest of them, she would understand the grief that Grace was dealing with. "Has she talked to Mom at all?"

"Not that I'm aware of." Makayla leaned forward to rest her arms on the desk. "I hate not knowing how to help her. The way she's acting, it's like she doesn't want us to be there for her. Every time I offer to go over or invite her to our place, she turns me down."

"It seems like she just needs her space," Bennett commented.

Makayla seemed to consider his words but didn't look convinced.

"I heard what you said the other day about her maybe being pregnant." Makayla's eyes widened at his remark. "Do you think it's really possible?"

"She says no." Makayla paused. "I just wondered since she's been having nausea and throwing up for no apparent reason."

"I can't imagine how she'd deal with that," Bennett said. "That would certainly be a shock."

"I would imagine it would be. She didn't say anything about her and Franklin trying to get pregnant. In fact, I'd kind of got the feeling that they weren't interested in having kids."

Bennett's mind was already churning with what they'd have to do to support her if she was really was pregnant. "Let me know if you hear anything."

Makayla nodded. "If she tells me."

When the phone rang, Bennett headed over to fill his coffee mug and then went back to his office while Makayla took care of the call. As he sat down at his desk, he realized that there had been no text messages or calls from Ellie so far that day. Since their conversation on Monday, she'd called him every day to try to convince him to give them a second chance.

Though he was relieved she had stopped calling, he was also sad that things hadn't worked out since he'd had high hopes for their relationship. They'd met at church when he'd volunteered to serve on a mission's committee for a conference the church was having. She'd been on the committee as well, and they'd ended up working together on the food for the conference. Her possessive and jealous tendencies hadn't shown themselves early on. They'd gone on several dates—almost a month's worth—before he'd introduced her to his family and friend group. And that had been where the trouble had started.

Her initial reserved and stand-offish demeanor had been understandable since his family could be overwhelming. But her attitude hadn't changed and then it had seemed to morph into jealousy in the last month or so. She'd been jealous of dumb things, like him taking his mom out for dinner. Or spending a Saturday afternoon helping his younger sister, Sammi, find a new car. Or volunteering to help someone from the church move.

He'd spent plenty of time with Ellie, so he had no idea why she was so jealous of the time he spent with the other people who were important to him. He'd invited her along a couple of times, but she'd declined his invitation, only to complain later that he hadn't spent the time with her.

How she had treated Grace, though, had just been the final straw. He hadn't expected her to be buddy-buddy with the other women in his life, but he had thought she'd at least be sympathetic to Grace's grief. With all he had going on, he just couldn't be with a woman who held herself so much apart from certain areas of his life. His family was important to him. His friends were important to him. And his involvement with the church was a necessity for him. His "perfect" woman would also welcome those things into her own life, just as he would welcome the important areas of her life into his.

When his phone chirped, Bennett sighed before lifting it up to look at it. When he saw Ellie's name, he just shook his head. It was as if his thoughts had brought on her text. He had no idea why she continued to try to push things. He thought he'd been quite clear when they'd talked the day after he'd broken up with her.

Ellie: *Can we go out for dinner on Friday? So we can talk?*

Bennett fought the urge to respond immediately in the negative. Instead, he set the phone aside and went back to work. He'd answer her text later.

GRACE LEFT THE BUILDING where she'd just spent the last hour and a half, not sure if she'd be returning. She'd wanted help dealing with the nightmares of the accident. The woman, however, seemed to have a different agenda. She'd wanted to talk about her relationship with Franklin and how she was dealing with his passing.

No.

She didn't want to talk about that. She was dealing with her grief in her own way. She didn't need the woman's help with that. All she wanted was to stop having the nightmares. The dreams about missing Franklin, she could handle. It was the ones about the accident that she wanted to stop.

Maybe she needed to find another counselor. Or a psychiatrist—one that could prescribe some drugs that might help.

Once she got home, Grace stood inside the door and stared around at the space she had shared with her husband. Since it had been Franklin's before they got married, it had a very masculine look to it with dark colors and big, leather furniture. His job as a successful real estate agent had afforded him a nice home. And now it was hers.

She wasn't sure how she felt about it. Franklin hadn't really given her the freedom to change much in the condo when they'd first gotten married, and as time went on, she'd just not cared to make any changes, so it wasn't truly her home. She thought of Makayla's offer to move back into the apartment they'd once all shared together, but she wasn't sure she could handle living in such close quarters again.

The one-bedroom apartment on the main floor of the Callaghan building was still empty, though, since Gabe seemed to prefer to stay at his parents' place whenever he was in town. The idea of living there—at least for the time being—was definitely becoming more appealing. Close enough to hang out with her friends if she wanted, and yet still be able to retreat to her own space when she needed it.

But was she ready to make any type of major move yet?

Grace pressed her hands against her temples. With everything going through her head, it felt like it was going to explode. Exhaustion plagued her as her fractured sleep from the previous night caught up with her, and she was relieved to crawl into bed after eating a quick supper. Thankfully, her thoughts left her alone long enough so she could fall asleep.

"HOW ARE YOU DOING, Grace?"

Grace winced at Bennett's question. It was one that she was getting especially tired of. When she'd been doing fine, she'd never had a problem with it. Now, however, *fine* was a lie, but no one had the time for a real answer. And she wasn't sure she'd give one to Bennett anyway.

"You know what," Bennett said, "That's a dumb question. Let me just say that it's good to see you in today."

"Thank you." Grace felt a sense of relief that Bennett understood how difficult that question was for her.

"We're going out for lunch today," Bennett said as he lifted his briefcase from where he had set it on her desk. "You know the drill."

And she did. So when eleven o'clock rolled around, she switched on the answering machine and prepared the sign that would go on the door to let customers know that the office was closed until one o'clock. Bennett came to the front of the office with Ethan and Tristan, followed a few minutes later by Makayla. The guys went in Bennett's truck while Grace went with Makayla.

"Tami has a date tonight," Makayla said as she steered her car out of the lot behind Bennett.

"What?" Grace had expected Makayla to talk to her about how she was doing, so her comment took her off-guard.

"I know, right?" Makayla shot her a grin. "I was surprised too."

"With who?" Grace suddenly felt totally out of touch with her friends' lives. It was a pretty stark reminder that life was still going on around her. Without her.

"Surprisingly enough, an athlete," Makayla said.

"Really? I thought that was a definite no-no on Tami's list. What changed her mind?"

"A soft-spoken wide receiver whose faith is important to him. Apparently, he's also persistent. Tami said he'd been asking her out for a few months now."

"Wow. Have you met him?"

"Yes. He's part of Bennett's Bible study, and I had a chance to meet him when Bennett hosted a dinner for the guys one night. He also attends our church when he's not playing a game."

"I guess Franklin would have known him as well?" Grace asked.

"Yes, probably," Makayla said. "He's been part of the study for three or four months now."

The revelation caused Grace's chest to tighten. It was a reminder of how poorly she and Franklin had always communicated and how, even with the changes in Franklin's life, they had still been learning how to improve that part of their relationship.

"Do you want to come hang out with me tonight while she's on her date? Then we can drill her for the details when she gets home. I'll order pizza, and we can watch a movie." Makayla reached out to lay a hand on her knee. "Nothing serious unless you want it. Just us hanging out like old times."

"Ethan doesn't want to spend time with you?"

"Not tonight. I think he and Bennett are helping someone from their group with a move or something."

Grace let the idea sit in her mind for a moment, weighing her reaction to it. The pros. The cons. "Okay. That sounds...good."

She waited for Makayla's happy exclamation, but instead, her friend just said, "You still want a Hawaiian pizza?"

No, her stomach quickly protested the thought of such a combo. "I think I'll just go for a cheese pizza this time around."

"Cheesy crust?"

"Yes, please." Now that her mind had focused on a pizza loaded with cheese, she felt like she couldn't wait until later to eat it. Hopefully, she'd be able to find something equally as appealing at the restaurant for lunch. It was weird how she could go from no appetite to starving within minutes—with bouts of nausea in between. "Guess Bennett picked the restaurant today, eh?"

Makayla laughed as she swung her car into a spot in the parking lot next to Montana's. "Yeah, although Ethan and Tristan didn't object."

They got out of the car and joined the men where they stood next to Bennett's truck. Inside the restaurant, they found that Steve and Emily were already there with Mitch—Makayla and Bennett's stepbrother—and had a table for them all.

"So good to see you, sweetheart," Emily said as she pulled Grace in for a hug. The soft scent of her perfume enveloped her. It was a scent that Grace would always associate with Emily. "Here, sit next to me."

Grace wondered if she was going to have to endure a lunch filled with questions about how she was doing, but she was pleased when Emily's conversation centered around Makayla and Ethan's wedding. She found herself laughing as Emily shared her ideas for what she thought Makayla should do.

"I think we could go to some florist shop—or maybe Michaels or even the craft aisle at Walmart—and make the bridesmaids' bouquets.

Wouldn't that be a nice touch? Making each one specifically for a bridesmaid."

"No, Mom." Makayla rolled her eyes. "No fake flowers. Absolutely no fake flowers. We can order special bouquets using real ones."

"I suppose you don't want my input on the bridesmaids' dresses either," Emily said.

"You're coming with us to try on dresses, so of course you'll have input. But no big fluffy dresses in bright pink."

Grace turned and frowned at Makayla. "But what if I want a big fluffy dress? I think we should go for a princess ballroom style for all of us."

Another eye roll along with a shake of her head. "I know you guys are just messing with me, but it would serve you both right if I took you up on these suggestions."

It felt good to laugh. For just a moment to forget that this wasn't just any Friday lunch with the people from the office. It wasn't unusual for Franklin not to be present at something like this. So the loss wasn't as apparent as they talked and ate and enjoyed their time together. Grace knew it wasn't something that would last. There would come another moment when the huge hole would come front and center again, but for right then, she would embrace the moment.

Later that evening, as she and Makayla sat on opposite ends of the couch, each with a plateful of pizza, Grace found that the moment had continued. They'd found a movie that made them laugh as they ate, but every once in awhile, a thought would cross Grace's mind.

Is it too soon?

Too soon to be having moments that weren't saturated by grief? Too soon to be smiling? Too soon to be laughing at funny movies?

She didn't know.

The only thing she *did* know was that if she didn't surface from the sea of grief every once in a while, she was going to drown. Maybe others knew how to survive under water in that sea, but she didn't. In some ways, it seemed to almost be getting worse. The numbness from the shock of everything was wearing off, which meant that the grief was deeper and larger than it had been right after Franklin had died.

She knew that Makayla would never judge her, and because of that, she relaxed and for the moment, pulled herself up out of the sea of grief to hang around the edge of it for awhile. It would be waiting for her at the end of the evening, and she would slip back into it because it didn't feel right in her heart to leave it completely just yet. Maybe she never would. Though she and Franklin's love hadn't been as deep or as strong as others', it had been growing and changing. She would probably forever mourn the loss of what it might have become.

"I took a pregnancy test," Grace blurted out as she looked at Makayla.

$\mathcal{M}$AKAYLA FROZE, the end of her slice of pizza drooping . "You took a pregnancy test?"

Grace nodded, picking at the cheese on her piece.

"And?" Makayla lowered her pizza back to her plate and turned to face Grace more fully. "Was it negative?"

Unable to hold her friend's direct gaze, Grace focused on the movie that was now more background noise than anything else. "I don't know."

There were a couple moments of silence. "You don't *know*?"

"I didn't look at it. I took the test but then turned it over and left it on my bathroom counter."

"Is there a chance it might be positive?"

Grace hesitated to nod because this was something she hadn't discussed with Makayla—the fact that Franklin had been eager to start a family. When they'd gotten married, one of the things that had been a definite point in Franklin's favor, when so many other things hadn't been, was that he hadn't wanted children. Grace hadn't really changed her mind about it completely like Franklin had, but she'd allowed him to convince her that they needed a child to complete their family. They'd been trying for a couple of months before the accident, so yes, it was possible she was pregnant.

She didn't want to be though. People would tell her how fortunate she was to still have a piece of her husband to hold, but she'd much rather have had him…or nothing at all. Did that make her a horrible person? Probably to a lot of people it would, but she had her reasons.

"Yes. There's a chance." Grace felt it then. The edge of the sea of grief lapping at her toes, eroding the sand beneath her feet and drawing her back in.

As if realizing that the chance of a positive pregnancy test didn't bring Grace joy, Makayla paused the movie. Then she reached out and grabbed Grace's plate and set it with hers on the coffee table. Next, she settled on her knees in front of Grace and took both her hands. And waited. When Grace looked up, Makayla was blurry through a wash of tears.

"When you decide to turn that test over, if you want company, you know I'm there." Makayla paused. "Do you want to talk about it?"

Grace shook her head, the movement spilling tears down her cheeks. "Not right now."

She felt Makayla's hands squeeze hers briefly before releasing them. "Then we won't. We'll keep watching our movie and eating our pizza. However, if you change your mind, you only have to say the word."

Makayla got to her feet, handed Grace her plate and sank back down onto the other end of the couch with her own plate. When the movie started up again, the sea of grief receded, leaving Grace to feel as if the ground beneath her was solid once again.

Once the movie ended, Grace didn't want to leave so happily sat with her feet tucked up under her, listening as Makayla chatted about things that were going on with her younger sister, Danica, and Ethan's younger sister, Sierra. Grace thought of the girls as her own sisters, so enjoyed hearing how things were going with them.

They were in the middle of discussing the roles the girls were going to play in Makayla and Ethan's wedding when the door to the apartment opened. Grace glanced over to see a sudden influx of people. Tami led the way followed by a large, dark-skinned man then Ethan and Bennett.

Ethan walked right to the couch and leaned over to give Makayla a kiss before holding up a bag. "I brought ice cream."

Tami came around to give Grace a tight hug before letting her go. "Well, I think Makayla made brownies earlier today so we could eat those with the ice cream." She turned to the man behind her. "Oh. Keenan, do you know Grace?"

The man shook his head as he looked at Grace. His brown gaze softened as he reached out to take her hand, grasping it between both of his. He dropped to his haunches beside her, bringing him to eye level with her. "We never had a chance to meet, but I did know your husband, and I'm so very sorry for your loss."

"Thank you." Grace had no idea what else to say to this giant of a man who was holding her hand so gently.

"I wasn't able to attend his funeral since I was out of town, but my thoughts and prayers were with all of you." He gave her hand a squeeze before letting go and straightening to his impressive height.

Grace gave the man a smile as she thanked him again then her gaze went to Tami. The expression on her friend's face as she stared at Keenan was something Grace hadn't seen from her in a very long time. After the heartbreak Tami had suffered in her early twenties, she had steered clear of serious relationships. It looked like maybe that was about to change.

Makayla pushed up off the couch. "Why don't you all have a seat, and we'll dish up some brownies and ice cream. Everyone up for that?"

Bennett settled into the recliner in the corner while Tami led Keenan to the loveseat. Bennett and Keenan talked about the upcoming football game, and Tami appeared far more interested in the sport than Grace had ever known her to be. Ethan and Makayla came back shortly carrying a couple of trays with bowls of ice cream and brownies. They set the trays on the coffee table and then handed out the bowls, spoons and napkins.

Grace took the bowl Ethan held out to her. "Would you like a cup of coffee, Grace?"

"Thanks, but no," Grace said. She wasn't sure that it was the best idea to keep drinking it without knowing the results of the pregnancy test for sure. She took a bite of the ice cream, relishing the cold as it melted on her tongue.

Once everyone had been served, Ethan settled into the opposite end of the couch while Makayla curled up between him and Grace. Conversation flowed around her as she took small bites of the brownie and ice cream. She looked around at the people in the room, her gaze settling on Bennett as he smiled at something Keenan said.

She wondered if he and Ellie were still together. It would seem that she should have been there with him that evening. Though Grace really didn't have the right to much of an opinion where Bennett and his girlfriends were concerned, she really felt that he deserved someone better than Ellie. The woman's distant and sometimes outright rude personality just didn't seem to jive with who she knew Bennett to be. He needed someone who would mesh well with his family, and Ellie did not seem to be that person.

Bennett looked at her, and their gazes met for a moment before she lowered hers to the bowl of ice cream and took another bite. There were times over the years when she missed the friendship that she'd once had with him. However, she had no one but herself to blame for the tension between them now.

BENNETT SCRAPED THE BOTTOM of the bowl for the last bit of ice cream and brownie. As he sat there surrounded by couples, he considered how things might have been different between him and Grace. That made him wonder if perhaps he'd made a mistake in agreeing to Ethan's invitation when the move they'd been helping with had wrapped up earlier than they'd thought it would.

Though he tried to relegate how he felt for Grace to the past, at moments like these, it was hard. He had long held feelings for her. From the day Makayla had brought Grace home with her from school so they could work on a project together, Bennett had fallen head over heels for her.

She'd had a beautiful smile and an infectious laugh. Once he'd learned a bit about Grace's background and the losses she'd endured, her smiles and laughs had made even more of an impact on him. There had just been something in her that drew him to her.

At first, he'd been happy to just have her friendship, but then he'd found the courage to ask her out. She'd agreed at first, but before they had a chance to spend time together, her grandmother had gotten sick, and Grace had pulled away from him. Not only had they not gone on a date, but she'd also backed away from their friendship as well.

To this day, Bennett didn't understand why. She'd still had a special place in his heart, for a lot of years now. Working together as well as having her around even during their social times had made it difficult to put distance between them. A clean break from Grace might have killed those feelings, but instead, he'd spent the years alternating between accepting that the feelings would always be there and searching for the one woman who would mean more to him than Grace did.

It hadn't happened yet.

If he were to be totally honest, he'd continued to have feelings for her even after she'd married Franklin. It had been a knife in his heart when she'd gotten married to the man. Bennett hadn't been able to grasp why Grace had chosen a man who had treated her the way Franklin had. If she'd married someone who had treated her the way Bennett would have, he might have been okay with her marriage. But since she hadn't, he had struggled to support the union.

When he'd seen Ethan come alongside Franklin and try to befriend him, Bennett had just shaken his head. Though Franklin and Ethan had had a few encounters that hadn't been positive shortly after the two of them had met, Ethan persisted. Bennett hadn't been sure what to make of it. He'd been a Christian longer than Ethan and had prayed for Franklin since he and Grace had gotten married, but honestly, he really hadn't believed that Franklin would—or could—change.

Seeing that metamorphosis had been a wake-up call for him. And it wasn't long after Franklin had started attending the Bible study he led that Bennett had finally made a real effort to put aside his feelings for Grace, and he'd begun to root for her and Franklin. It had been in just the last six months that Bennett had felt that he was truly free from the feelings he'd had for Grace for so long.

As he looked at her now, though, he tried to only think about how he could be a good friend to her. He had a feeling she'd need that more than anything in the months ahead.

"So you guys are really going to get married at the lake?" Bennett asked when the conversation—as usual—turned to the upcoming wedding.

"Yep," Makayla said with an excited smile. She leaned over to press her face against Ethan's shoulder, looking up at him with love clearly evident on her expression. "It was the one place that Ethan and I could agree on. It holds special meaning for us both."

Ethan nodded his agreement as he lifted a hand to brush against Makayla's cheek. Bennett loved to watch the two of them together. He hadn't really spent much time thinking about the type of man that he'd want for his sister. Given the intense aspects of Makayla's personality, he had wondered a few times if she'd find a man who could embrace all of her without trying to change her. Ethan was definitely that man. They complemented each other well.

Until he'd had a front row seat to Ethan and Makayla's love story, the type of relationship he'd hoped to have for himself had been rather vague. But seeing two people with obvious personality differences work through them to get to a place where their love was a solid foundation for their future together had made Bennett want that for himself. It was a good reminder of why breaking up with Ellie had been the right move. He didn't think that they would have ever had a relationship like what Ethan and Makayla had.

"It's going to be fairly small." Makayla glanced over at Grace. "The bridesmaids and I will be staying at the hotel the night before."

"What about the guys?" Bennett asked.

"In tents down by the marina," Makayla said.

"Say what?" Bennett looked over at Ethan. "Seriously, dude? You're gonna make me sleep on an air mattress the night before your wedding."

When Ethan shook his head, Bennett leaned over and held out his hand for a high five, but jerked it back when the man said, "Sleeping bags on the ground."

Keenan chuckled, his laugh low and deep. Makayla and Tami also laughed, and even Grace cracked a smile.

"You've grown soft, Bennett," Grace said with a glance in his direction.

"No…" Bennett started to object, but then he laughed. "Okay. Yeah. I must admit that the idea of sleeping in tents doesn't hold the appeal that it did ten years ago. So sorry, dude, but I'll be sleeping in the hotel with the girls if the alternative is a tent."

"Oh no you won't," Makayla said with a vigorous shake of her head. "I'll make sure you are not allowed to step foot into the hotel. You can rough it with the rest of the guys."

Bennett saw Ethan grin. "So you expect me to spend the night roughing it? I'll just go back to the house. I'm the favorite kid, so Mom and Dad will let me sleep there."

"Pretty sure I'm the favorite," Makayla stated. "The first to get married and bring a great new son into the family."

"Actually, I think I'm the favorite," Grace said. "After all, your mom agreed with me that we should be wearing poufy princess brides-maid dresses."

Bennett stared at Grace, an unexpected burst of happiness filling him at the smile on her face. "Nope. I'm definitely the favorite."

"Is this a common debate?" Keenan asked, directing a look at Tami.

Tami laughed. "There are so many kids in that family that I would imagine that on any given day, the favorite changes."

Keenan looked over at Bennett. "How many of you are there?"

"There are ten of us kids." When Keenan's eyes widened, Bennett went on to explain. "My mom and our step-dad, Steve, each had four kids when they got married and then they had two more. And then they've unofficially adopted a few along the way like Tami, Grace, and Ethan. We have an ever-expanding family."

"There is always room for one more," Makayla agreed. "Do you have family here, Keenan?"

Keenan shook his head. "Most my family lives in Chicago, but I've made my home here since this is where I've played football for five years now."

"Well, if you need a family, let us know. We're familiar with professional sports too since our brother, Kenton is in the NHL."

Though Keenan had been part of the Bible Study for a few months, they hadn't talked about family stuff too much, and Keenan's schedule had kept him from being available for the family get-togethers. Keenan had proved to be a man of solid faith with lots of insights that Bennett appreciated. He'd enjoyed having the man in the study, and now it looked like he might become part of their social circle as well which Bennett thought would be great.

Keenan's interaction with Grace earlier had also reinforced his admiration for the man. Honestly, anyone who treated Grace well was in Bennett's good books.

"To go back to our original topic," Ethan began when talk of their family trailed off. "Steve has actually helped me find a houseboat with enough space for all us guys. So we'll be out on the water, and even though we're not in luxury like the girls, we'll be comfortable."

"That sounds like fun," Grace observed. "You'll just have to make sure you get Ethan back to shore on time."

"Maybe you should be worried that your groom is planning to spend his last night as a single man on something that would allow him to escape easily if he should get cold feet," Bennett pointed out.

Makayla laughed. "Of all the details I'm worried about for this wedding, Ethan getting cold feet is not one of them. He'll be there."

The indulgent look on Ethan's face supported Makayla's claim. "Yes. I'll be there."

As the talk continued around the plans for the wedding, Bennett found himself watching Grace. He was glad that she was participating in the conversation even though her level of interaction was nowhere near what it would have been in the past. Baby steps, he supposed. But it was a sign to Bennett that Grace hadn't been totally lost to her grief. It eased some of the concern he had carried over the past month.

After about half an hour later, Bennett saw Grace lay a hand on Makayla's arm and then lean over to talk to her. Makayla nodded as she spoke then got to her feet, pulling Grace up as well.

When the others looked in their direction, Grace said, "I think I'm going to head for home. Thanks for the ice cream and brownie." She walked over to where Tami sat, the other woman coming to her feet as Grace approached. They hugged for a long minute, Tami talking softly in her ear. Grace nodded then smiled at her as they stepped apart. "It was nice to meet you, Keenan."

Keenan stood up, towering over Grace. "Can I give you a hug?" He grinned down at her. "I'm a huggy kinda person."

Grace stepped closer to him and allowed herself to be embraced by the gentle giant. "Thank you."

Bennett wished he could offer Grace a hug, but he was pretty sure that wouldn't be welcome. He didn't miss the look Keenan shot his way when Grace hugged everyone except him before making her exit from the apartment. Makayla went with her, returning a short time later, a thoughtful look on her face.

"She doing okay, babe?" Ethan asked when Makayla returned to her seat beside him. He slipped his arm around her shoulders and pulled her close.

"Better, I think, but still struggling."

"Losing a loved one is something you never truly get over," Keenan said, his voice soft, his expression somber. "You just have to adjust to a life that includes memories of them instead of their presence."

Tami rested a hand on his arm. "Who have you lost?"

Keenan's gaze lowered. "Grandparents. Parents. A brother."

"You sound like Grace," Makayla observed. "She's lost her grandparents and parents as well. It just doesn't seem fair that now she's lost her husband."

"Life isn't fair," Keenan said. "Before she passed away my grandmother always told me to never ask *why me* but rather to ask *why* not *me*. It's easy to get caught up in feeling sorry for yourself when bad things happen, but we can choose to rise above those circumstances, to embrace the lesson we will be taught as we go through those dark and difficult times."

"Grace has chosen to rise above what's happened to her in the past, but I can't help wonder if this one might just be too much," Makayla said, a frown marring her features.

"We'll just have to pray that it isn't," Keenan said, his determination clear. "I have been praying for her since hearing of Franklin's death and will continue to do so. In fact, why don't we pray for her right now?"

As the others nodded, Bennett leaned forward to brace his arms on his thighs, his hands clasped together, and bowed his head. For the next little while, each of them murmured prayers on Grace's behalf, asking God to give her the strength to face life without Franklin. It was times like this that Bennett appreciated the friends and family God had blessed him with. He just hoped that Grace knew that each of them was there for her too.

Once the prayer time was over, Bennett got to his feet. "I think I'm going to head for home as well."

"Me, too," Keenan said. "Thank you for letting me join you all this evening."

"I bet you didn't expect this to be how our date ended," Tami said as she smiled up at the man.

Keenan smiled back at her. "I thought I was just going to drop you off with a good night and hopefully a promise of another date. It's been a great evening, and I'm still hoping to leave with that promise."

"I think I can give you that," Tami said as she bumped her shoulder against his upper arm because he was that much taller than her. "Let me walk you down."

They all walked out of the apartment together, but Bennett walked down to the second floor with Tami and Keenan while Ethan lingered behind with Makayla. Bennett said goodbye to the couple when they continued down to the main floor.

In his own apartment, Bennett went to his fridge and grabbed a can of soda before heading to his computer. As he scrolled through his social media after checking his email, he saw a status update pop up from Grace.

So grateful for family, good friends, chocolate, ice cream, and pizza. Definitely in that order. <3

Seeing a positive status update from Grace gave Bennett a sense of relief. He'd thought she'd been enjoying the evening, but seeing proof of it in her own words was good. Of course he knew people could put one thing out on social media while something else was happening behind the scenes, but her words supported what he'd seen earlier at Makayla's. She hadn't posted a lot in the weeks since Franklin's death, so he had no doubt she'd get a lot of support from her friends who saw her status.

Bennett couldn't help but smile as he clicked the *like* button on her status.

Chapter Six

RACE SET HER OPEN LAPTOP down on the bed beside her—Franklin's side—then reached out to snap off the light on the nightstand. She turned over to stare at her Facebook page. Her profile picture was one that Makayla had taken of her when they'd been out at the lake earlier in the year—just a couple of weeks before the accident. She was laughing and looked truly happy. Part of her wanted to yell at her happy self. To tell herself to brace for the coming heartbreak.

Would she ever be that happy again?

Her cover photo was another one Makayla had taken at the same time as her profile one, but this one was of her and Franklin. They'd been sitting together, looking out at the water. Their times with the Callaghans and McFaddens had improved significantly when Franklin began to make positive changes in his life and attitude. She knew that they had all had issues originally with how Franklin treated her, but it hadn't bothered Grace. It would only have mattered if she'd loved him. She was so glad for Franklin's sake that he'd found peace, joy, and love in his life, but it would be hurting a whole lot less now if things hadn't changed between them.

She couldn't dwell on that, though. The fact was that they had enjoyed almost five good months together. She was grateful for that, but Franklin's death had left her determined to never be vulnerable to feeling heartache like that ever again. It was bad enough that she'd be devastated if anything happened to Tami, Makayla or any of the Callaghan-McFadden family. There was no way she was going to compound that by allowing herself to love anyone else.

The next morning, however, as she once again found herself in the bathroom being sick, Grace was forced to accept that quite possibly she wasn't going to have a choice in the matter. When the nausea finally eased, and she felt safe moving away from the toilet, Grace crawled on her knees over to the counter and reached out to grab the pregnancy test. Gripping it in her hand, she turned around and sat on the bathroom floor, her back against the vanity.

She inhaled and exhaled several times. It was time to face reality. A reality that could very well include being a single mother. For a moment, she wondered if she should call Makayla to come over. But them she realized that this was just the first of many things she was going to have to do on her own if this test was positive the way she thought it was likely to be.

Her hand trembled as she turned it over and opened her fingers to reveal the result on the wide stick.

Pregnant

3+

With a sigh that bordered on a sob, Grace let her head drop back against the vanity. What was she supposed to do now? She barely felt able to take care of herself these days. How could she take care of a helpless baby who would be totally dependent on her?

All she could think about was all the things she would need and what she'd have to do. How was she supposed to work and take care of a baby? She knew women did it all the time, but it hadn't been part of her life plan to be a parent, let alone a single mom.

A new fear suddenly filled her. For so long, she'd feared losing those she loved, but now she wondered what would happen to her baby if something happened to her. And if her child was too young, they might not remember her. Grace's memories of her own parents weren't very clear anymore, and she had been ten when they'd passed away.

She tried to take a deep breath, but the tightness of her chest made it difficult. As thoughts and worries tumbled through her mind, Grace pulled her legs in and wrapped her arms around them.

She was turning into Makayla with all her anxiety over something that may or may not ever happen. Okay, the baby was apparently definitely happening, but she had some time to worry about everything else. She would have to just take it one day at a time.

If she could.

The bathroom floor began to hurt her butt, so Grace pushed up to her feet. Turning, she braced her hands on the vanity and stared into the mirror. The circles under her eyes seemed deeper than before, but other than that, she looked the same. Her life had changed irrevocably— again—and yet, in looking at herself, it seemed as if nothing had.

Unable to continue looking at herself, Grace straightened and grabbed an elastic to pull her hair back. With one last look in the mirror, she left the bathroom.

Since it was Saturday, Grace didn't have to go to work, but she felt like she would go crazy if she stayed in the condo. She would have gladly ventured out into a yard if they'd had one or hung out with a neighbor if she had known any well enough, but since she didn't, her only choices were to stay in the condo or go to a mall or a park. She wished that this was a weekend that they'd planned to go to the lake. It would have been a great distraction, and she actually found herself craving the feel of the sunshine on her face. The breeze in her hair.

Without really thinking more about where to go, she got herself ready and left the condo. Sunshine greeted her, and the warmth of the day embraced her. It wasn't until she was pulling out of the underground parking at their building that a destination came to mind. She made a quick stop along the way, then pointed the SUV toward the north part of the city.

Before too long, she pulled through the open wrought iron gate of the cemetery where Franklin was buried. It had been a little over a month. A month during which her world had changed not once, but twice. Franklin should have been there to share it with her, but instead, she had to walk across freshly mowed grass toward a temporary grave marker.

She sank onto the grass at the side of the plot. The outline of the grave opening was still faintly evident, but the flowers from the internment had been cleared away. As she stared at the marker, she let out a long breath.

Franklin Moore

The black granite headstone, when it was ready, would also read: *Beloved husband.*

And now he had one more role, even in his absence. *Father.*

"We're gonna be parents," Grace said as she laid the small bouquet of flowers in front of the grave marker. "I hope I can do this without you." She tipped her head back and stared up at the cloudless sky. She knew that it was only Franklin's body in that grave and that he had another purpose in heaven that didn't include being aware of what was going on in her life, but she hoped that he knew. Pressing a hand to her stomach, she hoped with all her heart that he knew that he would live on in their son or daughter. "I miss you so much."

She found as she said the words that they were truer than they would have been a year ago. Tears pricked against her eyes and threatened to spill over. She hadn't understood why God had taken Franklin to begin with, but she had that question even more now that she knew about the life they'd created together. Though she hadn't asked the question aloud of anyone, it was definitely on her mind each and every day since his totally unexpected death.

Would she ever be at peace about this?

It just felt like her life had been ripped in half. A life interrupted. They hadn't had the chance to fully experience the love that had been slowly growing between them. Most people wouldn't—hadn't—understood why she and Franklin had married, but they'd both had their reasons. It was in the same way that people wouldn't understand how things had been changing between them in the past six months. Now it felt like a story unfinished...

Grace's fingers curled into the grass by her leg. Her life was just one unfinished story. As a daughter. As a granddaughter. As a wife. Every relationship she'd had except friend had ended before it's time. And now there was a new fear—the fear that the role of mother would also be cut short. She didn't think she could handle that one more time.

She stared at the grave for a bit more, wishing she had some assurances. Something that would help her face the days ahead without fear.

It wasn't until her shoulders started to heat under the sunlight that Grace realized she'd been sitting there for awhile. With a sigh, she got to her feet, brushing the grass from the seat of her capris. She let her hand rest on the marker for a second then headed back to her car. Instead of going home, she headed to the nearest mall and started to wander, not too surprised when she found herself in the baby section of one of the stores, looking at the furniture and clothing.

She didn't plan to buy anything, but it seemed like maybe this could be the first step to accepting the new direction in which her life was now headed

The next morning, Grace decided to go to church. She'd been attending the same church as Makayla and her family since shortly before her grandmother's death, but it was the first time she'd gone since Franklin's death. She just hadn't been prepared to face people outside of her small social circle.

It took her awhile to decide what to wear. She felt like people were going to be judging her on what she chose. Too bright and she wasn't mourning Franklin properly. Too dark and she was depressed. In the end, she settled on a pair of white capris and a navy blouse with a fitted bodice and capped sleeves. She skipped any jewelry aside from her wedding ring. Her makeup was just enough to cover the circles under her eyes, and she just left her hair curly instead of straightening it like she usually did.

She'd barely stepped into the foyer of the church before someone approached her to offer their condolences. Several more came alongside her as she made her way toward the sanctuary. She appreciated that people were praying for her and wanted to know how she was, but it was a bit overwhelming. All she wanted was to worship and be fed spiritually. And maybe to find some assurance that her life was going to be okay.

"Good morning, Grace." She looked up to see Bennett standing beside her, concern on his face. "Are you going in for this service?"

She nodded, grateful that he had engaged her in conversation. Maybe it would keep others from approaching her for a few minutes. She just needed a bit of a break. "Do you know if Makayla is here?"

"I saw her earlier with Ethan. They might be seated already." He held his hand out toward the doors leading into the sanctuary. "Are you ready to go in?"

She walked with him through the sanctuary doors then headed to the section where Makayla and Ethan usually sat. Tami was with them, but Keenan wasn't which likely meant he was playing a game that day. They all smiled at her as she slid into the pew beside Tami with Bennett behind her. She breathed a sigh of relief as she found herself encircled by her friends.

As the service progressed, Grace was grateful that she'd made the effort to come, and as they stood to sing the final hymn, she felt as if it had been chosen just for her.

Be not dismayed whate'er betide,
God will take care of you;
Beneath His wings of love abide,
God will take care of you.
God will take care of you,

Through every day, o'er all the way;
He will take care of you,
God will take care of you.

Through days of toil when heart doth fail,
God will take care of you;
When dangers fierce your path assail,
God will take care of you.

All you may need He will provide,
God will take care of you;
Nothing you ask will be denied,
God will take care of you.

No matter what may be the test,
God will take care of you;
Lean, weary one, upon His breast,
God will take care of you.

Once the service ended, Makayla gave her a tight hug then held her at arm's length. "You're coming out to the house for lunch, right? Mom told me to call you after the service if you weren't here."

Grace nodded, needing the beauty of the rural home that she'd been to more times than she could count. It had been her second home for many years. Many more years than she'd lived in Franklin's condo. It would feel more like going home.

"Good," Makayla declared. "I was pretty sure you'd want to. Dad is barbecuing."

Her stomach growled in anticipation. She'd been sick again that morning and hadn't dared to eat anything but a couple of crackers before leaving the condo. Hopefully, she wouldn't get sick again that day. So far, for the most part, the sickness was now only coming in the morning when she first woke up. She wasn't sure that she was ready to share the news just yet, and running for the bathroom to be sick would be a sure giveaway.

As she drove outside the north part of the city toward the Callaghan home, the chorus of the hymn continued to play through her mind.

God will take care of you,
Through every day, o'er all the way;
He will take care of you,
God will take care of you.

It was something she found herself clinging to, the promise that God would take care of her. She knew that He had taken care of her so far, but she sure wished that her life could just cease to be one of loss. The mantle of grief that had overshadowed her life was getting heavy. Too heavy. The grief from her family's deaths had eased over the past decade or so but had never completely disappeared. And now it was back, heavier than ever.

But as she pulled up to the sprawling country home, Grace wanted to just put the grief aside for a couple of hours. She just wanted to be able to feel the love of the family that had supported her before when she'd been lost and alone, and she knew they would do it again.

"GOOD AFTERNOON, MOM," Bennett said as he bent to press a kiss to his mom's cheek. He stole a pickle from the bowl she had in front of her.

"Hello, sweetheart." She looked up at him with a smile. He couldn't miss the signs of age on her face, and yet she looked as beautiful to him as ever. No small wrinkles by her eyes or strands of gray in her hair would ever detract from the beauty of her smile and the love in her eyes.

"Ben!"

He turned to see his youngest brother, Dalton, coming toward him, a wide grin on his thin face. He wore a white T-shirt underneath a plaid shirt with its sleeves rolled up to his elbows. His skinny jeans made him look…skinny, and Bennett was once again concerned for his young brother. He didn't remember any of them being as small at that age as Dalton was.

He wore a bracelet made up of several leather strands on his left wrist, and his hair was longer than it had been in recent months. No doubt it was because he was just about out of school for the summer so the school rules on hair length wouldn't apply for a few months.

"Hey, buddy," Bennett said as he slipped an arm around the teen's thin shoulders. "How's it going?"

Dalton returned his hug then hopped up to sit on a stool at the island counter. He reached across and also snagged a pickle from the bowl. "It's going good. Almost out of school, so I'm cool."

Their mom pushed the jar, bowl and a knife across the counter to Dalton. "Wash your hands, and you can cut the rest of the pickles since you insist on eating them."

"One for the bowl. One for Dalton," he said with a grin as he went to wash up. "You've been warned, Momma."

Though Bennett was happy to live in a space of his own, there were times he missed hanging out with his family in their home.

"Is Grace coming?" she asked as she handed Dalton a towel to dry his hands. "Makayla said she would ask her."

"Yes, and Tami's coming too, but we might have to turn the football game on for her." Bennett sat down on the stool next to Dalton and stole another pickle. "Keenan is playing."

"So they're serious then?" His mom looked up from the potato salad she had just removed from the fridge.

"Sure seems like it. You'll like him."

"I can't wait to meet him, but I guess it won't be on a Sunday, eh?"

"Not while it's football season most likely." Bennett watched as Dalton cut the pickles, following through on his promise to eat a piece of a pickle for every one that went into the bowl.

The noise of approaching vehicles drifted through the open window above the sink. The engines quickly silenced and were replaced by the sound of voices as the front door opened, and then Makayla, Tami, and Grace appeared in the doorway of the kitchen with Ethan right behind them. His mom moved to embrace each of them.

Bennett moved to a stool on the far side of Dalton, watching the group gathering in the kitchen. Most specifically, Grace. It had been awhile since he'd indulged in a little *Grace-watching*. He hadn't done it since Grace had started dating Franklin. Not that he sat and stared at her—that would just be creepy—but he allowed himself to notice things about her that he might not otherwise have.

Like how the dark smudges under her eyes hadn't lessened much in the month since Franklin had died. Or that the smile she gave people still didn't quite reach her eyes. She looked as lovely as ever. He'd always thought she was beautiful, even as a teenager, and that had definitely not changed over the years.

He had seen a similar sadness in her when her grandmother had passed away. It had taken a long time for that sadness to fade, only to reappear off and on over the years. He had a feeling that the sadness would be around much longer this time.

He hadn't been able to help her with the sadness after her grandmother's death, and she probably wouldn't accept his help this time either. So he'd do this time what he'd done the last, and that was to just be present. And to pray. He no longer doubted the power of prayer after seeing the changes in Franklin.

"Take this out to your dad, sweetie, please." His mom gestured to a tray covered in tin foil.

Chapter Seven

ITH ONE LAST LOOK at where Grace stood talking with Sierra and Danica, Bennett picked up the tray and went out to join his dad. He found him at the large barbecue in the outdoor kitchen area his dad had built when he'd built the house. Ethan eventually joined them as did Mitch and Tristan. Bennett loved it when the family was all together.

Unfortunately, it rarely happened anymore. Mitch's twin, Gabe, was off who knew where. Ryan, his younger brother, was currently in Minneapolis working with BlackThorpe Security. He was usually home for holidays and sometimes a weekend here or there. Kenton, of course, was in LA even though it was the off-season for him. The guy barely made it home for Christmas let alone any of the other holidays since his career in the NHL had taken off.

Bennett knew that Makayla was hoping that everyone would be there for her and Ethan's wedding. He was pretty sure that Gabe and Ryan would make the effort, but it remained to be seen if Kenton would tear himself away from sticks and pucks and whatever model he was currently dating, long enough to show up. Or maybe he'd bring the model along. Wouldn't be the first time.

"What's up, buttercup?" Mitch asked as he jabbed Bennett in the ribs. "You look like someone stole the last of your favorite ice cream."

Bennett relaxed the frown that had obviously come from his thoughts of Kenton. "If someone has stolen the last of my ice cream, they'd better hope they can run fast."

"Well, it wasn't me," Mitch said with such an innocent expression on his face that for just a moment, Bennett wondered if his brother had, in fact, raided his freezer.

"Will you please go tell your mom we can eat in about ten minutes, Bennett?" Steve Callaghan asked with a wave of the long, heavy duty spatula he held.

"Sure thing." Bennett headed back to the house, climbing the steps to the large porch that ran all around the house. He reached the back door that led into the kitchen just as the women were headed out. With a smile, he opened the door and held it for them as they walked out with food in their hands. Then he poked his head into the kitchen and passed on his dad's message. "Anything else that needs to be carried out?"

A few minutes later, he headed over to the food table to add the pitchers of juice his mom had given him. When his dad called out that the meat was ready, everyone gathered around the long picnic table, falling quiet when his dad had them join hands for prayer. Bennett took Tristan's hand in his right then held out his left to Grace.

His dad's prayer wasn't long, but as Bennett held Grace's much smaller hand in his, he was reminded of how fragile and delicate she was. But that was only how she appeared physically. He knew she was strong inside…much stronger than a lot of people. Maybe even than him. Though he had lost his dad at a young age, his memories hadn't been strong or plentiful since his dad hadn't been around much.

Being in the military had meant he was on deployment more than he was around. And unfortunately, the strongest memories he had of his dad were of his last time home when the man had spent the majority of his time yelling at all of them, particularly his mom. It had been a relief when he'd headed back out on deployment. So, while he'd grieved the loss of his father, his grief had more to do with losing the man he'd once been rather than losing the man he'd been at the end of his life.

As they sat together in the shade of the big tree in the backyard of his parents' home with only sounds of birds as nature's playlist, Bennett felt a deep sense of contentment. Franklin's sudden death had really brought home the fact that neither another day nor another hour was promised to any of them. He was grateful for his family—both those related by blood and those who had been absorbed into it.

He glanced down at Grace, noticing that she was pushing around the potato salad on her plate. The thought came back to him about Makayla's concern that Grace might be pregnant. There'd been no further mention of it, so he wondered if that had been confirmed one way or the other. Hopefully, if she was, she'd begin to eat more. He understood how her grief might rob her of her appetite, but if she was pregnant, she'd need to find a balance.

"Did Kenton get back to you about the wedding, sweetie?"

Bennett's attention snapped back to the conversation at the sound of Kenton's name. He looked past Grace to where Makayla sat in time to see her nod.

"Yep. He said he'd try to come in for that whole week." Makayla smiled then glanced at Bennett. "He said for sure for the wedding, but he hoped to spend the week before here too."

Bennett looked away from Makayla, only to find Grace watching him. He hoped that the frown that previous thoughts of Kenton had brought to his face was absent now. Over the years, family members had tried to dig and figure out what had happened between him and Kenton. He had never revealed what had led to their estrangement, and he doubted that Kenton would either. Though he tried to keep from letting the tension between them spill over too much into family get-togethers. It wasn't as if he wouldn't stay in the same room as the man. He just didn't plan to have long talks and share confidences with Kenton the way they used to many years ago. That ship had sailed not long after high school.

"You plannin' to talk to Kenton this time around?" Dalton asked, a dark brow arched as he stared at Bennett.

"I always talk to Kenton," Bennett said without looking away from his younger brother's gaze. He refused to be intimidated by a teenager. "Just because we're not best friends doesn't mean we don't talk."

Dalton rolled his eyes dramatically—as only Dalton could. "Yeah, right."

"Dalton," their mom spoke in a cautionary tone. It was one that Bennett had heard many, many times throughout his life, but Dalton seemed to have more nerve than he—and most his siblings—had ever had.

"What?" Dalton asked indignantly. "I was just asking a question. What am I supposed to do? Google for the answer?"

Bennett fought the smile that threatened to overtake his face.

"Well, Google is your friend," Makayla pointed out while keeping her gaze on her plate.

"Sure, I'll get right on that." Dalton propped his elbows on the table and pretended as if he held a phone between his hands and was tapping on a screen—because they weren't allowed phones at the table. "What did Kenton do to tick Bennett off?" He paused. "Huh. Look at that." He held the invisible phone toward his mom who sat across the table from him. "No answer."

His mother sighed as she regarded her youngest son. "Dalton..."

Bennett knew he wasn't the only one fighting the urge to laugh. If nothing else, his brother was always good for a chuckle. The guy liked to entertain and be the center of attention. Lucky for him, being the baby of the family guaranteed that he usually was.

"Fine." Dalton glanced around the table and let out a long sigh. "I'll just ask Kenton."

Bennett did laugh then. The chances Kenton would spill the details were even less than Bennett doing it. Dalton could certainly try, but he was pretty sure that if Kenton was going to divulge any details, it wasn't going to be to the person who could spill every detail of his life over every possible social media platform. Yeah, that was so not going to happen.

"Ryan and Gabe have also confirmed that they will both be there. Although Gabe gave me a lecture on springing it on him with such short notice." Makayla shrugged. "I told him to just suck it up and be here." She grinned. "And he said he would be."

He knew that there were likely a lot of people who wondered about the dynamics of their rather large, blended family, but the relationships between all of them—well, with the exception of him and Kenton—had pretty much continued on in the same vein in which they had started. Makayla had been the drama queen who had made sure all the boys— between the two families there had been six boys and two girls—had done her bidding whenever she could. Things hadn't changed a whole lot, only now Ethan was also there to do her bidding. Although, from the look on his face, the man was happy to pledge himself in servitude to the queen.

Maybe it would give the rest of them a break.

"I'll have a list of things for you to do, Bennett, since you're the best man," Makayla said, as if reading his mind.

Or maybe not...

"Your wish is my command," Bennett muttered.

"And don't you forget it," Makayla replied.

"Oh, I wasn't saying that to you, sis. I was hoping that Ethan would pick up on the line he'll be saying over and over once he says *I do.*"

"Wait," Ethan said, holding up his hand. "I was supposed to wait until *after* we were married to start saying that?" His shoulders slumped as he sighed dramatically. "Someone could have told me."

"Sorry there, bud," Bennett said with a shake of his head. "I tried to warn you."

Makayla's head whipped in his direction. "You tried to warn him about what?"

"That you were a 'special woman' who needed to be loved and cherished." Bennett made sure she saw his air quotes.

Before he could pull back, she'd reached around Grace and thumped him on the shoulder. "Just you wait. One of these days, you'll date someone who actually wants to be around all of us and then we'll have a ball filling her in on all dirt about you."

Bennett accepted the jab about Ellie without complaint. "Is that a threat or a promise? I mean, if you're willing to tell her all about me, it sure will save on having to carry on conversations. You like to talk so much more than me."

Their mom propped her elbow on the table and dropped her head forward onto her fist. "Where did I go wrong?"

Even Grace joined in when they all laughed at the woeful tone of his mom's voice. It was moments like these when he didn't understand how Ryan, Gabe and yes, even Kenton, could choose to stay away from home so much. Granted, Ryan came home the most of the three, but even in his off-season, Kenton rarely made an appearance. Of course, that could be partly Bennett's fault. A pang of guilt went through him at that thought. Maybe he needed to make more of an effort to not be so distant when Kenton was around.

Maybe…

Chapter Eight

August

G RACE STARED AT THE VASE sitting on the desk in front of her. When she'd walked in earlier, it was the first thing she'd seen. A crystal vase with three roses. One was blue, one pink and the other white. There was a small envelope held in place by a long clear plastic florist pick. She reached out and pulled the white envelope free but hesitated a moment before opening it.

Over the weekend, she had finally announced her pregnancy. She'd told Makayla and Tami not long after taking the test, but she'd sworn them to secrecy. It had been a difficult choice to keep it a secret, but she had wanted to make it through at least the first trimester before telling others. Although if she'd thought she could have gotten away without telling anyone until the baby was born and she knew it was healthy, she would have. She lived in fear of miscarrying because then she'd have to survive more condolences. And in this particular instance, she would prefer to grieve in solitude if she suffered yet another loss.

But she'd made it, so with Makayla's help, she'd spread the news. As she'd thought, most, if not all, the people that heard reacted with how fortunate she was to still have a piece of Franklin. And she was, but it was also difficult going through the milestones of the pregnancy without him by her side. Especially since he had been the one most eager to have a baby.

With slow movements, Grace opened the envelope and slid the small card out.

Congratulations on the baby, Grace!
You'll make a terrific mom.
Bennett

She reached out to touch the soft petals of the flowers, thinking of all the ways Bennett had helped her over the past three months. Just like every member of his family, he'd been there for her whenever she'd needed it. Given the nature of their relationship, most of his help had come as her boss, giving her time off when she needed it. He'd been super understanding on the days when she just couldn't make it into work. He hadn't known about her pregnancy but had given her the time off regardless.

The morning sickness had continued to plague her, but thankfully it had become more predictable so that she was able to work her schedule around it. Combined with the grief, however, the tiredness had been more difficult to deal with. It had been fairly constant while the waves of grief had come at the most unexpected times. She was grateful that both the morning sickness and the tiredness had eased off most days now as the first trimester had ended even as the grief had continued.

Sometimes it completely overwhelmed her that she was going to be responsible for a baby all by herself. Oh, she knew that Makayla and her family would always be there to help, but at the end of the day, the baby would be her responsibility.

Her crazy hormonal emotions had remained consistent, however. Whether it was a particularly touching movie or a funny commercial, her emotions could swing without warning. Thankfully, the nightmares had become less frequent since she'd found out she was pregnant. She still had dreams that left her emotionally wrung out, but the horror-filled nightmares didn't plague her like they had in the early weeks following Franklin's death. She had no idea why they'd pretty much stopped, but she was grateful.

"Mom said she has the dresses out at the house," Makayla said as she appeared beside her desk. "Oh, those are beautiful." She leaned forward to take a sniff of the roses. "Who are they from?"

"Bennett," Grace said as she laid the card and envelope on her desk.

"Really?" Makayla's brows lifted as she straightened. "Well, that was…sweet of him."

Grace nodded because it really had been sweet of him to do that for her. Flowers themselves were always nice, but to have him pick them out in that way with a color for each gender and then a white one said that he took the time to place the order, hadn't just grabbed what was on hand.

Makayla settled her hip on the desk. "So, are you ready for the big move?"

"Sort of. I'm still not sure what to do with Franklin's stuff. I just can't bring myself to give it away."

"You should just rent a storage unit and put it away for now. Maybe you'll feel better able to deal with stuff at a later date. There's no reason you have to rush to give it away or anything like that. I don't think anyone expects that of you."

Grace considered Makayla's suggestion, and it felt like an option she could live with. She didn't necessarily want to move all Franklin's things with her, but she didn't want to get rid of them yet either. Storing them, for the time being, was probably the best idea.

After the wedding—which was in two weeks—there would be a major shuffle at the Callaghan apartment building. Ethan and Sierra—who were staying in the two-bedroom apartment across from Bennett's—were going to be moving into the three-bedroom apartment on the top floor with Makayla. Tami had decided to take the vacant one-bedroom on the main floor. That left Ethan and Sierra's place for Grace.

She hadn't been too keen on moving back into the apartment with Tami and Makayla again when Makayla had first suggested it, particularly with the wedding not too far in the future. But as her pregnancy progressed, the idea of being close to Makayla, Tami and the rest of the Callaghan-McFadden family had started to sound appealing. So when Ethan and Makayla had proposed the apartment shuffle, she had readily agreed. Once the couple returned from their honeymoon, they would begin to move everyone around. Tami had already started to move her stuff into the vacant one bedroom, but Grace's move would wait until after the wedding.

"I called one of the agents Franklin worked with and met with him about listing the condo. He said I should have no trouble getting it sold for the price I want."

"That's good. A relief I'm sure."

Grace nodded. "Everything okay for the wedding? No last-minute glitches on anything?"

"Nope. We're all good," Makayla said with a wide smile.

Grace was looking forward to her friend's wedding, though she felt a little awkward being matron of honor since Bennett was the best man. It was hard not to think about the feelings she'd once had, and the decision she'd made all those years ago to never get into a relationship with Bennett. She felt guilty at times, thinking about her old feelings for Bennett even as she grieved for Franklin. But the feelings she had for Bennett went back so much further than the ones she'd had for Franklin.

She had truly come to love Franklin, and the feelings she'd had for Bennett had definitely faded...but apparently, they'd never gone completely away. And now that she was finding herself in situations where Bennett was present a lot more, memories of those feelings had begun to surface. The problem was that she didn't want them. They would be the last thing she needed on top of everything else she was dealing with.

"Well, I guess someone beat me to it," Mitch announced as he strode toward them, his gaze on the vase of flowers on her desk. In his left hand, he held a bouquet of roses. "These are for you, Gracie."

With a smile, Grace stood and took the flowers from him, motioning for him to lean over the desk so she could press a kiss to his cheek. "Thank you, sweetie."

Mitch had a grin on his face as he straightened. "So, who beat me to the punch?"

"That would be Bennett," Makayla informed him.

With a sigh, Mitch crossed his arms. "That dude is so on top of everything, I can't imagine why he thinks he needs his own secretary."

Grace frowned as she turned to look at Makayla. "Bennett is getting a secretary?"

Makayla was also frowning…at Mitch. She turned back to Grace, a placating look on her face. She held out her hands as she said, "It's just something that's being discussed. After all, you'll need to train someone to take over for you while you're on maternity leave."

Grace hadn't thought about how that would work. She couldn't really envision—at that particular moment—taking the full maternity and parental leave she was legally entitled to, which could be almost a year. This job was important to her. She'd had it since she'd graduated from the University of Winnipeg with a fairly useless degree in English once she'd decided not to tack on the necessary courses in order to become a teacher. Steve Callaghan had offered her the job of receptionist at their company when Makayla had stepped into the role of office manager with her business administration degree. It had worked well for the past eight years, but what if they brought in someone to cover for her who they ended up liking better?

"Hey." Makayla nudged her shoulder. "It'll be fine."

Grace clutched the flowers as she sat back down, not feeling at all reassured. Usually, she wasn't insecure about things like that, but right then with so much uncertainty in her life, she didn't need it in her job as well. It had been the one place she'd felt safe, and that was why she'd decided to come back to work after Franklin's death. Now she didn't know what to think. What to feel.

"Seriously, sweetie," Makayla said as she rubbed her back. "You're always going to have a place here. You're irreplaceable."

She nodded, needing for Makayla to move out of her reassuring mode. If Makayla kept up with it, she was going to end up crying. Grace looked up and gave her friend a smile. "Of course I'm irreplaceable."

Makayla stared at her for a moment then smiled back. "Well, we'd better get Mitch's flowers into a vase. Can't have them wilting by the end of the day."

"Sorry, I didn't even think about bringing a vase," Mitch said as he rubbed the back of his neck.

"I think we have something in the lunchroom we can use," Grace said as she stood back up, the flowers in her hands.

Makayla went with her, and they were able to find something that would hold the flowers. Once she'd set them back at Grace's desk, Makayla headed back to her office leaving Grace alone with her thoughts.

She tried to work through her usual morning routines. Email. Phone calls. Opening mail. Sorting it. All the while, her stomach churned, but it wasn't from the pregnancy for a change.

Finally, she pushed back from her desk and headed down the hallway to Bennett's office. She wasn't sure why she was coming to him. Maybe because she thought—hoped—he'd be straight with her while Makayla would keep trying to protect her feelings.

As she stepped into his open doorway, Grace stood watching Bennett for a moment. He had abandoned his suit coat and just wore his light gray button-down shirt with the sleeves rolled to his elbows. He was on the phone and looking down at his desk where he was making notes as he talked. She had just decided to come back later...if she still felt the need to...when he reached out to hang up the phone and spotted her. He froze for a moment, his brows drawing down over his dark eyes.

"Can I talk to you for a minute?" Grace asked before her nerve completely deserted her.

Her words seemed to shake Bennett loose from whatever had caused him to freeze at her appearance. "Yes. Of course. Have a seat." He got to his feet as he gestured to the chair across from him, waiting until she'd sat down before settling back into his own chair. "What can I do for you?"

"First of all, thank you for the flowers. They're beautiful."

Bennett smiled, the corners of his eyes crinkling. "You're very welcome. And congratulations again."

"Thank you." Grace shifted, pressing her fisted hands into her lap. "Uh. Mitch mentioned that you're going to be hiring a secretary."

Bennett's expression smoothed out as he grabbed the pen he'd been using just a few minutes ago. "Yes. We have been discussing that. Since Denton Homes had that scandal about the quality of their work, we've ended up with a lot more inquiries and potential work. That means we're going to get busier because we're not going to let this opportunity pass us by. Getting someone else to help you out will make sure you're not overwhelmed."

"You don't think I can handle it?" Grace asked, well aware of the defensive tone in her voice but seeming unable to control it.

"That's not it at all, Grace," Bennett said as he sat forward, resting his forearms on his desk. "We had been discussing it already, but the news of your pregnancy has just reinforced the fact that it would be a good idea. This way, you'll have help as the pregnancy progresses in case you need to take time off. The job as receptionist is always yours, Grace, but you may find your priorities shifting as your due date gets closer. This way you can feel free to focus on other things because you know there's someone who can cover for you."

It all sounded so logical, so why did Grace feel like covering her face with her hands and crying? It felt like decisions were being made about her life without even consulting her. She hated feeling so out of control—both of her emotions and her life. From the moment Franklin had died, her life had changed without her permission. And now she had to deal with this.

Taking a deep breath, Grace tried to gather her scattered emotions, so she didn't melt down in front of Bennett. "Okay. Thank you for your clarification."

Grace started to get to her feet, eager to escape Bennett's office as she questioned the emotions that had driven her to come there in the first place.

"Grace, wait a minute," Bennett said, getting to his feet.

She sank back into the chair, her gaze on her hands.

"Are you okay?"

Grace clasped her hands tightly together in her lap, hating herself for letting her emotions get the better of her. They were so near the surface all the time now, but she couldn't let them dictate her actions like this. She took a deep breath, glancing over when there was movement beside her chair. Bennett had dropped to his haunches beside her, one hand on the back of the chair, the other covered hers. She looked down at their hands then up at his face, meeting his concerned dark gaze.

When she blinked, the tears that had been pricking at the back of her eyes spilled over. Grace tried to get to her feet, but Bennett tightened his grip on her hands.

"What's wrong, Gracie?" His voice was low and heavy with concern. "Tell me what I can do to make this better."

She shook her head, unable to speak. Then, without warning, Bennett slipped his arm around her shoulders and pulled her close, her head coming to rest on his shoulder. Grace closed her eyes and pressed her forehead against his neck and let the tears flow. Although *let* might be an inaccurate description. She had no control over her emotions, and she didn't have the strength right then to fight them.

Chapter Nine

ENNETT REMEMBERED THAT one of the websites he'd visited after hearing news of Grace's pregnancy had said that an expecting woman's emotions could be all over the map. It was just such a shock to see her meltdown like this, especially in his presence. Even in the time since Franklin's death, he could count on one hand the number of times he'd seen her cry. And on two hands the numbers of times in total he'd seen her cry since they'd first met. Which was why it was a bit unnerving to have her crying in his arms.

It wasn't that Bennett thought she hadn't cried at all outside of those times he'd seen her, but it appeared that for the most part, she didn't feel comfortable letting him see her reduced to tears. That thought would have hurt him immensely as a teen, but now, Bennett knew that experiences could dictate actions in a way others might not understand. For sure he hadn't understood Grace's actions when everything had happened—or hadn't happened, as it were—between them all those years ago, but over time, he'd just stopped trying to figure it all out. It was less painful that way.

So while he understood that hormones might be fueling the current emotional meltdown, Bennett still wasn't sure what to do with the weeping woman he held. He'd meant to give her a hug, thinking then she'd pull herself together and move on with her day. Now he had to figure out how to give Grace what she needed while protecting himself. He'd accepted that the feelings he'd had for Grace were still present in his heart, but he'd been working to figure out the balance between being a supportive friend while not getting too emotionally involved.

"Bennett, have you seen…." Makayla's voice trailed off as Bennett looked up to see his sister standing in his doorway. "Grace? What's going on?"

Wasn't *that* the question of the century? He felt Grace take a shuddering breath before she began to pull away. Bennett made no effort to stop her movement, relieved that his sister was stepping in to help. He had absolutely no clue what to do with a weeping, pregnant woman. No clue.

"Are you okay, sweetie?" Makayla asked as she dropped to her knees beside Grace. "Is this about us hiring someone?"

Bennett watched as Grace brushed her fingertips over her damp cheeks. She looked over at Makayla. "Who knows?" Her shoulders slumped. "I guess that's part of it. I just…don't want to lose this job."

"You're not losing anything, Gracie," Makayla said. "But you have to admit that things are changing. You're going to have a baby who needs you, and this job will not be as important. It will always be here for you, but we need to prepare for the times when you can't be at the office. Whoever we hire won't be there to replace you but to assist you. And you'll be back at the apartment block with the rest of us. You're not losing anything, sweetie. Change may be coming, but we're right here with you."

Bennett had never been so grateful for his sister. Makayla was often a pain in the neck, but right then, she had all the right words for Grace. Perhaps they should have included Grace in more of their discussions about hiring an assistant for her. He realized now that they had caused her even more hurt by excluding her.

Grace nodded as she took a deep breath. "I'm sorry."

"Nothing to be sorry for," Bennett said as he got to his feet. "I realize now that we could have handled this all a little better."

She glanced at him, meeting his gaze for a couple of seconds. "Thank you for thinking of me."

Always.

That immediate thought took Bennett off-guard. He turned and walked behind his desk, not wanting to think too much about that. He sat down, watching as Makayla took the seat beside Grace.

"Why don't we have a meeting tomorrow," Bennett suggested. "We can discuss how to make this all work. Your input is important, Grace, so don't be afraid to give your thoughts. Okay?"

"Okay," Grace said with a nod. "I'll try to do it all without crying."

Bennett glanced back and forth between the ladies not sure if he should laugh or not. Relief flooded him as Makayla started to laugh and Grace joined in. He wasn't sure he was equipped to handle a woman who had raging pregnancy hormones. From tears to laughter in minutes. It was enough to give him whiplash. He could only imagine what it would be like when Makayla got pregnant. She had enough mood swings as it was.

"So we're good?" Bennett asked, just wanting to make sure that there was nothing else that might pop up without notice.

"We're good," Grace said, her usual calm, professional demeanor falling into place. "I just need to fix my makeup."

"Well, let's go," Makayla said. "I think Bennett is getting ready to have a meltdown of his own, having to deal with us."

Bennett didn't bother to deny the comment since it was fairly close to the truth. He was going to need a guys' night out after this. How did husbands deal with pregnant wives for a full nine months? Living with them, even, not just spending a few hours with them at work. It was definitely a mystery to him, but thankfully not one he would have to be solving since that wasn't his role in Grace's life.

"ARE YOU SURE THAT YOU should be doing this?" Bennett asked as he followed Grace into the amusement center where they had reserved the laser tag room for a joint bachelor/bachelorette party for Ethan and Makayla.

She stopped and turned around to look at him. "Why? Because I'm pregnant?"

"Well," Bennett began, uncertain if he should continue given the look on her face. The arched brow and questioning expression made him scramble to find another excuse since it appeared the pregnancy one wasn't going to fly with the expectant woman.

"I'm fine, Bennett. It might be different if I was nine months along or if I was playing against strangers, but I can still move relatively easily, and I trust everyone to not run me over." She turned back to look around the large entryway of the amusement center. "Let's find the guy I've been emailing about all this."

Bennett followed Grace as she walked toward the large front desk. When she'd come up with the idea of doing a laser tag party at the amusement center, Bennett had had his reservations—and they'd all centered around whether it was a good idea for Grace. He had to accept the fact that she knew what was good for her and wouldn't do anything that would jeopardize the baby.

It had been a busy few days since Grace's meltdown in his office. Now they were in the final countdown to the wedding which would be on Friday night at the cabin out at the lake. Ryan, Kenton, and Gabe had all arrived the day before and would be joining the rest of the people that had been invited to the laser tag party. Grace had wanted to be there early to make sure everything was in order once everyone else arrived.

"Everything is ready for you," the young man behind the desk assured her. "We also have the room set up as you requested."

"Thank you so much. May I put some things in the room?" Grace lifted the bag she carried. "We brought a few decorations and other things."

"Yep. Just follow me."

Bennett trailed behind Grace and the young man, his thoughts all over the place. Ever since Kenton had arrived a couple of days earlier, he'd fought to be civil and not let the feelings from the past spill into the space he kept between the two of them. He'd resolved to not let anything overshadow Ethan and Makayla's wedding.

"Can you help me with this stuff?" Grace asked when the man had left them alone in the room.

"Sure. What have you got?"

She came to stand next to him and fished through the bag she held. "Plates."

Bennett took the plastic wrapped paper plates and looked at them. They were plain, but in the burgundy color Makayla had chosen for her wedding. He worked the plastic off them. "Did you want me to set them on the table or put them around the table at the seats?"

"We'll just put them at the end of the table and then put the pizza and chips in the center. Erin is bringing a bunch of cupcakes."

"Hopefully it's a big bunch," Bennett said as he set the plates onto the table. "I can never eat just one."

"Well, you can have my share," Grace offered then handed him a pack of napkins. "This baby has decided it doesn't like sweets this week. Can you believe that?"

Bennett turned away to hide his smile. Grace sounded so appalled at the idea, which wasn't surprising given that she usually loved anything sweet. "I'll be happy to eat your cupcakes in addition to mine. Does what the baby likes change frequently?"

Grace dropped down into a chair as she continued to pull stuff out of the bag. "Sometimes it's daily. Sometimes it's weekly."

"Any pickles and ice cream cravings?"

"Not yet, but I made sure to pick up a jar of pickles and some ice cream to have on hand just in case the craving hits in the middle of the night. I can't be out chasing down craving ingredients at one in the morning."

Bennett paused in ripping the plastic off the cups she'd handed him. Her words were a stark reminder that she was doing this on her own. Other pregnant women had husbands who would go out to get them what they craved. Grace didn't.

"Well, you know that once you've moved back into the building, Tami, Makayla or I will be more than happy to do a craving run for you. Just give one of us a call."

Grace stopped her rummaging and sat with her hands resting on the bag as she looked at Bennett, her face serious. "Why? That's not any of your responsibility."

"It's not about responsibility. It's about friendship."

"I get that about Tami and Makayla, but what about you?"

Bennett stared at Grace for a moment, trying to decipher her words. Did she not consider him a friend? While they certainly hadn't been close, and for awhile he had kind of avoided her because of the hurt she'd inflicted on him years ago. However, in recent years, he'd thought that they had come to a place of friendship—not as best friends, for sure—but friends nonetheless. That she didn't feel the same hurt him more than he'd thought possible.

Without responding, Bennett returned his attention to the cups. It felt like his world had shifted just a bit. He really hadn't dwelled too much on the roles they played in each other's lives, especially since she'd married Franklin, but if his reaction to her words proved anything, it was that he'd at least assumed they were friends.

"Bennett—"

"Is this where the party's at?" Gabe's booming voice cut Grace off, which was just fine with Bennett. He had a feeling that he wouldn't want to hear anything more that Grace had to say about their non-existent friendship.

He glanced over at his brother and spotted Kenton standing behind Gabe. Kenton was frowning, his gaze bouncing between Grace and Bennett. "Uh, Gabe…"

Bennett gave Kenton a subtle shake of his head and set down the pile of cups he'd finally freed from the plastic and picked up the next set. He resisted the urge to take his frustration out on the innocent party ware.

"How are you, Gracie Lou?" Gabe asked as he stooped to give her a hug. "I hear congratulations are in order."

Grace reached up with one hand to grasp Gabe's shoulder. "Thanks, sweetie. It's good to see you again."

"Wouldn't miss this wedding for the world." Gabe dropped down onto a chair next to her. "Are we eating before laser tagging?"

"No. I just wanted to get everything set up beforehand. We'll be coming back here when we're done."

"What's with the joint party, dude?" Gabe asked as he got back to his feet. He slapped Bennett on the shoulder.

"This was what Ethan and Makayla wanted." Bennett glanced at Gabe and shrugged. "Since it's their wedding, we do what they say."

A few more of the guests drifted in before Ethan and Makayla showed up. Bennett was happy to see James Dawson walk in with his wife, Erin. And it had nothing—well, almost nothing—to do with the fact that they were carrying bakery boxes filled with cupcakes.

"How are you doing?" James asked once he'd set his boxes down on the table. "Keeping busy?"

Bennett had finally finished up with the party ware, so he stepped away from the table with James. "You know it. It's been a bit crazy. We've been picking up business because of the issues Denton Homes had." He crossed his arms, watching as his younger sister, Sammi, and Tami helped Grace finish setting up the table. "We've been doing interviews this week to get a little more help on the admin side as well as some guys for construction."

"We heard that Grace was pregnant."

Bennett nodded. "It was a surprise for all of us. Her most of all, I'm sure."

He was glad for the conversation with James and a few of the other men that showed up. They usually had more socialization, but over the past month, he'd been so tied up with work, they hadn't had much time with each other. Plus, with it being summer, quite a few people had been on vacation. James and Erin had gone to Scotland for three weeks with Erin's foster sister, Noella and her Scottish husband, Finn. Even their small Bible study group had been on hiatus for the summer. It felt good to be back together again, even if they were going to be shooting at each other.

It wasn't long before everyone who'd been invited was in the small room. One of the employees came in to explain how the laser tag would work and soon they were suiting up and taking possession of their weapons. They had planned to have two teams, but it couldn't be girls against guys since their family and friends group tended to be testosterone heavy. Instead, they just counted off and split up.

As they filed into the laser tag area, Bennett put aside the incident with Grace and focused on having some fun with his closest friends and family. He and Kenton ended up on the same team, which surprisingly, didn't bother him as much as it might have.

Chapter Ten

*E*VERYONE WAS IN HIGH SPIRITS as they made their way back to the room where the food and cupcakes waited. There were six extra large pizzas in the middle of the table, and it didn't take the group long after grace was said to make a significant dent in them.

Grace stood for a moment staring down at the pizzas, trying to figure out which one the baby would tolerate the best.

Ham and pineapple? *No.*

Veggies? *Nope.*

Meat Lovers? *Definitely not.*

Plain cheese it is.

Grace reached for a slice and put it on her plate. Truthfully, she wasn't very hungry at all, but it had nothing to do with the baby. She just hadn't been able to get her conversation with Bennett out of her head. Her comment had been a knee-jerk reaction to keep Bennett at a distance. When he'd mentioned being willing to do midnight runs for her cravings, she'd had a sudden moment of imagining what that might be like. That had taken her thoughts to a place where she wasn't comfortable going.

Not yet.

Not ever.

Moving around the table, Grace found an empty seat between Sierra and Mitch. She was happy to be able to sit down. She was already starting to feel weird twinges in parts of her body. According to the pregnancy books she'd been reading, it was only going to get worse. Six more months and then everything would once again change for her future. Her job wasn't going to be hers for much longer. And then what?

"Earth to Gracie. Earth to Gracie."

Gracie glanced over at Mitch. "Hey, sweetie. What's up?"

"I think that's my question for you," he said as he peered down at her plate. "I thought you were supposed to be eating for two. It seems like you're barely eating for one."

"Baby isn't feeling it for pizza today." Grace stared down at her slice of pizza seeing only how the grease sat in puddles on the cheese's surface. She swallowed hard, wondering if she should have just stuck to the potato chips someone had brought. Her morning sickness might not be as gone as she'd hoped. Or maybe now she had just moved on to food aversions. Ever changing food aversions. At this rate, she wouldn't have to worry about having to lose weight after the baby was born.

"What does baby feel like most days?" Mitch asked as he reached over and took the pizza from in front of her. Apparently, he wasn't taking any chances that her lack of appetite might lead to an upset stomach or worse. He knew all about her pregnancy induced vomiting.

Grace picked up her glass and took a sip of water. And then another. "Water?"

"You're gonna need more than that. You need to have a talk with that child of yours. Tell her that she needs to let you eat or else."

"First of all, she?"

"Well, yeah, I happen to think it's a girl," Mitch said with a shrug.

"And second...or else?"

"That's what Mom always used to say when we were acting up. You better do this or else."

"Ah... I'll make sure to have a conversation with...her." Until that moment, Grace hadn't thought too much about whether she'd be having a girl or boy, but Mitch's comment brought the thought of her baby's gender to the forefront of her mind.

As Mitch turned to talk to whoever was on the other side, Grace let her gaze search the room until it landed on Bennett. He stood talking to James, and if someone hadn't known better, they might have taken them for brothers. Both were tall with dark hair and strong features. They were even dressed similarly in jeans and polo shirts.

Working with Bennett as best man and her as matron of honor had been a challenge for Grace. Every day she lived with the knowledge that she'd hurt him and that—as she'd proven again earlier—she just kept hurting him. She wondered if it would make any difference if he knew that she hurt too.

She looked over to where Kenton sat with two family friends—Forrest on one side and Tennyson on the other. Inadvertently, she'd dragged him into things she never should have, and she was pretty sure that what had transpired all those years ago between the three of them was the reason that Bennett and Kenton were estranged.

It was just more of the guilt she carried. Would Makayla still be her friend if she knew what she'd done to Bennett? And how she'd used Kenton?

Tension and anxiety churned within her, and Grace tried to keep her breaths even and steady. All of the sudden, it felt like everything that had been even slightly worrying her pressed down on her. Everything going on with Bennett and Kenton. The new person starting work at the company on Monday. Makayla's wedding. The move. The pregnancy.

Life.

She was not prone to panic attacks. In fact, she had never had one. But that didn't mean she didn't recognize what was happening to her. However, the last thing she wanted was to have a panic attack at what was supposed to be a fun event for her friends.

Thankfully, conversations continued on around her which gave her the chance to slowly get her panic under control. One day at a time. That's all she could do.

"Chips?"

Grace stared at the bag Mitch held out to her, running the idea of chips by her finicky stomach. Deciding it was worth the risk to get something into her system, she took the bag and dumped a handful onto her plate. "Thanks."

Finally able to push aside her anxieties, Grace tuned into the conversations going on around her. Sierra was talking with Danica and Dalton about their upcoming school year. They had just a few weeks remaining until classes started up again. Mitch was joking with Tami about her continuing relationship with Keenan who, once again, hadn't been able to join them because he was playing an out of town game. Grace was happy to see Tami open to having a relationship once again. She'd been turned off dating after a not-so-great relationship while she'd been in university and had continued to keep men at arm's length through university and even after she'd started working.

When they'd been seniors in high school, before Grace's grandmother had died, the three of them had come up with a wedding plan. Tami was going to be maid of honor for Grace, Grace was to be maid of honor for Makayla, and then Makayla was to fulfill that role for Tami. After Tami had sworn off relationships, she had offered to give up her role in Grace's wedding so that Makayla could be maid of honor for Grace. Makayla had declined and insisted that Tami still be Grace's maid of honor. Their wedding pact was still in place which was how she'd ended up with her role in Makayla's wedding.

"Did you and Bennett have a hard time coming up with a plan for this?" Mitch asked.

Grace glanced over to where Bennett still stood. "No. I came up with a few different ideas to present to him and let him make the final decision. I had paintball, laser tag, bowling or roller skating."

"Roller skating?" Mitch asked with an arched brow.

"Well, I figured since you all ice skate so well, roller skating would be a breeze."

"Knowing our luck, one or more of us would have ended up with broken bones. Just a few days before the wedding." Mitch grinned. "I think Makayla would have killed you."

"At least I wouldn't have been one of them since you wouldn't catch me on skates at the moment. Bennett wanted something that everyone could do even though he still wasn't convinced that laser tag was safe for me."

"Over-protective Bennett in action once again," Mitch commented as he dumped some chips on his plate. "I'm surprised the guy doesn't have a head of gray hair courtesy of all the worrying he does about us younger sibs."

Grace picked up a chip and nibbled on it. That one trait was what had attracted Grace to Bennett so long ago. She'd met him for the first time when he'd come to pick Makayla up from school one day early in their junior year. Bennett and Makayla had been arguing over Makayla's plan to hang out with Tami, Grace, and a few other girls and guys from their class. She'd wanted him to come back an hour later, but he'd been certain that their mom and dad wouldn't approve since they didn't know the other kids.

The concern on Bennett's face, even as he had finally relented, had struck a chord with Grace. Though her grandmother certainly cared about her, she hadn't been overly concerned about who her friends might be. Before Bennett had shown up, Grace had called her grandmother to let her know she was hanging out with friends, and she'd just told Grace to let her know when she was on her way home. She knew it wasn't that her grandmother didn't care, it just seemed that the older woman had raised a teenager in a different time and perhaps didn't understand how things were different now from when Grace's mom had been a teenager.

So seeing Bennett's obvious care for his sister, Grace had found herself wanting that for herself. But Bennett had had a girlfriend at the time, so Grace hadn't even been on his radar as his sister's friend. He'd asked her out on a date finally, and she had accepted, but before they'd had a chance to go out, her grandmother had died unexpectedly. Her grandmother's death had brought with it a realization that whoever she loved, died. Not wanting to take a chance with Bennett's life, Grace had told him she couldn't go out on their date after all.

And then she'd put the nail in her own coffin by asking Kenton to be her date for her graduation. He'd been offseason with his first NHL team and had said yes without hesitation. Grace knew that her emotions would never be invested in Kenton the way they were with Bennett. If she'd have let him, Bennett could have become the most important person in her life. She wasn't sure she could have survived losing him. So instead of taking that chance, she made the decision to exist on the edge of his life.

Maybe people would have thought she was crazy if she'd voiced how she felt, but she didn't really care. Most likely, they hadn't lost their whole family either. Everyone they loved. If they had, maybe she'd be willing to listen to them, but if not, then they had no right telling her that her fear of losing more people in her life was invalid or crazy.

"How about we all head out to Mom and Dad's?" Bennett suggested. "Dad said he'd start up a fire in the pit and we can roast marshmallows for s'mores."

"Well, you don't have to ask me twice," Forrest exclaimed as he got up from the table.

It seemed that the others shared his sentiments because soon all the stuff in the room was packed up and the garbage was cleared away. As everyone climbed into their cars and began to head out of the parking lot, Grace sat in hers, waiting. She stared down at her phone, debating if she felt up to going or not. There was no doubt that she was tired from the day, but she couldn't decide if she was too tired or if she could still go and enjoy herself.

A knock on her window made her jump. She looked over to see Bennett, bent down next to her door. After a brief hesitation, she started her car and then lowered the window.

"Are you planning to come out to the house?" he asked, his brow concerned.

"Thinking about it. I'm feeling kind of tired."

"I think Makayla would worry if you didn't. We'll make sure you have the most comfortable chair, and you won't have to do anything. Mitch or Gabe would even roast all the marshmallows you want."

Grace looked into his serious dark blue eyes. She still wasn't sure what to do, but she knew that he was right. Makayla would worry if everyone else showed up, but she didn't. Especially since if she went home, she wouldn't be close enough for Makayla to check up on her after their time out at the house.

"Okay. I'll come for a little while," Grace said with a nod. "But I probably won't stay too long."

"Sounds good." Bennett tapped the edge of the window before straightening. "See you in a bit."

Grace watched in her mirrors as he walked to where his car was parked. She sighed as she put her car into reverse and slowly backed out. Was there anything Bennett could ask her to do that she'd refuse?

BENNETT FOLLOWED GRACE'S CAR through the traffic heading north out of the city. He hoped that she really did feel up to spending some time at his folks' place. Though he hadn't meant to guilt her into going, that's probably how it had come across. He just hadn't liked the idea of her going back to her condo and being by herself while the rest of them were together. It was important for her to know that they were all there for her.

His phone rang as he was driving, and he tapped the screen to accept the call through the Bluetooth. "Hello!"

"Hi, sweetheart." His mom's voice filled the cab of the truck. "Are you on your way out?"

"Yep. Just a little bit behind the rest of the gang."

"Good. I'll have your dad get the fire going." She paused. "Is Gracie coming out too?"

"I don't think she was planning to, but I kind of talked her into coming for a little while. Make sure that people leave a comfortable seat for her. I promised her that."

"No worries. I'll make sure that they leave her a good spot," his mom promised before ending the call.

The parking area in front of the house was pretty full, so Bennett had to double park behind Mitch's vehicle. Grace had already parked behind Ethan's truck but hadn't gotten out of her car yet. Bennett hoped that she was feeling okay. It was so hard for him to know anymore if her behavior at any given time was related to Franklin's death or the pregnancy or just how she was going to be from now on. Even though he hadn't been that close to her, he could see the differences in her now. He hoped, for the sake of the baby, that she would find the joy with which she used to live her life once again.

Even though she'd hurt him earlier with her revelation that she didn't really even view him as a friend, Bennett couldn't help but worry about her. As he rounded the bed of the truck, he spotted her climbing out of her car.

"Did everyone end up coming out here?" Grace asked as they headed for the steps leading to the porch.

"Looks like it." Bennett motioned her away from the front door. "Mom said Dad was starting a fire in the pit, so why don't we just head on around to the back?"

They walked together along the wraparound porch and found the rest of the group in the large back yard. Bennett could smell the smoke and with the slight chill in the air, he knew it would feel good to sit around the fire.

Grace moved away from him to where Makayla stood with Tami and some of the other women. Bennett watched her go before turning to find Kenton watching him. Their gazes met for a moment before Kenton looked over at Grace. Bennett felt the slow burn of anger that he always had when he was around Kenton briefly flare to life. He pushed it down, though, because he was doing his best to keep from letting his feelings about Kenton color this special time for his sister and Ethan.

"Are we gonna sing around the fire?"

Bennett turned to see Dalton standing beside him, his guitar clutched in his hands. The boy was all about music and art and all things creative, so it didn't surprise him that Dalton would want them to sing. Dalton flicked his head to swing his long bangs out of his eyes, a relatively futile effort since his hair always slid right back to cover part of his face. The one bright blue eye that Bennett could see was peering up at him in expectation.

Bennett slid an arm around his narrow shoulders and gave him a quick hug. "I think we could probably sing a few songs."

"Thanks, Ben!" Dalton darted off toward the pit where their dad stood with Mitch and Gabe building up the fire.

"I've got the s'mores' fixins," his mom said as she moved through the group with a large tray in her hands. "But it looks like it might be a bit before the fire's ready for the marshmallows."

As if drawn by a Pied Piper, people followed her toward the fire and the chairs set up around it. Bennett considered making sure that Grace got the best seat there but held back. That wasn't his responsibility. She could take care of herself, and something told him that any effort on his part to aid her would be frowned upon.

Bennett stood behind the circle of chairs, hands on his hips as he stared at the flames. Life was going to change...even as it stayed the same. With Ethan and Makayla getting married and Grace having a baby, life was going to be different. The business was expanding, even with his dad having retired. Makayla was usually the one that resisted change, but Bennett found that he was not really looking forward to those changes. Maybe it was because the changes weren't actually happening to him. Yes, he'd gotten a new position when his dad had retired, but he'd already been doing a lot of the work in preparation for that change.

Now that he and Ellie had broken up, he didn't even have the prospect of a serious relationship. Same job. Same apartment. Same relationship status. Single... And with things getting busier at work, he wouldn't have the time or energy to devote to a relationship. There was no one that he currently knew that he was interested in pursuing a relationship with, and the prospect of having to get to know someone from scratch just seemed to require too much effort.

Bennett heard Dalton begin to quietly strum his guitar. The teen sat on a stool back a bit from the fire, the guitar on his knee. Bennett still wasn't sure where Dalton had gotten his musical talent and creative gene from. Aside from singing, the rest of them had no interest or ability in playing an instrument. When someone called out a title, Dalton lifted his head and immediately began to play the song.

Though there were seats in the circle, Bennett chose to settle on the picnic table a short distance away. He sang along with the group but found that right then, his heart wasn't really engaging with the music. It was a frustrating feeling for him because it was so out of the ordinary. Normally he was focused and strong and able to handle everything, but the upcoming changes were affecting him in a way he hadn't anticipated. Maybe he was more like Makayla than he'd ever thought.

"What are you doing back here, sweetheart?" His mom's arm linked with his and she pressed her head against his shoulder. They were back far enough that she could speak to him without disrupting the song. "Everything okay?"

Chapter Eleven

ENNETT COVERED HIS MOM'S HAND with his as he kept his gaze on the fire. There wasn't a day that went by that he wasn't grateful for his mom and her decision to stay strong even when she'd been left a single mom. And then Steve had come into their lives and been the male role model that they had needed. All of them. Even Sammi and Makayla. They'd needed a good example of how a man should treat a woman. By the time he'd passed away, their own father had been a pretty poor example of that.

"Everything's fine, Mama." Because really, in the big picture, it was. He had a family who loved him, a job he enjoyed and a roof over his head every night when he went to bed. He had no reason to be down or to complain about anything. He needed to remember that when he was tempted to feel discouraged or frustrated with certain areas of his life.

Knowing that he was causing his mom unnecessary worry, Bennett began to sing along a bit more enthusiastically with the rest of the group. These were moments he should be treasuring. His family was all together—yes, even with Kenton there, he should be treasuring it. His sister was getting ready to marry the man she loved, and their family was going to expand. These were good things. And even though Franklin was gone, he lived on in the child Grace carried. That too was a good thing.

As the song ended, Bennett took a deep breath then let it out, pushing aside his negative thoughts and feelings. Now was not the time or the place for any of that.

Though he didn't move any closer to the circle, he joined in with the singing as Dalton moved them from song to song, sometimes responding to a request from someone in the group. When the fire had finally died down to hot coals, Bennett and his dad began putting marshmallows on sticks while his mom and Sammi got the chocolate and graham crackers ready.

Even though it hadn't been that long ago since they'd eaten Erin's cupcakes, people still happily indulged in more food. Grace included.

"Guess the baby was in the mood for s'mores, eh?" Mitch said as Bennett moved past where Mitch and Grace sat to hand Sierra another stick with a marshmallow on it.

"Yeah. Go figure. Sticky, chocolatey mess is baby's fave at the moment." Grace held out her s'more toward Mitch who lifted his in response. "To chocolate!"

Bennett wondered what it must be like having moods and food cravings dictated by someone you hadn't even met yet. If a pregnancy could do this to someone as upbeat as Grace normally was, he couldn't imagine what it would do to someone already naturally moody like Makayla. He hoped that Ethan knew what he was in for. At the moment, however, it seemed that the sun rose and set on Makayla as far as Ethan was concerned. Maybe that admiring attitude would carry them through the first pregnancy.

All pregnancy thoughts aside, Bennett was just glad that Grace seemed to be enjoying herself in spite of him basically guilting her into coming. It helped him feel a bit better about it all. If she hadn't been enjoying herself, he would have felt badly. Of course, he'd had little to do with her enjoyment, but that was beside the point when it came right down to it.

"You ready to play at being the best man at the wedding?"

Surprised to hear Kenton's voice so close to him, Bennett glanced over his shoulder from where he'd been putting more marshmallows on sticks. "No playing *at* it, man. I'm definitely going to be the best man there."

"And so humble too," Kenton remarked as he leaned a hip against the picnic table where Bennett was working.

"I learned humility from watching you," Bennett informed him.

"When you're as talented and good looking as me, humility is highly overrated."

Bennett straightened and turned to look at Kenton, not entirely sure the man was joking. They didn't know each other well enough anymore for him to know for sure. And the way the guy always had one model girlfriend after another, it appeared that they, at least, thought he was attractive. Or maybe it was his money. He was just lucky he'd managed to avoid getting the "hockey smile." So far.

"If all else fails, you could buy yourself a good dose of humility." Bennett turned back to the marshmallows. "Did you have a s'mores or does your trainer forbid you from enjoying the simple pleasures in life?"

"I'm off-season—in case you've forgotten the hockey schedule— so I can indulge. Maybe it's *your* trainer that should be keeping *you* from indulging."

"You're making the assumption I *have* a trainer. And I've been too busy loading up sticks with marshmallows to do one for myself."

"Always the martyr, Ben. No wonder you're still single. Who could compete with that?"

Bennett hoped the darkness and the fact that he had his profile to Kenton hid his frown. "Certainly not you."

"Boys!"

Though the sharp tone of his mother's voice snapped him back to where he and Kenton were actually having words, he didn't look in her direction. He finished the last stick before turning around. "Who needs another marshmallow?"

Without meeting anyone's gaze—not hard to do when it was basically dark—he made his way around the circle, handing out the sticks to anyone who wanted one and collecting the ones they were done with. "Do I need to make some more?"

"Can I make one for you, Ben?" Dalton asked when he appeared at his elbow. "I promise not to burn it."

Hearing the earnest tone of Dalton's voice, Bennett said, "Sure thing, buddy. Let's get a stick."

Dalton grabbed onto his arm as they headed for the picnic table. Bennett had a strange feeling that his younger brother was taking a side in what he saw as a conflict between him and Kenton. He had specifically avoided talking about what had initially caused the strife between them and usually went out of his way to not bring it up when they'd been together over the years, but since Kenton had initiated the conversation, Bennett wasn't going to just let him take his jabs. Unfortunately, everyone gathered there had had a front seat to their verbal sparring match.

He didn't want to create division in the family, especially with a wedding in the offing. Part of him was angry at Kenton for choosing this night to fan the flames of their conflict. The guy could have just left things alone like they had done every other time they'd been in the same vicinity as each other. Of course, Bennett realized, he could have chosen to react differently. He'd also fanned the flames, and no doubt made the situation uncomfortable for the people who had heard them.

"Here you go," Bennett said as he handed Dalton a stick. "Remember. Golden brown. No burning."

"You betcha." Dalton took the stick and headed over to sit next to Sammi.

Kenton had taken a seat beside Gabe and Mitch which also meant he was sitting near Grace. When Bennett looked at her, however, he found that she was watching him. He wasn't sure if she'd ever realized what had triggered the distance between him and Kenton.

After being nearly inseparable once their parents had married, cliché as it was, conflict over a girl had driven them apart. He had no idea what it would take to get them back to being the best friends they'd once been. If that was even possible because that type of closeness required trust, and that was something he just didn't have for Kenton anymore.

"Here you go." Dalton returned with the marshmallow done as Bennett had requested.

His mom appeared with two graham crackers and a piece of chocolate. Dalton put the marshmallow into place. When his mom handed the s'more to Bennett, she reached out to place a hand on the back of his neck to pull him down to her level. "We will be having a conversation about what just went down with you and Kenton. I understand that he started it, but I expected better of you."

Though she placed a kiss on his cheek before releasing him, Bennett felt the burn of disappointing his mom like acid in his stomach. And she was right. While Kenton appeared to have left behind the faith they'd been raised with, Bennett hadn't, and he should have known better than to spar with Kenton verbally like that.

He would be glad to see the end of this day.

Once it appeared that everyone had had their fill of s'mores, Bennett helped his mom put everything back on the tray and carried it into the kitchen for her. His dad had added a few more logs to the fire, causing the flames to leap back up again, and Dalton was once again strumming on his guitar. All of that fell behind him as Bennett walked into the kitchen.

"Do you want to tell me what that was all about with Kenton?" his mom asked as she unloaded the tray.

"I'm not sure what prompted him to say what he did tonight." Bennett crossed his arms as he leaned back against the counter. "We hadn't spoken earlier."

"Maybe that's part of the problem, sweetheart. You two aren't talking. At all."

Bennett could hardly argue with her there, but he still sighed. "True, Mom, and I doubt that's going to change anytime soon."

"I wish I understood. You used to be best friends."

"He took something I told him—something I hadn't told anyone else—and he betrayed that confidence. A best friend wouldn't have done that."

"That's a long time to hold a grudge. It will continue to eat at you."

"It really only comes to mind when we're actually in the same city. And since that doesn't happen very often, I really don't think about it that much."

"Maybe if you got this sorted out between the two of you, Kenton would come home more frequently."

Bennett didn't like the implication, but yet again, he could hardly argue with it. He had prided himself on being the responsible one in the family. The one that would take care of everyone else—both friends and family. Instead, today, he'd seemed to have failed on several fronts. "I'm sorry all this has come out now. I'll try to make sure it doesn't overshadow what's going to happen this week."

His mom sighed. "I just want you all to be happy and get along."

"I'm sorry, Mom, but that's not gonna happen tonight. I think it's best that Kenton and I keep our distance, and since he's staying here, I'll be the one to leave." Bennett straightened then gave his mom a kiss. "I'm gonna head out."

His mom frowned. "I hate to see you go. Are you going to be okay?"

"I'm fine, Mom. I just don't want to escalate things tonight." He fished his keys out of his pocket. "I'll see you at church tomorrow."

"Okay, sweetheart. Love you."

"Love you too." Bennett gave her a reassuring smile before heading to the front of the house and then out into the cool August night. Though he should probably have said goodnight to the group, he was actually relieved to just be leaving. Tomorrow would be another day. One where he'd hopefully have his spirit re-energized and have the ability to put this day behind him.

GRACE KEPT GLANCING at the back door of the house. She'd watched the interaction between Kenton and Bennett with a sense of dread. It was the first time since their falling out that she'd seen them talking to each other. And she wished that she hadn't witnessed it. No doubt she wasn't the only one who felt that way. It hadn't been a pleasant interaction. Obviously not for them and certainly not for those gathered around the fire as a captive audience.

When Emily returned to the back yard a short time later, she was alone. The older woman made her way to her husband's side, leaning against him as his arm wrapped around her. He looked down at her, obviously listening as she talked to him though Grace couldn't hear what she said. Steve lifted his head, looking in Kenton's direction. He pressed a kiss to the top of Emily's head and wrapped his other arm around her in a tight hug.

Feeling as if she was an interloper in a private moment between the two of them, Grace shifted her gaze to the fire. Her emotions were all over the place once again. Concern for Bennett and Kenton. More so for Bennett since he hadn't come back out to join them. But then she had a longing for what Steve and Emily shared. And alongside that was the sense of loss because her chance to have it had died with Franklin.

Makayla went to her parents and, after a quick conversation, she headed over to where Grace was sitting. She dropped into the seat that Gabe had vacated to go talk with Forrest and Kenton.

"What's going on?" Grace asked.

After letting out a long sigh, Makayla said, "Bennett left. And I'm sorry, but I'm so mad at Kenton right now. They've managed to be in the same place together without confronting each other for years. But could Kenton just leave well enough alone and keep the peace for this visit? No.... He had to go and needle Bennett. Makes me so angry."

Grace wondered how the family would feel if they knew that she was likely the reason for the breakdown of Bennett and Kenton's relationship. Her stomach hurt at the thought of revealing that. Maybe she needed to have a conversation with Bennett about what had happened back then. Why she'd done what she had. Kenton wasn't to blame for what had happened. He hadn't known any better.

"Maybe they'll be fine for the rest of the week," Grace suggested.

"One can only hope because I don't want tension for the wedding. And I don't want Bennett avoiding the get-togethers we have planned because you know he will if he thinks it will keep the peace. But frankly, Bennett has been there for me more than Kenton has in recent years. I deserve to have him by my side for all of this." Makayla paused. "Can you make sure he's there?"

"Me?" Grace turned to look at her friend. "How am I supposed to do that?"

"Just when you're talking with him, make sure that he doesn't make excuses. And if he tries to, remind him that his favorite sister is getting married, and he needs to be there for me."

"Use a guilt trip, you mean?"

"Well, when you put it that way…yes. If that's what it takes. I want my wedding and everything surrounding it to be perfect, so he has to be there. I'll talk to Kenton and make sure he's on his best behavior too."

Grace was glad that Makayla hadn't tried to get her to do that. She really didn't know Kenton very well anymore. And despite what she'd said to Bennett earlier—and what she needed to talk to him about too—

she did consider him a friend. Just not one that she was likely to call for a craving run in the middle of the night.

"I'll do my best, but you do know your brother, right? He can be stubborn."

"Yeah, he can be, but I think he'll do it if you ask him to. Matron of honor to best man. If you don't do anything else as my matron of honor, make sure that Bennett is were I need him."

Grace agreed once again, hoping that Bennett would really listen to her.

"Are you ready to have an assistant on Monday?"

She wasn't sure how to respond to Makayla's question since she had mixed feelings about it. "As ready as I'll ever be. I just hope I can get her comfortable enough to be left on her own for two days."

"I was a little surprised by the one you ended up wanting to hire. What was it about her that made you think she was the best person for the job?"

Grace pondered the question, trying to figure out how to convey what it was about Maya St. James that had drawn her. "She seemed brave."

Makayla shifted in her seat, hooking her arm on the back of the chair. "Brave? You thought she needed to be brave?"

"It's not that she *needed* to be brave, but just applying and coming to the interview seemed brave of her. She had a real earnestness about her. I think she'll work hard."

"I found her timid," Makayla said. "Will she be able to handle the stronger personalities in the company?"

"Like who? Tristan? Mitch?"

Makayla laughed. "Okay. Maybe me?"

"I think she'll be fine. I don't really see her as timid. Reserved, yes, but not necessarily timid." Grace had warmed to the idea of an assistant during the interview process, a feeling that had really solidified when she'd spoken with Maya.

"I hope you're right," Makayla said. "This is supposed to help alleviate stress for you, not create more."

"She'll do that, I think."

Before the conversation could continue, people around them started to get up and say their goodbyes. Grace followed suit, and soon she was heading out as well. It wouldn't be long before she'd be driving back to the apartment instead of the condo. That would be a bit of an adjustment…making a home of her own for the first time. She'd gone from living with her grandmother to living with the Callaghans after her grandmother's death. Then Grace had moved into the apartment with

Tami and Makayla and finally in with Franklin when they got married. Though each place had been her residence, none had truly been her home, but now at twenty-six, she was going to have her own place. A home for her and her baby. It was exciting…and scary.

Going to the condo made her feel a little lost these days. The person whose home it truly was, was gone. Her connection to the condo had been severed. Though those feelings would definitely make it easier to move, it still filled her with sadness to think that what she and Franklin had had would never be anything more than it was now. Because of the baby, she needed to focus on the future. If it had just been her left, she might have stayed in the condo, surrounded by all the things that Franklin had chosen for his home. But the condo wasn't an ideal place for a baby. Franklin had promised her that when she got pregnant, they would move to a place that was more child-friendly. A home where they could grow as a family.

So she knew that Franklin would approve of her decision to move out of the condo. The apartment at the Callaghans' building wasn't as good as a house with a yard, but it came with an instant support system, and there was a big park across the street that was a good substitute for a yard.

The pending move stressed her out a bit when she allowed herself to dwell on it, but first, she had a wedding needing her attention. And her role in the wedding had now been expanded to include making sure Bennett was where Makayla wanted him, regardless of what Kenton was or wasn't doing.

Chapter Twelve

*T*HE FIRST TIME GRACE NEEDED to herd Bennett in the right direction came mid-week.

"What do you mean you're not going to the cabin tonight?" Grace asked.

Bennett looked up from his phone. "There's no reason for me to be out there tonight. The rehearsal is tomorrow night, so I'll be up there in time for that."

"There is a reason, Bennett," Grace said firmly. "Your sister wants you to be there. We've cleared the schedule, so there is no need for you to stay here in the city."

With a sigh, Bennett slid his phone into his inner suit coat pocket. "I don't think it's a good idea for me to be in close quarters with Kenton right now. Not if we want to keep the tension low for the wedding."

Grace hesitated, once again thinking that maybe the three of them— her, Kenton and Bennett—needed to sit down and have a conversation. "Makayla wants you there, Bennett. You're her brother. You're Ethan's best friend. You deserve to be there."

Bennett looked at her, his expression tight. "I'll see what I can do, but I make no promises."

Grace watched him walk away from her desk. The man had been more subdued and reserved than usual since the confrontation with Kenton on the weekend. She hoped that she'd convinced him to come because she really didn't want to let Makayla down. If it appeared that she'd failed, she'd have to sic Tami on him.

"Grace? I'm not sure what to do with these?"

At the sound of the new employee's question, Grace turned around. Maya St. James stood there with a couple of files in her hands. Grateful for the distraction, Grace helped Maya with the files. The young woman had been eager to learn and had made relatively few mistakes. She'd even gotten the hang of their phone system quite quickly. That was important since she was going to be manning the phones for two days on her own. The office was going to be closed, but Bennett had wanted someone to answer the telephones and take messages if necessary.

When the office closed at five, Grace once again approached Bennett. "Did you decide to come out tonight?"

Bennett regarded her, his dark blue gaze serious. "Why are you being so insistent about this, Grace? What does it matter to you whether I'm there or not?"

Grace felt her stomach clench at his questions. They made her think of things she didn't want. That she didn't feel she should be thinking about at this point. So she settled on a truth...not the truth she'd ever tell anyone else, but *a* truth. "Makayla told me to make sure that you were where she wanted you. She said that if it seemed you were going to back out of something, I was supposed to remind you that she wants you there."

Bennett ran a hand through his hair in a rather uncharacteristic move of apparent frustration. Usually, he was the picture of control, so seeing this side of him struck Grace as wrong. "I understand that, but I also don't want to create tension by being there."

"Then just come and steer clear of Kenton. Makayla said she was going to talk to him about what all this means to her and what she expects of him. I think it will be okay."

Bennett reached for the suit coat that hung on the back of his chair. As he shoved his arms into the sleeves, he said, "I'll be there a bit later. I need to run home and pack a bag. Are you leaving from here?"

"Yes, I brought all my stuff with me."

"This is just the family tonight?" Bennett asked as he closed down his computer.

"Well, yes, and me."

He glanced over at her. "You're family."

Strangely enough, Grace had felt that way about everyone in the Callaghan and McFadden clan except Bennett. When he came to mind, Grace had never thought of him as a brother the way she had the rest of the guys. But she'd never told anyone that because she hadn't wanted to explain why she felt that way. And that wasn't about to change now.

"Then I guess I'll see you out there later tonight." Grace gave him a quick smile before leaving his office.

Makayla and Ethan had headed up earlier in the day, and Steve and Emily had been there since the day before. She wasn't sure what the rest of the family had planned for arrival times at the cabin. It was just family for the night, and then over the next two days, the rest of the people who had been invited to the wedding would begin to arrive. Grace was grateful that they included her as part of their family. Belonging was truly a blessing.

It took her two hours to drive north of the city to the large cabin that belonged to the Callaghans. She'd spent a lot of time out there over the years, but this was going to be the most memorable time for sure. When she'd started the journey out to the cabin, she'd called Makayla to tell her about the conversation with Bennett and then had spent the rest of the time listening to praise and worship music as she drove.

It was soothing for her soul and helped to make sure that her mind was in the right place as she prepared to deal with a happy—and yet still sad, for her—time.

BENNETT SLOWED THE TRUCK as he approached the driveway that led to the cabin. He'd debated the wisdom of coming out for this night. If Grace hadn't come to talk to him about it, he would have waited and gone up the next day. He huffed out a sigh. No matter how many years had passed since he'd first had a crush on Grace, she still could get him to do things that no one else could. He wondered if Makayla knew that.

Still, he'd taken his time coming. He'd gone back to the apartment and did a workout in the gym they had in the basement of the building. It was almost seven by the time he'd left the city which meant it was nearly nine by the time he made it to the cabin.

There were a lot of cars already there. It didn't look like very many had carpooled. Since it was all just family, he didn't care that he was blocking someone in as he parked. They all hung their keys by the door when they arrived so that if someone needed to move a vehicle, they could find the key.

After shutting off the truck, Bennett got out and pulled his suitcase and garment bag from the back seat. Warm light spilled from the windows of the cabin, and Bennett paused to take in the beauty of the scene. He loved the cabin and had lots of happy memories of times spent there. He hoped that this time there would add to those memories, not overshadow them.

When he pulled open the door to walk inside, laughter and conversation greeted him. He hung his keys up then ventured further into the cabin.

"Bennett!" His mom came toward him with her arms spread wide, a welcoming smile on her face. She pulled him into a tight hug. "Are you hungry? I've some food set aside for you."

"What did you have?" Bennett asked when she stepped back. "I did grab a bite to eat before leaving the city, but I might be persuaded to eat something more."

His mom smiled. "We had ham, potato salad, and everything that we usually have with that meal."

"Okay. I think I'm hungry." He smiled down at her. "Let me run up to put my bags in the room."

Bennett wasn't looking forward to sharing a room with Kenton, but he had no choice. The way the cabin was set up, there were two large rooms that had bunk beds to sleep the boys in one room and the girls in the other. Thinking ahead, his dad had made sure the bunk beds would fit them into adulthood, so they were longer and wider than the average bunk bed plus they were heavy duty. Certainly sturdy enough to hold them as they grew into adults. There were a few other rooms that had beds for couples, but that wasn't where he and Kenton would be sleeping.

There was one lower bunk without a bag on it, so Bennett dropped his bag there and hung his garment bag in the closet. No one else was in the room, so he wandered over to the windows that looked out over the back of the cabin. The small garden lights that his dad had draped in the trees were twinkling softly in the darkness. In two days time, Ethan and Makayla would be getting married out there. With the setting sun as their backdrop, they'd be exchanging vows to start their life together. The first of their family to marry.

He wasn't surprised it was Makayla. It had never really crossed his mind that he or Kenton—being the eldest of the family—would be the first to marry. Though he dated, he hadn't ever felt the desire to marry any of those women even though he had always hoped that one of them might turn out to be the love of his life. And goodness knows Kenton went through women like water. He wasn't sure the man had ever had a relationship that lasted more than a few months. If that.

When he walked back downstairs and saw his family—some gathered around the table, some stretched out on the sofas in the living room—he was glad that he'd made the decision to come out. The next night more people would be out at the cabin for the rehearsal, but tonight it was just his family—and Grace—and he was grateful to be there.

"Here you go, sweetheart." His mom was standing at the counter with a plate and food.

"Thanks, Mom," Bennett said as he dropped a kiss on her head and took the plate she held out. "It all looks good."

After he'd filled his plate, he headed to the table and sat down next to Tristan who was doing something on his phone. He glanced over and smiled before looking back down.

"I was beginning to wonder if you were actually going to show up," Makayla said as she lifted a mug to her lips once he'd finished saying a prayer of thanks for his meal. "When Grace said you had agreed to come out, I didn't think it would be so late."

"Just be glad I'm here. I could be at home sleeping on my king size memory foam topped bed in peace and quiet instead of a single bunk bed surrounded by snoring chuckleheads."

"Hey," Tristan protested beside him. "I don't snore."

"Says you," Mitch chimed in from the couch behind the table. "I may or may not have evidence to the contrary."

"Shut up, Mitch," Tristan muttered as he slouched down, his focus back on his phone.

Bennett listened as they all bantered back and forth while he ate. It was a good reminder of how they had once been before life had taken them in many different directions. Since they had been able to get together the summer of the previous year, it wasn't like they hadn't all been together recently, but it was unusual for it to just be them without non-family members. Of course, that didn't apply to Sierra, Ethan or Grace. They were all considered family.

He looked down the table where Grace was sitting with a pile of candy, a spool of ribbon and some sort of netting. She and Makayla were working together to assemble something for the wedding apparently. Makayla would put a pile of candy into the circle of netting and then Grace would put a loop of ribbon around the netting and tie it up.

When Grace looked up, and their gazes met, she gave him a quick smile before returning to her job. Bennett held his breath for a moment, trying to ignore the way his heart had skipped a beat at her smile. He exhaled as he gave himself a talking to about how allowing himself to feel anything for Grace would just make things difficult. Again.

This was not the time to be thinking of anything like that because Grace was still grieving. She might always be grieving and not ever ready for another relationship. And even if she ever was interested in another relationship, it wouldn't be with him. He'd managed to accept that years ago, so now he just needed to remember that. Even if he had to remind himself about that over and over.

"So as the best man for this gig," Bennett began, "what do you need me to do tomorrow and Friday?"

Makayla glanced up at him. "Oh, I have a list of things that are your responsibility. I just wanted to wait until you got here to email it to you."

"Is that because you're going to have Ethan steal my truck keys so I can't leave when I see how long the list is?"

"Who told you?" Makayla asked with a glare around the table before she dissolved into laughter. "That's partly true, but I'm not going to make Ethan do something as shady as stealing your keys. Expect to find the list in your inbox when you wake up tomorrow."

"Good thing I plan to sleep til noon." Bennett finished the last of his potato salad. "How big of a list can you really have? You're getting married behind the cabin."

"Oh, there are plenty of things to do. Setting up chairs. Arranging flowers. Putting out candles."

"You're having candles outside? They're never going to stay lit," Mitch pointed out.

"We've taken that into account," Grace said as she plunked a newly tied candy bundle into a box beside her. "They will be in glass jars and, lucky for all, they're battery operated."

"Yeah, Mitch, they're battery operated," Bennett said over his shoulder. "How could you imagine they'd be anything but?"

"Shut up," Mitch said just before Bennett felt something soft hit his back. "Like you assumed they were battery operated."

"I did," Kenton piped in. "I mean, really, what else could Makayla have possibly used to light her way down the aisle?"

"You shut up too," Mitch said with a laugh. "I can't wait until one of you gets engaged. I'll be sure to let your fiancées know that you'll each be in charge of the candles for the ceremony."

"Well, thanks to Makayla, I'll know what to do," Bennett said as he got up from the table and carried his plate and silverware to the sink.

"Like anyone is ever going to marry you, dude," Gabe chimed in for the first time.

"Boys," their mom cautioned. "Let's be nice to each other."

"We *are* being nice, Mom," Gabe said. "I was going to help Bennett understand why he'd never be having to worry about a candle problem at his wedding."

"Well, at least I know I'm not having a candle problem at *my* wedding," Makayla said. "And that's because Grace and Bennett will make sure that all of them work properly."

"Here are some brownies if any of you want dessert," his mom said, peeling back the cling wrap that was covering the large plate.

Bennett could tell his mom was trying to diffuse what she saw as a potentially explosive situation. They had always teased and joked like that without her getting after them, so her fears were obviously grounded in the confrontational conversation that had taken place between him and Kenton. He slipped an arm around her shoulder and gave a squeeze.

"They look good, Mom," Bennett said as he snagged a brownie.

The rest of the guys came over to grab some for themselves while Makayla and Grace continued to work with the candy at the table. Bennett pulled a couple of sheets off the paper towel roll and then put a brownie on each before carrying them over to the table.

"Sustenance, ladies," he said as he set them in front of Makayla and Grace.

They both glanced up and grinned at him.

"Thank you," Grace said as she set down the ribbon she held and reached for the brownie. "Luckily, Baby is okay with chocolate and sweets today."

"What are you going to blame your cravings on once the baby's born?" Makayla asked with a laugh as she picked up her brownie. "You just need to own your love of chocolate and sweets, girl."

Bennett took one of the seats vacated by the guys and settled down across the table from the ladies. "How many of those are you making?"

Makayla glanced at the box where they'd put the completed ones. "One for everyone who's going to be at the wedding."

"How many people are you actually anticipating?"

"Around fifty or so."

"Fifty?" Bennett leaned forward. "And the reception?"

"It's just a dessert reception here at the cabin. Since it's a sunset wedding, we aren't going to have a meal following it. The sunset is happening around eight-thirty these days."

"You're lucky," Grace commented. "You're going to be able to get a good night's rest and have all day to get ready. Since my wedding was at two in the afternoon, I had to get up early to get ready."

"We all had to," Makayla reminded her.

Bennett thought back to Grace and Franklin's wedding. He had woken that morning with a pit in his stomach that hadn't gone away at all that day. Listening to Grace say her vows with Franklin had made it the worst day of his life. He'd allowed himself to feel bad that day, but only for that day because then he made himself move past it.

But now Grace's vows to Franklin had been fulfilled, and Bennett hated that the feelings he had managed to suppress were threatening to resurface. And there was no guarantee that he'd be any more likely to have those feelings returned this time around than he had been the first time he'd dealt with them.

"So what's the first thing you're going to need me to do tomorrow?" Bennett asked. "I understand you're going to send me a list, but I'd like to know what time you want me up."

As he listened to Makayla outline the plan for the next day—which was surprisingly not as busy as he'd anticipated—Bennett realized he'd be spending a chunk of the day with Grace. And then he would be heading out on the houseboat with the guys while the ladies were at the hotel for the night and getting ready the next day.

"Here." Makayla shoved the bags of candy across the table at him. "I want to talk to Ethan before we all call it a night."

"So what exactly are we doing here?" Bennett asked.

"Put six of the kisses in the middle of a piece of tulle, and then I'll tie them off." Grace gave him a demonstration that he didn't really need, but who was he to stop Grace when she was actually talking to him.

They worked in silence for a few minutes before Grace said, "I was beginning to wonder if you were going to show up."

"I told you that I'd be here. I just felt it might lessen the chances of confrontation if I came a bit later."

"I think Makayla gave Kenton a strict lecture. He'll behave."

"And so will I," Bennett assured her.

Silence fell between them once more, and Grace was the one to break it again. "Have you ever told anyone what happened between you and Kenton?"

Chapter Thirteen

ENNETT PAUSED, HIS HAND hovering over the piece of netting. "No. That's just between him and me."

"And yet it's impacting your whole family," Grace pointed out. "You aren't one big happy family like you used to be."

Bennett focused on counting out six candies then pushed the netting circle toward Grace. "I don't hate him, but I'll never trust him."

"Sometimes you just need to forgive, so you can move past it," Grace said.

"This isn't about whether or not I forgive him, I'll never be able to forget. A trust betrayed is hard to recover from."

Bennett shifted in his seat, glancing over to where Kenton sat talking with the twins and Ryan. At one time, he would have been right there talking and laughing with them. He turned his gaze back to the job at hand. Even if he wanted to move past this with Kenton, he wasn't sure where to start.

"I think it would be good for the sake of your family for you to somehow get past whatever happened," Grace said softly.

He glanced up at Grace, but her gaze was on the ribbon she was tying around the netting. Would she want him to resurrect the past if she knew the role she played in all of it? Something told him that she wouldn't. In order to make peace with the past like she wanted him to, he'd have to bring up how his feelings for her had led to what had later happened with Kenton.

"I'll keep that in mind." Bennett knew, on one level, that she was right, but given that he knew he had no future with her, it felt best to just leave it all in the past. He probably should still talk to Kenton and try to get to the point where they could hold a civil conversation. They owed at least that much to their parents.

THE HEAVY CURTAINS COVERING the windows kept the sun out even though her phone had told her it was just after eight in the morning. There were still lumps under the blankets on the other beds, so it appeared Grace wasn't the only one getting a slow start to the day.

She curled on her side, a hand pressed against her stomach, hoping it would stay calm. The day ahead was busy, and she didn't want to be sick to start it off. Feeling sick wasn't her only concern for the day.

She wasn't sure what had prompted her to talk to Bennett about his feud with Kenton. Goodness knows she didn't want to have to deal with the stuff in *her* past. Maybe it was because she was almost one hundred percent positive that the feud somehow involved her. It wasn't pride or an over-inflated sense of her own worth that made her think that.

It just seemed to make sense given that it all happened almost immediately after she and Kenton went to her prom. In pressing for him to deal with it, she could very well be opening up stuff that she didn't want to deal with. It was risky, but she just hated the look on Emily's face when tensions began to rise within the family. She could see the hurt and stress on the older woman's face, and Grace just wanted her to not have to deal with it. Emily wanted her family to be as close as they once were. She wanted them all to get along—that much was very clear. What mother wouldn't want that?

Grace would never have to deal with that as it was highly unlikely she'd ever have a child beyond the one that she carried. When Franklin had asked her to reconsider having a family, she'd only agreed because she'd known he'd be by her side. Only now he wasn't there. She didn't feel equipped to be a mother. Especially a single mother. But it was too late for anything else now.

There was movement beside her and then an arm jabbed her lightly in her back. "You awake, Gracie?"

"Yep." Grace reached behind her and patted Makayla's arm. "How are you feeling today? Less than two days now."

"Yay! Finally!" Makayla's voice was loud enough to disturb the others in the room.

"Kayla…" Sammi's sleepy voice drifted over to them. "Go back to sleep."

Grace grinned. "I doubt that's going to happen, Sammi. She's not going to sleep much between now and the wedding."

A loud groan let them know that Sammi wasn't pleased with that revelation.

"You have to cut me slack, Sammi," Makayla said. "It's not every day a girl gets married. So chill, sis. Your turn will come."

A pillow landed on them, and suddenly there were giggles coming from the bunk beds where Sierra and Danica had slept. Then Makayla started laughing, and Grace couldn't help but smile. She was grateful for the distraction from her thoughts. It was a time to focus on her friend and the happy occasion that had brought them all together. There would always be time for her to think about her own life and grief after all this was over.

She was going to give herself permission to have fun. To smile. To laugh. To enjoy herself in a way she would have if Franklin had still been alive. Her friend deserved to be surrounded by people who were happy on her special day.

"Let's get up," Makayla said. "I'm hungry for some breakfast."

"Don't eat too much or you might not fit in your dress," Sammi said.

"Why do you think I choose a style that wasn't tight?" Makayla flipped the covers back over Grace.

She turned over onto her back as Makayla got out of the bed. She was barely a shadow in the dimly lit room as she moved around. Then the lamp on the nightstand snapped on, flooding the room with light. Grace threw her arm over her eyes as a chorus of groans filled the room. There would be no going back to sleep now.

"C'mon, guys. Up and at 'em."

Grace slowly lowered her arm and blinked a few times before shoving the blanket off and pushing herself up to sit on the side of the bed. Sierra and Danica were also moving around, but Sammi laid on her stomach with a pillow over her head. While Makayla went into the bathroom, Grace dug through her bag and pulled out a pair of capris with an elastic waist and a loose-fitting T-shirt.

She swapped out her pajamas for the clothes and then went into the bathroom to do her morning routine. Knowing that there were people arriving throughout the day and with the rehearsal scheduled for the evening, Grace took the time to put on some makeup and curl her hair before heading downstairs for breakfast. Normally, Steve banned makeup at the cabin, but he'd made an exception for their time there for the wedding.

By the time she was ready, the teen girls had already left the room. Sammi still hadn't pried herself out of bed, but Makayla was ready and led the way downstairs. It appeared, from those already gathered for breakfast, that Sammi was the only one who was still in bed. Breakfast had been spread out on the island and people were filling their plates and finding seats around the large table.

Grace hesitated at the bottom of the stairs as the aromas of bacon, sausage, pancakes and maple syrup assaulted her senses. She pressed a hand to her stomach, willing it to stay calm. There was no way she wanted to be running to the bathroom to toss her cookies.

Please, baby, just leave Mama's stomach alone for one morning.

"Feel up to eating, sweetheart?" Emily ran a hand down Grace's arm. "I can make you some plain toast if you'd like."

Grace shook her head. "I want everything but especially the bacon. Really want some bacon this morning. I would happily make deals with this baby in order to be able to enjoy this breakfast."

Emily slipped her arm through Grace's and pulled her toward the island. "There's plenty here, but I don't want you to force yourself to eat."

Grace nodded as she stood there, waiting to see which way her stomach was going to go. While she felt slightly nauseous, her stomach wasn't in full revolt like it was some mornings. Hoping for the best, Grace picked up a plate and followed Makayla around the island. She didn't load her plate up since she didn't want to waste the food if her stomach wouldn't let her eat after a few bites. There was plenty of food though so if she decided she wanted more, she could come back for seconds.

She ate slowly, focussing more on swallowing each bite than on the conversation around her. Once she was done, she decided she wouldn't press her luck with a second helping of anything. She, along with several others, helped to clear up the breakfast before gathering in the living room for a wedding meeting.

"We have several deliveries coming in today and tomorrow," Steve said. "So we need to coordinate to make sure that everything goes smoothly."

Grace knew that they were going to go ahead and set up a bunch of stuff in preparation for the rehearsal later. Thankfully, there was no rain in the forecast for the next forty-eight hours. The more they could do that day, the better.

"Why don't you let me do that?" Bennett said a couple of hours later as she picked up a folding chair from the stack that had been recently delivered.

Grace straightened, leaning the chair against her hip. "They're not that heavy. I think I can handle setting up a few."

Bennett frowned as if deciding whether he should chance saying something more. "I guess you're right."

"I am." She smiled at him. "I think I know what I can handle. I won't overdue it."

He hesitated again then nodded. "How about I carry the chairs to you, and you can set them up?"

She knew he was just concerned about her overdoing it while being pregnant and was likely trying to find a compromise between his concern and her desire to help out. "Okay. Sounds like a plan."

Bennett looked relieved, probably glad that she hadn't snapped at him. "Good. Why don't you head down there, and I'll bring you the chairs?"

Grace led the way down the steps of the layered deck. There were others working on setting up the chairs, so she really didn't need to help out, but it felt good to lend a hand. Steve had instructed them on how to arrange the chairs, so as Bennett brought them to her, she opened them up and set them on the deck. Mitch and Gabe were helping as well, while Kenton and Ryan had been sent to a nearby town to pick up some food that Emily had ordered for part of their rehearsal dinner. Grace had heard Emily tell Makayla that Steve had insisted that she outsource as much of the cooking as possible so that she could enjoy the wedding with a minimum of stress.

They had just finished the chair setup when Tami showed up. The minister and his wife, along with the musicians, were also supposed to arrive before the rehearsal at four. The next day James and Erin were supposed to arrive with the wedding cake and cupcakes, and Finn and Noella were going to pick up the flowers from the florist.

"Is this lined up properly?" Bennett called out as he and Mitch positioned the large white arch in the open area in front of the chairs.

Grace joined Makayla in the aisle and looked at the arch's position. "To the left a little, I think."

"Yes," Makayla agreed. "Shift it about half a foot to the left."

The guys moved it as requested, and Grace regarded it once again. "Bennett, bring your side toward us just a bit."

Once he'd shifted forward with his side, Makayla said, "Yep, that's perfect."

Grace turned in a circle, taking in the set-up that would be the scene of the start of Makayla and Ethan's life together. Thoughts of her own wedding came to mind unbidden. It hadn't been a time of excitement and anticipation like this was for Makayla. She hadn't been nervous about it either. At the time, people had commented on how calm she was. How unflappable she'd been through all the planning. Franklin had wanted a big wedding and had sent invitations to anyone he'd ever done business with.

It really had been more of a social event than a celebration of the start of a marriage. There had been no unique parts of the wedding that reflected who she and Franklin were. No specially written vows. They'd just let the minister use whatever he wanted for their vows. Neither of them had needed the wedding ceremony to be a personal event. Grace had an idea of what Makayla and Ethan's wedding would involve, and it kind of made her a bit sad, but she also knew that she and Franklin wouldn't have been able to have any other sort of wedding at that point in their relationship.

And she also had to acknowledge that it didn't matter what type of wedding a couple had, it was the marriage that followed that was more important. So while they hadn't had a deeply meaningful ceremony, they *had* been working on building a better marriage.

"Do you have flowers for that?" Bennett asked as he joined them in the aisle between the rows of chairs.

"Finn and Noella are bringing them tomorrow."

Bennett folded his arms. "We're gonna be working like crazy to bring this all together, aren't we?"

"Not me," Makayla said. "I have a spa appointment then hair and makeup."

"What about Grace, Tami, and Sammi?"

Makayla nodded. "Yes, they'll be working like crazy with you."

"So we're your slaves," Grace observed. "What else is new?"

"Yeah, we are all Makayla's slaves," Tami agreed.

Before they could continue to needle Makayla, Emily called for her to come to the house. Ethan was standing with Emily and the minister from their church. While the couple talked with the minister, Grace and Tami discussed where the flowers and candles were to be set up the following day. Bennett hadn't been exaggerating when he'd said they'd be working hard the next day. Thankfully, they would have more help once Erin, Noella, and their men arrived.

Grace escaped upstairs to her room just after lunch to lay down for a bit. The day had warmed up, and her normal tiredness was weighing on her. She knew if she was going to make it through the rest of the day, she'd need to rest for a bit.

When she ventured back downstairs a couple hours later, there seemed to be controlled chaos in action.

"You doing okay?" Bennett asked when she walked near where he stood.

"Yep. Just need to take a nap every once in awhile. Growing a baby is hard work," she said with a small smile. "But Bennett, unless you see me prostrate on the floor, you need to assume that I'm okay. Every time you see me, you're asking if I'm okay."

Bennett frowned as he puts his hands on his hips. "Am I really?"

"Yes, you are. Unless I give you some real reason to be concerned, like I'm just coming around after fainting, I think you can assume I'm okay." She paused then asked, "Is there something that prompts you to keep asking me that?"

Chapter Fourteen

*U*H…YOU'RE PREGNANT?" Bennett said by way of explanation. "I'm not sure what else to ask you, I guess."

"I'm not the first person to ever be pregnant," Grace pointed out. "And aside from a little tiredness and some nausea, I'm doing fine."

"Alright. So no more asking if you're okay," Bennett said.

Grace considered his words and then had to figure out why she was slightly disappointed at the thought of him not expressing concern about her anymore. "Why don't we compromise?"

Bennett lifted a brow at her. "A compromise?"

"Yes. You're allowed to ask me once a day if I'm okay." She held up one finger. "Just once. Not every time you see me."

When Bennett smiled, it made Grace happy that she had suggested the compromise. "I will try my very best to only ask you once a day. So I'm done for today."

"Yes, you are." Grace turned away from Bennett, crossing her arms as she looked at where the others were gathered around the kitchen island folding bulletins for the ceremony. "I guess the rehearsal will be starting soon."

"Yep. The pastor is outside with Makayla and Ethan. The musicians are just at the hotel getting settled in. The houseboat was also delivered to the marina. Everything is falling into place just like Makayla wanted."

Grace was happy to hear that. When they were younger, of Grace, Makayla and Tami, Makayla was the one who had talked the most about getting married. It was good to see that she was getting the wedding she had always dreamed of.

"Hey, you two," Tami said as she approached them. She slipped her arm around Grace and gave her a hug. "Ready for the big day?"

"As long as Makayla doesn't change her mind, everything should be good to go," Bennett said. "So, Tami, is Keenan coming up for the wedding?"

Tami smiled as she nodded. "Since he played on Wednesday, he's free to come up."

Grace watched her friend's face as she talked about the football player. She wouldn't be surprised if there was another wedding in the next year or two. From what she'd seen, Keenan seemed to be a great guy and perfect for Tami.

For a moment, she felt a pang of grief at the realization that her two best friends were now part of couples. An evening out, if they included her, would be the two couples and Grace. Yeah, she'd be the fifth wheel. That would be challenging, and she'd have to fight the urge to turn down any such invitations. Add to that, she'd have a little one she'd have to take into consideration. When she'd been married to Franklin, she'd been willing to hang out with Tami and Makayla just like the three of them always had since Franklin had no problem with her going off with them. Since she had been the only one with a husband then, it had never been a problem for just the three of them to hang out together.

But in this case, Ethan and Keenan were good friends so it stood to reason that the two couples would be going out together. Double dates. Not double dates plus one.

"Hey." Bennett's hand came to rest on her back. "Are you…uh…why the sad face?"

She gave him a small smile. "Nice save."

"I know, right?" He chuckled. "I have a feeling I'm going to be having to save myself a lot in the next six months."

Grace couldn't help but laugh as well, glad to feel the dark thoughts that had been settling over her lift. If she'd been alone, she had no doubt that she would have allowed that darkness and grief to overtake her completely. Instead, all she felt was the underlying grief that was always present but not overwhelming.

She stood elbow-to-elbow with Bennett as they finished folding the last of the bulletins, and then they moved outside to begin the rehearsal. Since she was the matron of honor and Bennett was best man, they were paired to walk down the aisle and then back up the aisle at the end of the ceremony. They had decided to have Ethan walk in first followed by the other pairs and then Grace and Bennett would come right before Makayla. Since none of the family or close friends had little ones, they'd decided to forgo the flower girls and ring bearers. And while it would have been cute to have little ones as part of the wedding, if they didn't know the bride and/or groom well, it might lead to more toddler drama than including them was worth.

As Grace walked down the aisle, she held tightly to Bennett's arm. The step at the edge of each section of the deck was shallow, but she was determined not to do anything that would make her fall in front of people. Behind the wedding arch and the minister, the water sparkled and gleamed in the afternoon sun. It was a little warm, but there was a breeze coming off the lake that helped to cool things down. Thankfully, the sun would be setting when the wedding took place the next night so they wouldn't have to worry about heat. In fact, it might end up being a little chilly.

Once they reached the lowest level of the multi-tiered deck, Bennett covered her hand with his and gave it a gentle squeeze before letting go and moving to stand next to Ethan. The string quartet finished with the music for the processional and began to play the bridal march. Grace once again found herself swamped with memories at the sound of the music. She hadn't expected these emotions from just the rehearsal and had to look down at the deck so she could blink rapidly and keep the tears at bay.

She tried to think of other things—anything else—to keep the memories at bay. The last thing she wanted was for her emotions to overshadow the happiness of this occasion.

BENNETT KEPT AN EYE on Grace throughout the rehearsal. He felt a bit like she needed to have someone watching out for her since she was on her own. Of course, he was kind of hampered now that she'd called him on constantly asking her if she was okay. He'd just have to be more inventive in the ways he asked how she was doing.

After the rehearsal was done to Makayla's satisfaction, everyone headed inside where his mom and the minister's wife had started to set out the food for the rehearsal dinner. Though they had the money for a more elaborate wedding, both Ethan and Makayla had decided that they wanted to keep things simple and spend the money they saved on the wedding on a nicer honeymoon. Bennett had been a bit surprised when Makayla had decided to do things like that because she'd always talked about having a big elaborate wedding. It was just one more way that it seemed she'd changed since Ethan had come into her life.

When he had filled his plate with the pulled pork, buns and salads, Bennet sat down next to Ryan. He hadn't had much opportunity to chat with his brother since he'd arrived. Of course, of the three siblings who didn't live in Winnipeg, Bennett was in contact with Ryan most frequently. They video messaged at least once every couple of weeks and texted a lot in between.

"Are you heading home on Sunday?" Bennett asked as he put the top on his pulled pork bun.

"Yep. Back to work on Monday." Ryan took a bite of his food.

"So, any girlfriend yet?"

Ryan rolled his eyes. "You ask me that every time we talk."

"I know. I keep hoping your answer will change."

"Fine. There's no girlfriend, but there is someone I'd like to get to know better." He paused. "We'll see. How about you?"

"I'm pretty much the same. I haven't really had the time to date since Ellie and I broke up."

"Are there many single women at your church?" Ryan asked.

Bennett shrugged. "There are several, but so far I've found them to be a better fit as a friend than a girlfriend or potential wife."

"With a wedding this small, the chances of one of us catching the garter tomorrow is pretty high. Maybe it will be you."

Bennett laughed. "I hope Keenan catches the garter, and Tami catches the bouquet. Then they can be the next to get married."

"He does seem like a pretty decent guy. Good enough for Tami."

Bennett looked across the table when Grace sat down there, a loaded plate in front of her.

"Baby liking pulled pork today?" Bennett asked.

Grace smiled. "Yes. The baby is starving."

"Do you know yet if it's a boy or a girl?" Ryan asked.

"No. It's a little too soon for an ultrasound to be able to tell."

"Are you planning to find out?"

Grace swallowed the bite she'd been chewing then took a sip of water. "I keep going back and forth on that. I think Franklin would have wanted to know, and it would be nice to know for buying things."

"Do you have a strong preference?"

Grace sighed. "I know I should say I don't, but given my situation, I think having a girl would be easier. Raising a boy by myself would be more challenging, I think."

"You do know that a little boy would always have us guys around to help him out. We'd all be there to help teach him the important things about being a boy like learning to skate and play hockey." Bennett smiled. "If you have a little boy, he'll have lots of uncles. You wouldn't be doing it alone. Hey, even if you have a girl, we'd teach her things like skating and how to beat guys at hockey or football."

"He's right," Ryan said. "You're not doing it alone. Boy or girl, we're all gonna be there for you. Well, I'll be supportive from a distance. But others, like Bennett and Mitch, will definitely be there to help you out."

"I know," Grace said with a nod. "But the baby is ultimately my responsibility. I feel like I need to be able to do this parenting thing on my own."

"Gracie," Bennett said with a shake of his head. "It's great that you want to do it on your own, but when you don't have to, it seems a bit...ridiculous to resist others' efforts to help you. We're all excited about the baby."

Grace's hand dropped below the edge of the table to rest on her stomach. "You're excited?"

"Sure. Why wouldn't we be? The first baby in the family. And really, my mom has always felt that every baby is worth celebrating. So yeah, we're all excited."

Without responding, Grace continued to eat her dinner. Bennett hoped that he hadn't upset her, but everything he'd said was the truth. They were excited, and they were definitely going to be supporting Grace however they could.

Once the dinner was over, the guys loaded up in two of their vehicles and headed for the marina to begin their night on the houseboat while the ladies went off to the hotel for their night in luxury. The minister and his wife were staying at the cabin with Steve, Emily, and Dalton. The teen had opted not to go with the rest of the guys, stating he'd rather stay at the cabin where he didn't have to deal with talk about sports and business.

It appeared that he was correct in his assessment of what they'd be doing. It wasn't long after the fellows had settled on the houseboat that they began discussing the latest football game, analyzing how Keenan and his fellow teammates had played. Talk eventually turned to hockey as Kenton shared what was happening in his world.

They were all seated on the top deck of the boat, enjoying the sun as it slowly sank below the horizon. They had lots of cold soda and junk food, and even after the big dinner they'd enjoyed, they didn't hesitate to eat some more. Once it was fully dark, they turned on the deck lights and continued to talk. They seemed to touch on almost every topic as the evening slipped past. Thankfully, they didn't have to be up super early the next morning for the wedding.

As Gabe talked about his latest adventures and what he had planned for the future, Bennett found himself wondering how Grace was enjoying her evening. He had heard Makayla talking about visiting the spa at the hotel, so he hoped that Grace was able to relax and have some fun. He had no idea where she was in the grieving process. It had only been about three months since her husband's death so he had to imagine that her grief was still pretty fresh. He hoped that the upcoming move would help her focus more on the future.

When he'd asked his mom how long she'd grieved for his dad, she'd said that her grief had started before he was even dead. She'd grieved for the person he'd once been. The person he no longer was by the time he'd died. But she'd said that while she'd never forgotten his dad, she'd found that the overwhelming grief had begun to ease fairly soon after she'd received word of his death. She'd been alone on the military base with no family close by, and she hadn't had much time to grieve as she prepared her family for a major move. Having four kids that needed her, had helped to keep her grounded in the present.

She'd said that there had still been times she'd grieved deeply, but it could never last long since he and his siblings needed her. The one thing that had stuck with Bennett was how she said that everyone's grieving process was different and that they showed their grief in different ways. Some grieved very privately. Others were more open about it.

Her answers kind of frustrated Bennett even though he knew that wasn't a good reaction, but he wanted things to be more easily explained. He wanted to have some specific time frames. Like at what point would the grief have lessened enough for a person to move on?

Even as the thought formed in his head, Bennett frowned. The idea of Grace moving on filled him with equal amounts of fear and anticipation. He didn't like either feeling, but he didn't want to have to analyze why that was.

"Where are you?"

Bennett glanced over at Ryan. "Here. Just thinking through a bunch of stuff."

"Well, don't. We're supposed to just be having fun tonight. Put the serious stuff aside for the time being."

Bennett knew he was right, but it seemed like he just couldn't get Grace off his mind. No matter what he was doing, thoughts of her lingered on the edges of his mind. He was reminded of how he'd been in high school when he'd had a crush on her. He really didn't want to go back to that place. It had ended up leaving him heartbroken, and he didn't want to chance that again. Was it possible for him to just be concerned about her without his heart getting involved?

Chapter Fifteen

G RACE WATCHED AS EMILY HELPED Makayla with her veil. After they'd spent the previous night at the hotel, they'd had some time in the spa that morning. Now they were back at the large cabin, in the girls' room, putting the final touches on their hair and makeup. There were five of them—her, Tami, Sammi, Danica and Sierra—attending Makayla as well as five guys standing up with Ethan. In addition to Bennett who was his best man, Ethan had chosen Mitch, Tristan, Ryan and Tennyson, who had become a good friend to him after having met him through Gabe. Ethan had felt badly about not having all Makayla's brothers, but Makayla had told Grace that she'd assured Ethan that choosing the men that he felt closest to wasn't going to be a problem. Kenton and Gabe would just have to understand that, since they hadn't visited much over the past year, Ethan wasn't as close to them.

There was a knock on the door, and Danica went to answer it.

"They sent me to tell you we're almost ready," Dalton said.

"Okay. We'll be down in a few minutes," Danica told him then shut the door.

Since they were on a deadline with the sunset, they all took one quick last look in the mirror before picking up their bouquets and heading for the door. Emily led the way since she would the first to go down the aisle to be seated. Sierra followed, then Danica, Sammi, Tami and finally Grace. The guys, including Ethan, were waiting on the main floor. Because Ethan didn't have a family of his own, they'd decided to have him walk down the aisle with Emily. He would walk her to her seat and then take his place next to the minister while the rest of them walked down the aisle.

Once he and Emily had left, Makayla came downstairs to join the group. Bennett came to stand next to Grace and gave her a smile.

"How are you doing this fine day?" he asked.

Since it wasn't technically *Are you okay?,* Grace wasn't going to count it as his once-a-day question. He wasn't looking at her in concern, which helped as well. He—as well as the other groomsmen—wore dark gray pants with light gray, long-sleeved shirts. Their ties were a soft rose color that matched the girls' dresses which were somewhat sixties style with a fitted bodice and a flared skirt that went to just below their knees. Grace was glad that she wasn't further along in the pregnancy or the dress probably wouldn't have fit.

Ethan wore the same dark gray pants and light gray shirt, but he also wore a vest and a silver tie. Makayla's white dress had a fitted bodice like the bridesmaid dresses. The satin bodice had a sweetheart neckline that was visible beneath the lace that covered it and gave the dress its capped sleeves. The skirt of the dress flared out, covering the strappy sandals that were perfect for a casual wedding. Her hair was partially up and the rest fell in long curls down her back. And as usual, her makeup was done to perfection.

At first, Grace had thought it was weird to have a sunset wedding, especially when the bride and groom weren't planning to see each other before the wedding to take pictures. But then Makayla had shown her pictures of other weddings that were photographed at night, and they had been beautiful.

All in all, the wedding was going to be full of meaning for them and so beautiful. Grace held tight to Bennett's arm as they waited their turn. He pressed his hand over hers and gave her a reassuring smile just before they began to walk down the aisle.

Grace, along with most of those present, shed a few tears as Ethan and Makayla spoke their vows to each other. She was glad that Emily had insisted that they all wrap tissues around the handle of their bouquets. It hadn't been long into the service before she'd needed them.

Hearing Ethan talk about his love for Makayla had made her chest ache as if a vise had tightened around it. A longing once again filled her to experience that sort of love. What she'd had with Franklin had been moving in that direction, but they had still been in the process of really learning about each other. Learning to love each other. They hadn't really ever fallen in love, but they had made the choice to love each other.

It was too soon to even be contemplating another relationship—and most the time she didn't even want one—so that longing caught her off-guard at the strangest moments. Well, maybe a wedding wasn't a strange place to be having thoughts about a relationship, but Grace didn't want to be thinking about that right then.

The chairs they'd set up were nearly all full, which was surprising considering the venue was a two-hour drive from the city. She did know that Steve had arranged for a block of rooms at the hotel to be available at a reduced rate. Keenan was there, sitting with James, Erin, Noella, and Finn. There were a few people who were there because of their work connection, but most were from the church and family friends.

Once the vows were said, the rings exchanged, and the bride and groom had kissed, the happy couple led the recessional from the wedding arch back up to the cabin. Soon people were congratulating the beaming couple and standing in groups chatting. Not long after the end of the ceremony, the photographer took Ethan and Makayla back down to the wedding arch and the area looking out over the water. It was the same spot where they'd gotten engaged earlier that year.

After the pictures were done, they cut the cake and tossed the bouquet, which Grace stayed away from and Tami caught. Bennett ended up catching the garter when Ethan threw it. He and Tami joked good-naturedly, and Keenan pretended to be jealous, fending off comments about his inability to catch the thing considering what his job was.

Grace had settled on a seat off to the side, happy to be off her feet for a bit. She knew it was all just wedding lore, but the thought that Bennett could be the next to marry did funny things to her heart. It kind of hurt to think of him getting married to someone. Someone that wasn't her. It couldn't be her because she wouldn't do that to him. Wouldn't cut his life short by loving him.

So she would smile and be his friend, and when the day came that he got married, she'd congratulate him. And his bride. Hopefully, it would be in the distant future, so she wasn't in the same vulnerable emotional state she was currently in.

Once the wedding traditions were completed, Ethan and Makayla said their goodbyes and left for the hotel. Their plan was to overnight there, and then the next morning they were planning to head into the city and catch a flight to some island paradise for a ten-day honeymoon. That was something else that she and Franklin hadn't really had. He'd had a couple of big listings and hadn't wanted to be away from the city for very long, so they'd ended up going to Banff for four days. At the time, she hadn't minded not having a long honeymoon, but now she wished they'd taken some time away together once they'd started working on their relationship.

Regrets.

It seemed that lately, every time she thought of Franklin, in addition to the grief, there were always feelings of regret. She didn't want that, though. She wanted to be able to remember Franklin and the happy times they'd shared together. While they hadn't had a lot of those times, they had been working toward having more.

It didn't take long for everyone to clear up the remnants of the cupcakes and other food they'd had at the small reception. It seemed most the guests were staying the night at the hotel, while Grace was back at the cabin to once again stay in the girls' room with Tami and the other girls.

It was almost midnight by the time everyone but the family and her and Tami had left. They all dropped into the couches and chairs in the living room and seemed to let out one big breath. It was kind of hard to believe that the wedding was over. Even though it hadn't been that long between engagement and wedding, for her, the time had seemed to have flown by and yet at the same time, to have dragged on.

It really depended on what she was thinking about. In terms of the wedding, it seemed like the time had flashed past. But when she thought about Franklin, it felt like time had dragged on forever. Three months felt more like three years sometimes.

"Well, if I can move," Emily began, "I'm going to head up to bed. I'm beat."

Her comment seemed to spur the rest of them into motion, and soon they were all meandering upstairs to the bedrooms. Grace changed out of her bridesmaid dress then cleaned off her makeup and brushed out her hair before crawling into the large bed she was sharing with Tami since Makayla wasn't there. She let out a long breath and closed her eyes, grateful to have made it through the day without a total emotional breakdown.

"You doing okay, sweetie?" Tami asked in the darkness once they'd all settled down.

"Yeah. It was a good day. I thought it might be worse, but it ended up being good. I just tried to stay focused on Makayla and Ethan. I'm so happy for them. They are perfect for each other."

"Yeah, they are," Tami agreed. "It was beautiful."

They both lapsed into silence because that basically covered it all. It had been beautiful. And now it was time to sleep.

BENNETT WOKE BEFORE ANYONE else in the guys' room. He lay there for a few moments before rolling out of bed. He pulled on a pair of shorts and a T-shirt and headed out of the room. As soon as he took his first step into the hallway, he smelled coffee which made him jog down the stairs.

"Didn't expect to see you guys til around nine at least," his dad said when Bennett joined him in the kitchen.

Bennett poured himself a cup of coffee. "I couldn't get back to sleep, so I figured I might as well get up. Is Mom still sleeping?"

"Yep. Want to sit outside?"

Bennett nodded and followed his dad as he walked out into the cool morning air. They settled into two Adirondack chairs on the deck. The view was still a bit obstructed by the chairs and the wedding arch. They'd be clearing that all up a bit later.

"Hard to believe it's over," Bennett said as he lifted his mug to his lips. He savored the warmth as it slid down his throat.

"One down. Nine to go," his dad announced. "And it looks like you're up next."

"Me? I don't think so."

"The garter says differently."

Bennett chuckled. "I don't think the garter is a good indication of anything."

"You just never know."

"I'd need to find a potential bride first." The thought was actually wearying. Every relationship he'd had, had felt difficult. Not that he expected a relationship to be easy and not need work, but sometimes it had just felt like more work than was worth it. And often it had seemed that in the relationship he was the only one making an effort. With everything going on with the business, he just didn't think that he would be able to devote the time and energy to a serious relationship.

"Sometimes what you need is closer than you might think," his dad commented cryptically.

Before Bennett could respond, the back door of the cabin opened, and Kenton came out with Tristan right behind him. They settled into the other two chairs that had been pushed up near the back of the cabin to make room for all the wedding chairs. Their conversation was slow as they talked about the wedding, the weather, and the plans for the day.

"Up first for me is starting breakfast. I told your mom that I'd take care of it, but I wouldn't turn down some help."

They all groaned at being volunteered for breakfast helpers, but Bennett really didn't mind. He knew that his mom had worked hard over the last few days to give Makayla the wedding she wanted, so if helping his dad with breakfast meant his Mom could take it easy, Bennett would be happy to help out.

Once they were back in the kitchen, they began the process of cooking pancakes, scrambled eggs, and bacon, and cutting up fruit. His dad and Kenton took care of the pancakes and eggs while Bennett did the bacon and Tristan cut up the fresh fruit. They had begun to put the first of the pancakes and bacon out when others began to make an appearance.

Bennett found himself keeping an eye out for Grace, but even after everyone else had made an appearance, she was still absent.

"Is Grace okay?" Bennett asked Tami as they sat down together at the end of the table.

"She's fine," Tami said with a smile. "Just super tired from a busy week. I think Sierra was going to take her up a little bit to eat, and I wouldn't be surprised if she went back to sleep. Between wedding stuff and growing a baby, I think she's just drained."

"I know several are feeling that way, and they're not even pregnant," Bennett commented as he cut his pancakes.

"Yeah, that letdown after something like a wedding can be physical as well as emotional. I think it's a bit of both for Grace, but her pregnancy is fine, so you don't need to worry about that."

"Good to know," Bennett said, then decided he should probably change the subject. "So is Keenan hanging around for awhile today?"

"Yeah, I think so. James brought his boat out, and I think they're planning to stay on until tomorrow. Might be our last time out on the lake this year. Are you going to get your boat out on the water?"

"I might if enough people are interested."

It was almost noon before he got a text from James asking about the boats. A quick check with the people hanging out at the cabin revealed that most were up for some time out on the water. Grace still hadn't made an appearance, but since Tami—who was a nurse—wasn't concerned, he tried to keep his own concern reined in.

He'd thought that Grace might show up before they left for the dock, but she hadn't. His mom was staying behind, so at least she wasn't alone.

They ended up staying out on the boats for several hours. A few people—like Noella and Finn—had come for an hour or so before heading back into the city. James had said that he and Erin along with Tennyson and Forrest were staying another night. It was great to be surrounded by friends and family, and he and Kenton even managed to keep the conflict between them from raising its ugly head.

They were all pretty tired and hungry when they finally called it quits around four. Everyone headed back to the cabin after pulling the boats out of the water. When they got there, Grace told them that Emily and Steve had headed into a nearby town to pick up pizzas for supper. By the time they'd showered and cleaned up, the couple was back with a ton of pizza and soda. Bennett found he was starving so took several pieces of pizza before sitting down at the table across from Grace.

After his dad had said a prayer for their meal, Bennett said, "So Tami said you were pretty wiped out from everything. You feeling okay now?"

Grace nodded. "Just being able to sleep and relax helped a lot. I know you guys had fun on the boats, but I enjoyed the peace and quiet here with your mom. We had fun decompressing together."

"Are you ready for the big move?" Bennett asked. He was glad that he was staying put in the big apartment shuffle, but he planned to be available to help however it was needed.

"I think so. It's nice that I don't have a deadline to be out of the condo, but I should be able to get most of my stuff out fairly quickly. Thankfully, Ethan has decided—with Makayla's help, no doubt—to leave most of his furniture. The condo needs to be staged for selling, so I'm glad to leave the furniture there for the time being." Grace took a bite of her pizza, chewing and swallowing with a thoughtful look on her face. "And once it sells, I'll put the furniture into storage for a bit and then maybe try to sell it a little later on."

"Are you going to set up the nursery right away?"

Grace shrugged. "I don't think so. I'm not sure if I'll set anything up until I'm six months along or so. The move is enough for now."

"I'm sure that's true."

"Who's organizing the move?" Mitch asked as he settled into the seat beside Grace. "Is Makayla really trusting us to move Ethan's stuff?"

"Sierra told me that Makayla went through their apartment and put a post-it note on everything to tell people where stuff is supposed to go." Grace laughed. "I'm surprised that she trusted you guys not to 'lose' a couple of the notes."

"Don't give them ideas," Bennett said with a grin. "I'll follow the notes, but you know how the others are."

"Hey now," Mitch protested. "I'd rather not incur the wrath of Makayla, so I won't be losing any notes. Tempting as it may be to do so. She'd just make us move it all to the right places when she got back."

After having a good chuckle at Mitch's words, they discussed other aspects of the move which would happen the next weekend although Bennett figured that he and Mitch would begin to move things from Ethan's up to Makayla's throughout the week. That way, come the weekend, they could get Grace's stuff moved into Ethan's old apartment. Tami had already made the move down to the one-bedroom apartment on the main floor across the hall from Mitch.

Bennett was glad that the moves were finally happening. While he would never say it to Grace, he really felt that she needed to be closer to them. To the people who were willing to make up her support system. He knew that she would say that she didn't need help, and that was fine, but Bennett also knew that with his personality, he would always feel the need to take care of her. If Franklin had still been around to support her through her pregnancy, Bennett wouldn't feel that need to protect her.

But Franklin wasn't there to watch over Grace and the baby, so there was no way he wouldn't try to do what he could to help her. And then just pray that his protectiveness didn't lead to any other emotions for him. Grace had already made it clear that she wasn't going to let him into her life in any way except as a friend. So he needed to make sure that he kept his heart from falling for her once again. Any more than it already had.

Once they'd consumed the pizzas, his mom brought out brownies and ice cream for dessert and one of the teens pulled out some games. Bennett enjoyed times like this with his family and friends. And it was good to see Grace having a good time as well. And Tami looked happy with Keenan by her side. He hoped Makayla and Ethan were having fun where they were.

Contentment was a beautiful feeling. One he hoped he would always have.

Chapter Sixteen

*E*XHAUSTION PULLED AT GRACE, and she was so tempted to head into the bedroom and flop down on her new bed even though it had no sheets on it yet. She had returned to the city on Sunday and then on Monday had started to seriously pack up her stuff.

While she was leaving the larger furniture and some of the paintings, and sculptures that Franklin had decorated the condo with, she was taking all the dishes and other kitchenware, so that had all needed to be packed. And of course, all their personal stuff. She'd tackled her stuff first since she could come back after the move to finish getting Franklin's things put together and ready to go into storage until she could figure out what to do with them.

It was hard to think about giving away any of his things just yet, but at the same time, she didn't want to take all of them with her to the new apartment. She had chosen a few mementos of the happier times they'd had in recent months. Also, she had a framed picture of her favorite photo from their wedding that she had kept by her bedside. Other than that, most the things in Franklin's condo held significance for him but not for her.

"Why don't you sit down, Grace?" Bennett asked from behind her.

Grace turned to see him watching her with a look of concern. Though there were times when he didn't wear that expression around her, it seemed that he always thought she was pushing herself too hard.

"There's still so much to do," Grace said as she folded her arms. She gazed around the room at the stacks of boxes that awaited her attention. "If I sit down now, I probably won't get back up again."

"But maybe that's a sign that you should, in fact, sit down." Bennett gestured to an easy chair in the living room. "Put your feet up for a little while and boss us around. We're here to help."

"Listen to Bennett," Emily said as she walked out of the kitchen. "You may feel like it's your job to unpack everything, but your most important job right now is to growth that baby."

Grace sighed. Some days she missed having control of her own life. "Just let me grab some water, and I'll sit down for a few minutes."

Emily flopped her hands in a shooing motion. "Just go sit yourself down, I'll bring you something."

Grace knew better than to argue with the woman. Instead, she made her way over to the recliner Ethan had left behind and sat down. She toyed with the idea of lifting the footrest, but just sitting in the chair felt lazy enough.

"Get those feet up, sweetie," Emily said as she walked into the living room with a glass of water in one hand and a plate of cut up fruit in the other. "It'll help keep your feet from swelling. You've been on them all day."

Grace groaned but obeyed Emily's directive. She pulled the lever that would lift the footrest then took the water and fruit from Emily. "Thank you."

"You're very welcome." Emily kissed the top of her head. "You're growing our first grandbaby! We want to take care of you both."

Emily left the living room as if she had no clue of the impact of her words. And maybe she didn't. But Grace sat there, hands full, unable to wipe away the tears that slid down her cheeks.

"Grace? What's wrong?" Bennett quickly set the box he was carrying on top of a stack of others before coming to her side. Only his feet and legs visible from her head bent position.

"Nothing," she mumbled as she stared down at the fruit, trying to get herself back under control.

Bennett's legs moved out of view, and Grace glanced up to see him walking down the hallway to where the bedrooms were. She sniffled and lifted the glass of water to take a sip. The hormonal surges that brought her emotions so close to the surface were just another delightful aspect of her pregnancy. But still, her reaction to Emily's words had caught her off guard...just like the words had.

A couple of white tissues waved in front of her face. "Here you go."

She looked up to see that Bennett had returned. After setting the plate of fruit on her legs, she reached out to take the tissues from him. "Thanks."

He dropped to his haunches beside her. "Want to talk about it?"

Grace was a bit embarrassed as she swiped at the wetness on her cheeks before picking up a slice of apple. "Not really. Just having an emotional moment. They're happening more frequently these days."

Bennett seemed to consider her words before getting to his feet again. "I'm sure that's true. When Mom was pregnant with Dalton, she cried at the drop of a hat. I remember once when Tristan brought home some picture he'd drawn of our family, and Mom burst into tears. Poor Tris had no idea what was going on and started crying too."

"Sure, tell the story that makes me sound like a cry-baby," Tristan groused as he added another box to the pile in the living room. "How about the time you made Mom cry just by telling her you loved her? Making women cry since he was twelve years old."

Grace felt a surge of affection for the two guys as they teased each other. It felt like her ride on the emotional roller coaster was taking her up to the peak, but no doubt it was only a matter of time before she was over that peak and back down in a puddle of tears.

As she ate her fruit and drank her water, Grace directed the guys where to take the boxes. She was grateful that in the end, Ethan had decided to leave most of his furniture for her. Apparently he hadn't been as attached to his furniture as Makayla had been to hers. When it had come to merging households, about the only things—furniture-wise—that had gone from the second floor to the third floor had been Sierra's bedroom suite pieces and Ethan's favorite recliner—which wasn't the one she was sitting in. So though she had a lot of boxes to deal with, at least she hadn't had to worry about wearing the guys out with moving heavy furniture.

"Finish it all up, sweetie," Emily called out as she walked past, heading for the hallway.

Grace didn't even bother to argue that she was getting full. The strawberries, apples, and grapes had hit the spot. She had definitely been trying to eat better since finding out she was pregnant. Thankfully, her cravings so far had been fairly healthy. Well, as long as lots of ice cream was healthy. *Calcium, baby, calcium.* And the occasional day when all the baby wanted was sweets.

When the food was gone, and the glass was empty, Grace pushed the footrest down and got to her feet. She headed for the kitchen and put the glass and plate into the dishwasher. Her first dishes in it.

Emily had obviously known what she was talking about because the short break and the food had rejuvenated her. For how long, she had no idea, but she was going to enjoy this burst of energy while she could.

Grace headed down the hallway to where the bedrooms were. There was a bathroom on one side of the hallway and opposite that was the room that would be the nursery. Right now it was empty. At the end of the hallway was the entrance to the master bedroom with its own bathroom. Inside her bedroom, she found Emily and Danica making up the bed.

"You didn't have to do that," Grace said.

"I know, but we're no good at carrying boxes, so we do what we can." Emily smoothed her hand over the duvet. "Did you buy this new? It's so beautiful."

Grace went to stand next to Emily and touched the material. "Yes, I found it on sale and fell in love with the colors. I hope to find more things for the bedroom that will have these colors."

"I'm going to go see how Sierra is settling in upstairs," Danica said as she put the pillows at the top of the bed.

"Okay, sweetie. I'll be leaving in about an hour so make sure you two are ready to go."

Tristan and Bennett came into the room with a couple more boxes, making the room suddenly crowded.

"These have bedroom written on them," Tristan said. "Do you just want them with the rest in here?"

"Yeah, thanks," Grace said. "Is there much left? It seems you guys have brought in a lot of boxes already."

"There are a few left," Bennett said. "And then it's just the unpacking."

"I marked the boxes that hold the most important things, so if it takes me a bit to unpack the rest, I'm still good."

After finishing in the bathroom, Emily helped her unpack a few of the kitchen boxes, making sure that she had plates to eat off of and pots and pans to be able to cook. Emily also tackled a couple of the boxes that held Grace's towels and other bathroom things. The woman seemed to understand that Grace needed at least the basics around her to feel like she was in her own home.

"Don't do too much," Emily cautioned as she was getting ready to leave. "You've done a lot today. I think you need to just relax for the rest of the day."

That sounded amazing, so Grace had no problem agreeing to it. "Thank you so much for all your help."

Emily gave her a tight hug. "It was fun. I'm glad you're back close to family."

Grace hadn't been sure about the move initially, but now that she was settling in, she was so grateful for the opportunity to move back into the building. The condo had been a place to live, but it hadn't really been home. The house that she and Franklin had been talking about buying would have been home, Grace was sure of that. It would have been a place they'd chosen together. A place that would have reflected both of them instead of just Franklin.

After everyone had left, Grace opened a couple of boxes but didn't end up unpacking much beyond that. She went to the fridge and stood there, staring at the nearly bare interior. She'd cleaned out the fridge at the condo, but there hadn't been much there.

There was a knock on the door that pulled her attention from her food search. Walking over, she opened the door without even looking through the peephole. No one could get into the building without buzzing first, so this was either Bennett or Mitch. She wasn't surprised at all to see that it was Bennett.

"Hey," he said with a quick smile. "I was talking to Mom a minute ago, and when I told her that I was going to the store, she mentioned that you might need some stuff as well. Can I pick you up anything?"

Grace thought about the state of her fridge and how many things she needed. It wouldn't be fair to make Bennett pick those things up for her, but maybe she could get a ride with him and pick up the stuff herself.

"Would it be okay if I just came with you?"

Bennett's eyes widened briefly, but then he said, "Sure, that would be fine."

Though she normally wouldn't impose on him, the fact was that if she went with Bennett, he could push the cart and carry the groceries, making things a lot easier for her. It felt like she was using him, and in a sense, she was, but he *had* offered. Well, okay, he hadn't offered to take her, but he was always offering to help her.

"Thank you. I appreciate that. Are you going now?" When he nodded, she said, "Hang on a second. Let me just grab my purse."

When she came back from grabbing it off the kitchen counter, she found Bennett looking at his phone. "Okay. I'm ready."

As they walked down the stairs—that wasn't something she was looking forward to tackling with a baby in a car seat—Grace began to think of what exactly she needed to buy.

"Do you have a list?" she asked Bennett as he backed out of his spot a few minutes later.

"If I say yes, does that make me a nerd?"

"Haha. No. It means you're organized." Grace tapped her phone to bring up her notepad app, and she began to make a list. "I don't have one like I usually do, but I do need a few things to tide me over until I can do a bigger shop."

When they got to the store, Bennett took care of getting the cart, and then they headed inside. It was odd to be grocery shopping with someone else. Franklin had never been that into shopping unless it had been for clothes and such for himself. Otherwise, he would just tell her to order online if she wasn't interested in going shopping. So she'd usually just gone by herself, dashing in to get what they needed for the week. It wasn't something she had really enjoyed.

"So, are we going for pickles and ice cream?" Bennett asked as they headed for the fresh fruits and vegetables section.

"Ugh. No. Ice cream definitely but not pickles. That is not something I'm craving at the moment."

Bennett pulled out his phone and stared down at it. "Good to know. I'm in the market for ice cream too, but first, the healthy stuff."

"Well, that's no fun," Grace said, even as she searched for a decent hand of bananas. She found that they were something she usually grabbed in the morning to eat before heading to work.

Bennett put a bag with some apples into the cart. "You can put your stuff at the front of the cart if you want."

Grace nodded and set her bananas where he indicated. She also got herself some apples and a couple of avocados.

"Avocados?" Bennett wrinkled his nose.

"You don't like them?"

"Not even a little. The texture is just..." He shuddered. "Nope."

"You don't know what you're missing." Grace gave him a smile as she headed for the tomatoes.

As they worked their way around the store, Grace found herself enjoying it more than she usually did. And it was great to have someone who could reach the items on the top shelf. She ended up getting more than she had planned to, but Bennett seemed to be in no rush, so she went ahead and grabbed enough to last her through the next week.

"Do you have to drink a lot of milk now?" Bennett asked as he picked up some cream.

"I should probably drink more, but I'm not a huge fan of milk unless it's in a shake."

"Or frozen?" Bennett asked as they finished up their shopping in the ice cream aisle.

"Only if it's ice cream. I'm not an ice milk fan." Grace opened the freezer door and pulled out a container of chocolate chip cookie dough ice cream then went looking for some rocky road.

"How many are you planning to buy?" Bennett asked as he stood there with a container of chocolate fudge brownie.

Grace turned to face him with a lift of her brow. "Are you judging me?"

Bennett chuckled and put his ice cream into the cart. "Never. You're eating for two after all, so it makes sense that you have to buy two—one for you and one for the baby."

"That sounds good to me. The rocky road is for the baby."

"Have you wandered through the baby stuff yet?" Bennett asked as he pushed the cart toward the checkout.

"No. I figure I'll be doing enough of that in a few months." For some reason, Grace was in no hurry to start buying stuff for the baby. She knew that part of it was that she was still grieving for what a pregnancy should have meant in her life. Moving into a new chapter with Franklin. Instead of that, she was grocery shopping with Bennett and trying to figure out how she was going to balance everything as a single parent.

Suddenly, the fun of the evening slipped away. She fell quiet as Bennett began to unload his groceries from the cart to the conveyor belt. "I'll put my stuff through first, so I can get to bagging it and then I can do yours."

Grace didn't argue with him, and she started to unload her items once he was done with his. When he moved up to pay for his groceries, she pushed the cart forward to get the last of her things onto the conveyor. As she waited, Grace looked over at the display next to her and decided the baby wanted chocolate. She grabbed a KitKat bar and then added a second one because she could never have too much chocolate.

Bennett bagged up his groceries and then began to work on hers while she watched the cashier put the items through. By the time the cashier was done and waiting for Grace's debit card to go through, Bennett had all the groceries bagged up. He was definitely more efficient at bagging than she was. Without fail, she was still bagging her groceries when the cashier started on the next person.

"Ready to go?" Bennett asked as he put the last bag into the cart. "Did you need to stop anywhere else?"

"No, I'm good to go." In fact, she was more than ready to be home. Even though it was still filled with boxes that needed to be unpacked, the apartment was already feeling more like home than Franklin's condo ever had. She hated herself for making that comparison so frequently because it had been something they were working on changing. It pained her that she didn't have memories of a home with Franklin that was truly a reflection of them both.

Bennett seemed to realize that she had retreated into herself and didn't press for conversation on the drive home. After he had parked in his spot behind the building, he said, "Why don't you grab a couple of the lighter bags and head on up. I'll take care of the rest."

Grace considered arguing, but she suddenly found that her energy was gone, pushed away by memories and sadness. "Thank you."

Bennett chose a couple of bags for her, then grasped the handles of several others. Grace unlocked the door to let them into the building and led the way up the single flight of stairs to their floor. After she opened the door to her apartment, Bennett followed her in with the bags he carried.

"I'll be up with the rest in a minute," he said as he put the bags on the counter.

Grace appreciated that he didn't put everything on the floor. Not that she couldn't bend over, but doing that wasn't as comfortable as it used to be. She found the bag with the ice cream in it and stuck the two containers into the freezer. Next came the bag with the refrigerator things. Bennett had definitely packed strategically. He could give bag packing lessons. She always started out trying to pack strategically, but as soon as she realized she was falling behind, she'd just start tossing things into bags in order to not hold things up for others in the line.

"Here's the last of them," Bennett said as he carried a couple of bags into the kitchen and set them on the counter. "Did you need help putting things away?"

"I think I can handle this part, but thank you." Grace gave him a smile. "And thanks for letting me tag along tonight."

"Anytime. I usually make a grocery run on Saturday evenings. Feel free to come along or give me a list." Bennett paused. "I guess I'll see you tomorrow."

Grace walked with him to the door. "Good night."

After watching Bennett head back for the staircase, Grace shut the door and locked it. She turned around and leaned back against it for a moment. Exhaustion was pulling at her once again, but she knew she couldn't let herself relax just yet because if she did, she wouldn't get done what she needed to do. Pushing off the door, she headed for the kitchen to finish putting away the groceries before crawling into her new bed.

Chapter Seventeen

ENNETT AND ETHAN WERE THE LAST to leave the room where they'd met with the men's class before the service. It was their first class back after taking the summer off, and Bennett found himself excited about the upcoming year. He was glad that Ethan was in the class with him. They had agreed to co-lead it, and he was so encouraged by the growth the other man had shown since they'd first met over a year ago.

"That was a great class," Ethan said as they headed toward the foyer.

"I was surprised at the turnout. It is amazing to get that on a Sunday morning." Bennett spotted Makayla in the foyer and followed Ethan as he headed in that direction. "I hope they all continue to come."

"I suppose the attendance will fluctuate, but it would nice to stay that size or grow." Ethan greeted Makayla with a quick kiss when they reached her. "Hey, sweetie."

Bennett saw Grace standing a little past Makayla talking to Danica and Sierra. The two teenagers had probably been the most excited about Grace's pregnancy. They were always giving her name ideas and talking about how they were going to be the best babysitters ever.

Though he wasn't altogether sure why, Bennett got the sense that Grace was doing her best to ignore the impending birth. She was dealing with the pregnancy, but it seemed odd that she wasn't interested in looking at baby stuff or setting up furniture for the nursery. Of course, he couldn't discount the role her grief might be playing in all of it, but at the same time, he would think that a grieving woman would be looking forward to the birth of the child that would carry on her deceased husband's legacy.

But what did he know? When it came to women in general, let alone Grace in particular, he had no clue. Grace's grief mixed with her pregnancy was new ground for all of them.

After their little trip to the grocery store, Bennett had hoped that Grace would actually let him help her out more, but aside from when they were at work, he hadn't seen much of her. In fact, he saw about as much of her now as he did when she had lived at the condo.

He followed the others into the sanctuary, stopping to talk briefly with one of the ushers before continuing down to the pew where Makayla and Ethan were sitting. After taking a seat beside Ethan, he stared at the front of the sanctuary and let out a long breath.

He was tired. He clasped his hands loosely between his knees and let his shoulders slump. It was odd how coming into the sanctuary often brought to the surface the things he tried not to focus on the rest of the time. Like just how tired he was.

It had been a hectic couple of weeks, especially with Ethan being away. Without a family of his own, he knew he had a habit of working more than he really had to, of taking on extra commitments at the church, or helping out friends and family members, often at the expense of doing things he enjoyed. But doing that often brought an inner sense of fulfillment even though it could be physically draining.

As he watched, the worship team filed out onto the stage. When he saw Dalton there with his guitar, Bennett smiled. Seeing his youngest brother using his talents at church made Bennett happy.

As the music started, he put away the thoughts that were weighing him down. He usually left a service refreshed, and he expected nothing different this time.

WORKING ON A REPLY to a business email, Bennett paused when his cell phone began to ring. He recognized the ringtone as Makayla's, so he reached out and picked the phone up from where it lay on his desk.

"Hello," he said after he put the phone on speaker and returned to his email.

"Bennett, I have a huge favor to ask of you," Makayla said, her words coming in a rush.

Bennett glanced over at the phone, hesitant to respond. In the past, Makayla's huge favors had gotten him in trouble.

"What's going on?" he asked with a bit of trepidation because he usually couldn't say no to her.

Makayla gave an audible sigh. "I was supposed to go with Grace to her ultrasound appointment today. But I had an appointment of my own this morning which is running much later than I thought it would." She hesitated for a moment. "Would you be able to take her?"

Bennett sat back in his chair. He ran his hand across the back of his neck as he tried to formulate a response. "Not to be insensitive, but does she really need someone with her for this?"

"Bennett," Makayla said, her voice laced with exasperation. "Of *course* she needs someone to go with her. Normally, it would've been Franklin, but he's not here, so someone needs to be there with her."

"And why exactly has this fallen to me?" It wasn't that Bennett didn't want to take Grace. In fact, the opposite is true. But he had to factor Grace's feelings into the scenario, and when he did that, it didn't seem like a situation that she would be happy with. "Why can't Tami or even Sammi take her?"

"Tami is working, and Sammi is sleeping since she had an overnight shift, and she'll be working again tonight," Makayla said. "If Mom were here, I would ask her. But since she's with Dad in Vancouver, that kind of just leaves you. Trust me, I did try to consider other options before I got to you."

Bennett leaned forward to rest his elbows on the desk, his fingers massaging his temples. He still didn't think that Grace was going to be happy with the solution Makayla had found to her problem. "Have you actually talked to her about this? Or were you just planning to have me surprise her with the change in plans?"

Makayla sighed again. "It's not that I want to surprise her with it, but I just want to let her know there is another plan in place when I call to tell her that I can't be there."

"And what's to stop her from just deciding to take her car and go on her own?"

"She doesn't have her car with her today. Ethan dropped it off with Finn's mechanics early this morning for an oil change, so she came to work with me. I had planned to take her by the shop to pick up her car after her appointment was over."

Bennett let out a sigh. He would agree to go with her, but he would also be willing give her the keys to his truck if she objected to having him come along.

In the months since Franklin's death, Grace's interactions with him had blown hot and cold. One day she would be happy to have him help her out with something, and the next she would barely speak to him. Bennett had given up trying to figure out what prompted her mood swings — aside from her pregnancy. He had no idea which way she was going to swing when she heard the news that he was Makayla's substitute.

"So I'm assuming her appointment is sooner rather than later?" Bennett said.

"It's at two o'clock. I haven't even gotten into my doctor's office yet. I'm still sitting around in the waiting room, and my appointment was for eleven-thirty."

Bennett heard the faint sound of Makayla's name being called.

"I gotta go," Makayla said. "Guess you'll have to be the one to tell Grace about the change of plans."

Before Bennett could say anything, the line went dead. He let out a frustrated sigh and reached up to rake his fingers through his hair. Though he did his best to try to accommodate Grace's moods, he hated to put her on the spot. But unfortunately, he had no choice.

He pushed back from his desk and reached for his suit coat from the back of his chair. He slid his arms into it and pulled it up onto his shoulders before grabbing his phone and keys off his desk. After taking a moment to brace himself for Grace's possible reaction, Bennett left his office and headed for the foyer. Grace looked up as he stopped beside her desk. He could see that she was ready to go. Her purse sat on the desk along with her sunglasses and a water bottle.

"I just got a call from Makayla," Bennett began. He saw her brows draw together in a frown as she glanced at the clock on the wall.

"She was supposed to take me to my ultrasound appointment," Grace said.

Bennett nodded. "That's why she called me. She said that her appointment was running late, and she'd only just now been called into the doctor's office while on the phone with me. She asked if I would be willing to take you to your appointment since your car is in the shop."

Grace's frowned deepened. "You don't have to do that. I know you're busy. I can just call a cab instead."

Bennett shoved his hands into the pockets of his pants. "I'm willing to take you, Grace. I was only answering some emails."

Grace got to her feet, an uncertain expression on her face. "Are you sure? I hate to impose on you in this way."

"It's not an imposition," Bennett tried to assure her. "And we can swing by and get your car at the garage when your appointment's over."

"As long as you're sure." Grace picked up her purse, sunglasses, and water bottle. "I don't mind taking a cab, but I'd rather not." She glanced around then said, "Just give me a minute. I need to let Maya know that I'm leaving."

Bennett gave a nod and went to stand next to the door. It didn't take long before Grace reappeared with Maya at her side.

"I probably won't be back today, but I'll see you tomorrow." Grace gave Maya a parting wave then headed in Bennett's direction.

Bennett opened the door and held it for Grace. He followed her out into the cool fall afternoon. The leaves on the trees around the building had begun to turn beautiful shades of yellow, orange, and red. Fall was probably his favorite season of the year because of its beauty and the cooler temperatures.

He opened the door to the truck and waited as Grace grabbed hold of the handle above the door and stepped up into the cab. When she was secured in the seat, Bennett closed the door and walked around the bed of the truck to get to his door.

Once they were buckled in, Bennett backed out of his spot. "Where are you having the ultrasound done?"

"It's at the Women's Hospital at the Health Science Centre," Grace said, her voice soft. Bennett glanced over at her, dismayed to see the worried look on her face.

"Is this just a routine ultrasound?" Bennett asked, concerned that perhaps this appointment could have some potentially devastating news.

"Yes. It's just to check to make sure everything's okay with the baby. That it's grow is on track for my due date. My doctor tells me that it's routine." Grace paused then said, "But of course something can start out as routine and quickly change into something not so routine."

Before Bennett could stop himself, he had reached over to take one of her hands. He gave it a quick squeeze before releasing it. Gripping the steering wheel tightly in both hands, Bennett tried to reassure her. "We'll just have to pray that this stays a routine exam. There's no use borrowing trouble from the future."

Grace was silent for several minutes before speaking again. "I've spent the last couple nights imagining the worst. Preparing myself for the worst. I just haven't been able to let myself believe that this pregnancy is going to be trouble-free. That this baby is going to be born healthy."

Bennett wanted to reassure her that everything was going to be fine, but he couldn't guarantee that. He wanted to. More than anything else in the world, Bennett wanted to be able to tell Grace that the rest of her life would be free from heartache and sorrow. But he just couldn't do it. And he respected her enough to not offer her empty platitudes.

When he got to the hospital, Bennett parked his truck in the pay parking structure then followed Grace as she led the way into the Women's Hospital. She checked in at the information desk and was given directions to where she needed to go.

Though there was a waiting room in the general area, Bennett chose to follow Grace as she walked down a wide hallway to another waiting area. There she gave her name and appointment time to the woman sitting behind the desk.

This waiting area was much smaller, with only a handful of people waiting. A man who looked to be about his age sat beside a woman who looked ready to deliver at any moment. Seated at the other end of the group of chairs were two women, with the pregnant one looking closer to Danica's age. He couldn't imagine having a baby at such a young age.

Grace walked over to the chairs and sat down, settling her purse in her lap. She watched Bennett as he sat down beside her but didn't say anything to him.

As Bennett made assumptions about the others there in the room with them, he wondered what they might be assuming when they looked at him and Grace. No doubt they thought he was the father of her baby and that they were there together for the ultrasound of their little one.

If only they knew the truth. It was a reminder that so often the outward appearances of people or a situation could be completely off-base.

A nurse stood in the doorway and called out a name. The couple on the other side of Grace got to their feet and followed the nurse out of the room. Not long after that, someone else came in and gave their name at the desk then took the recently vacated seats, but still, Grace said nothing to him. Because of that, he didn't know if Grace wanted him to go with her into the ultrasound or if she preferred for him to stay in the waiting area until she was done.

By the time the nurse came to call Grace, Bennett still wasn't sure what to do. He got to his feet when Grace did, and when she turned to look at him, he finally asked, "Do you want me to come with you?"

Chapter Eighteen

*T*HERE WAS A MIX OF FEAR and vulnerability on her face, so Bennett wasn't surprised when Grace nodded. Without hesitation, he followed her as the nurse led them down the hallway to another door.

Once inside the room, the technician pulled the curtain to give them privacy. She instructed Grace on how to position herself on the bed. Bennett took Grace's purse and water bottle then helped her onto the bed before settling into a nearby chair.

"I'll just have you lift your shirt over your belly," the technician said. "I'll tuck a towel here to protect your pants from the gel."

Bennett kept his head bent, gaze on the floor, trying to figure out why he hadn't realized sooner what exactly this ultrasound would involve. Much like his sisters, Grace had adopted a more modest approach to her clothing. Even her swimsuit—at least the ones he'd seen her in—had always been one piece. So Bennett felt a little uncomfortable to be in the room with her as she bared her stomach. It created a feeling of intimacy that he didn't want because it was fake.

He wasn't there as her husband, and no doubt she didn't really want him there either. They were both trapped in the situation. He had no idea if she'd thought through what having him in the room meant. Or maybe he was the only one sensitive to the situation.

"The gel's going to be a little bit cold," the technician said, and then Bennett heard a squirting sound. "Now, let's just see how the little one is today."

Bennett tried to keep his attention on the floor, but when he heard the technician begin to point out body parts of the baby, he couldn't resist looking up at the monitor. He listened as the technician explained that that particular ultrasound was a 3D one, which allowed them to see the baby in much greater detail. Bennett stared at the screen as the technician worked, moving whatever she held in her hand around on Grace's stomach.

"Were you wanting to know the sex of the baby?" the technician asked.

Bennett glanced at Grace, curious to hear what her response would be. For some reason, he really hoped that she said yes because as he looked at the figure on the ultrasound, Grace's baby had become very, very real to him.

Grace stared at the monitor in silence. Bennett met the technician's curious gaze as she looked between the two of them. Finally, Grace gave a slow nod, and Bennett felt a rush of relief. Excitement grew within him as he stared at the monitor once more, waiting for the technician to tell them if it was a boy or a girl.

"Well, I hope you like the color pink because it looks like you're having a girl."

Once again, without thinking, Bennett reached for Grace's hand. He meant to just give her a quick squeeze, but her fingers tightened around his and held on. And in that moment, Bennett realized that a connection had been made within him to the child that Grace carried. He might not have been the one to contribute to the baby's DNA, but he had been there when they'd found out she was a little girl.

And while she might not be his biological child, she was always going to hold a special place in his heart. He just hoped that Grace would allow him to have an active part in her life.

"I'll just print off a few of these pictures for you," the technician said with a smile.

"Thank you," Grace said, her hand still clutching his.

Bennett wondered if she was aware that she still held it. He was in no rush to end the contact between them. He found that—right or wrong—he wanted a connection with Grace just as much as he did with her daughter.

The technician stood and began to wipe the gel from Grace's stomach. After she was done, Grace let go of Bennett's hand and worked her top down to cover her stomach. When she struggled to sit up, Bennett reached out and helped her into a sitting position.

"Here you go." The technician held out a strip of paper. "Congratulations on your little one."

"Will I need to have another ultrasound?" Grace asked as she slid off the examination table to stand next to Bennett. She took her purse back and tucked the ultrasound into it.

"That will be up to your doctor," the technician replied. "But normally if a pregnancy is going well, there's no need for any further scans."

Bennett wasn't sure if Grace wanted to have another ultrasound or not, but she nodded her head and thanked the technician before heading to the door. Bennett followed behind her, amazed at how much had changed for him in the past half hour.

Grace was quiet once again as they walked the wide hallway and then exited the building. Bennett didn't bother to say anything, knowing that if Grace wanted to talk to him, she would.

Bennett paid for the parking, and then they took the elevator to the level where they had parked the truck. He opened the door for Grace once more and waited for her to get settled. She was still quiet when he slid behind the wheel and backed out of the parking space. So many questions were on the tip of his tongue as he guided the truck out of the parkade and onto the street to take them to their next stop.

The drive to the garage didn't take long and soon Bennett was parking in the small lot attached to it. He got out of the truck and walked around to open Grace's door and help her out. Though he knew he didn't need to hang around to help Grace since this was her car and she could handle it on her own, Bennett still followed her into the office.

"Hello there, you two," Finn Kinnaird said with a smile. "I guess you're here for your car, Grace."

Bennett nodded his head at the man in greeting but didn't say anything further.

"So everything was okay? It just needed an oil change?" Grace asked.

Finn nodded. "Your car's in fine shape. Just keep bringing her back for regular maintenance, and you'll be fine."

"So are Makayla and Ethan back from their honeymoon?" Finn asked as he settled the bill with Grace.

"Yep, and boy, am I glad," Bennett said. "I hadn't realized how much I rely on Ethan, and just how much he does for the company until I had to do it all while he was gone."

Finn chuckled. "I know how that is. I had my main mechanic off for a week at the beginning of June, and it felt like none of us could pick up the slack. It made me very grateful to have the man working here."

"That's definitely how I feel about Ethan, too." Bennett watched as Grace put her debit card back into her wallet then slid her wallet into her purse.

Grace took the keys when Finn held them out to her. "Thank you again for your work on my car."

"Anytime," the man replied with a broad smile.

After asking him to pass on their greetings to his wife, Noella, and saying goodbye to Finn, Bennett and Grace left the office. Bennett was reluctant to say goodbye to Grace, but he figured that she wanted to get home.

"I guess I'll see you later," Bennett said as they stood together in the middle of the lot.

Grace nodded and looked like she was going to move toward her car, then paused. She turned to look at him, her brows drawn together. "Thank you for taking me to my appointment."

"I know I wasn't your first choice," Bennett said as he gave her a smile to take the edge off his words. "But I'm really glad that I was able to be there with you for this."

"I appreciate your support. I didn't realize how much I actually wanted someone to be there with me."

There was so much Bennett wanted to say to her, but he was pretty sure that she wasn't in a place to be willing to hear it. So instead, he nodded and assured her that the news they'd heard about the baby's gender wouldn't be something he'd tell anyone else. That was her news to share, not his.

As he drove back to the office, Bennett had to fight his natural tendencies to want to help Grace even more than he had been since Franklin's death. It was so reminiscent of how he'd felt not long after they'd met when he'd found out that her parents had passed away and then again when her grandmother had died. But she hadn't let him help her then, and Bennett was pretty sure that she wouldn't let him help her now.

Bennett had no sooner set foot in his office than Makayla appeared in his doorway.

"Thank you so much for covering for me with Grace," Makayla said as she dropped into the seat across from him. "My doctor is usually much more punctual than she was today. I thought I'd have the time for my appointment and then Grace's."

"Don't worry about it," Bennett said as he removed his suit coat and hung it on the back of the chair. He sank down into the chair and leaned back. "We didn't have to wait too long once we got there and the ultrasound itself only took about half an hour."

Makayla stared at him for a moment then asked, "Did you go into the ultrasound with her?"

Bennett hesitated a moment before nodding. "It didn't seem like she wanted to be alone, and she didn't tell me no when I asked if she wanted me there."

Again, Makayla stared at him, her brows drawing together. "Is there something that I should know about?"

Bennett knew that there were lots of things she probably *wanted* to know, but right then there was absolutely nothing that she *should* know. "Everything was fine as far as the technician could tell. You'll need to talk to Grace if you want more details about it. All I know is that the technician said that everything looked good and that she probably wouldn't need to have another ultrasound if her pregnancy continues to go well."

Makayla had a thoughtful look on her face as she regarded him. "I think I'll give Grace a call just to make sure that she's okay. I know this would've been something that Franklin would've done with her to."

"She seemed alright when I dropped her off to pick up her car, but I think we both know that she's good at hiding her feelings," Bennett said with a sigh. He sat forward and grabbed the pen that was sitting on his desk. He slid it through his fingers, the smooth surface gliding easily. "I'm sure she would appreciate a call from you."

"I'll do that now." Makayla got to her feet. "Thanks again for filling in for me on such short notice."

Though Bennett would've like to continue thinking about his time with Grace and the news she'd received, he decided that it would do more harm than good, so he set those thoughts aside and focused on the work he'd abandoned when he'd left earlier.

GRACE PULLED HER CAR into her parking spot and gathered up her things before getting out and heading into the apartment building. With a sigh of relief, she walked into her apartment and shut the door on the outside world. She went right into the bedroom and changed out of her work clothes into a pair of loose shorts and a baggy T-shirt. Then she went in search of food because she'd been too nervous to eat the lunch she'd brought to have before going to her appointment.

She'd been dealing with a tremendous amount of fear in the days leading up to the ultrasound. There was a part of her that didn't believe that the baby would be born safely and healthy. Until her conversation with Bennett earlier, she hadn't shared those fears with anyone because she knew they'd all just try to reassure her. She had been pleasantly surprised—and thankful—when Bennett hadn't. As she'd laid on the bed in the ultrasound room, all she could think about was what the ultrasound would find wrong with the baby she carried. So, to get through it without any bad news and, in fact, to hear some good news, had been unexpected.

She pressed her hand to her stomach. *A girl.* She was going to have a daughter. Though she hadn't felt a strong preference either way, she had wondered if she'd be able to be a good mother to a boy. After all, what did she know about boys? Pretty much nothing until they reached adulthood.

As she let the thought that she was going to have a girl settle into her mind, Grace opened the fridge and begin to pull out what she needed to make a salad. Since moving into the apartment, she'd been trying to make a real effort to eat healthy for the sake of the baby. It was hard, at times, when her cravings were for things that weren't exactly the most nutritious. But, hopefully, the salads and fresh fruits she'd been eating would offset the ice cream and chocolate bars.

After she had made her salad, Grace sat down at the table next to the window that overlooked the park. If she continued to live there after the baby was born—and so far she planned to—that would be where she would take her daughter to play.

Though she had told herself over and over again to not build up her hopes where the baby was concerned, Grace just couldn't seem to help having those mental flashes of what was yet to come. Depending on her mood and the situation, those wonderings could either be good or bad. Today they happened to be good, but just as quickly they could be dragged down if she let herself dwell on the fact that there was still plenty of time for something to go wrong.

Instead of focusing on that, Grace focused on what she was going to do with this newfound knowledge. Knowledge shared by only three people. Her, the technician, and Bennett. It was the last person that gave her pause. It felt strangely intimate to think that she shared that knowledge with Bennett. Out of everyone she knew, he was now the one that shared her most precious secret. She wondered if she would walk into work the next day to find a bouquet of pink roses on her desk.

Grace laughed at the idea, though. Bennett had promised not to reveal her secret to anyone, and having a bouquet of pink roses at her desk the day after her ultrasound would be a sure giveaway. She still wasn't sure if she wanted everyone to know or not. In fact, she hadn't been sure if *she* wanted to know until the moment she saw the baby on the screen and then the technician had asked her. Grace savored the knowledge now. Would Franklin have been disappointed? He had made no secret of the fact that once he decided he wanted children, that he'd really hoped for a son. Someone he could do things with.

Grace knew from experience that girls could do things with their dads just as much as boys could. Steve Callaghan had proven that, but she wasn't sure that Franklin had embraced that idea for himself.

She had barely finished her salad when her phone rang. It didn't surprise her to see Makayla's name on the screen.

She'd no sooner accepted the call and said hello when she heard Makayla's voice, full of apology. "Oh Grace. I'm so sorry that I wasn't able to go with you. My doctor was late seeing me, and I got tied up. I hope it's okay that I asked Bennett to take you."

Grace still wasn't entirely sure how she felt about Bennett's presence at the ultrasound, but she wasn't going to make her friend feel bad about something that was beyond her control. "It's fine, Makayla. Everything went well."

"So, there was nothing wrong with the baby?"

"No. The technician said that everything looked good. Although I do realize from having read other people's experiences that ultrasounds don't catch everything."

"Don't think that way," Makayla said. "I'm sure everything is just fine with your little one." She paused then said, "Did you find out if it's a boy or a girl?"

Grace contemplated keeping the information to herself, but in the end, she just couldn't. "I'm having a girl."

There was an excited squeal from Makayla, and Grace couldn't help but smile at her friend's excitement.

"Are you planning to tell people?" Makayla asked. "Because I'm not sure that I can keep this secret until your due date."

"You managed to keep the fact that I was pregnant a secret," Grace reminded her. "But no, I don't think I'll keep this a secret."

"How are you planning to let everyone know?"

Grace felt a twinge of sadness as she thought of all the reveal videos she'd seen on Facebook. The ones where the couple had opened a box of balloons or cut into a cake to see what color was revealed. There wouldn't be anything like that for her. "I think I'll announce it to your family the next time we're all together but just tell other people as they ask me."

"That sounds like a good idea. I know Mom is going to go nuts buying everything pink."

Grace once again stared out at the park across the street. She was thankful for the people in her life who were willing to fill the roles left empty by the deaths of her loved ones. Their excitement over the upcoming birth also helped to buoy her up when grief pulled her down.

"I can't believe that I'm the first one besides you to know that you're having a girl." Makayla paused. "Oh, right. I guess I'm not. Bennett knows, right?"

Grace wondered if Makayla knew that Bennett had been in the ultrasound room with her. Or did she just assume that Grace had told him afterward? "Yes. Bennett knows."

"Well, I think we should have a dinner to celebrate. I'm sure Mom would love to have something out at the house. Do you think you'd be up for that?"

With her phone in one hand, Grace picked up the empty salad bowl in the other and headed for the kitchen. "That sounds fine. When were you thinking of?"

"Let me check with Mom, but maybe we could do it on Friday."

"Do you think you can keep it a secret for three more days?" Grace asked as she put her plate in the sink.

"Oh I can, but I'm not sure if Bennett can."

Grace smiled at Makayla's dig at her brother. "He managed not to tell you, didn't he?"

"Not fair. I can't believe that my doctor's appointment screwed all that up. I could've been the first one to know instead of Bennett."

As she filled a glass with milk from the fridge, Grace realized that she was kind of happy that Bennett had been with her instead of Makayla. She really didn't want to think too much about why she felt that way, so she happily engaged in conversation with Makayla over the best way to let the rest of the family know the sex of the baby.

Maybe she'd get her reveal after all.

Chapter Nineteen

G RACE WALKED INTO THE KITCHEN of the Callaghan home a week later, surprised that she, Makayla, and Bennett had managed to keep from spilling the beans on the baby's gender. She found that she was excited for the evening and couldn't wait to share the news with the people gathered there.

In addition to the Callaghans and McFaddens, Makayla had also invited James, Erin, and a couple other friends who had known both her and Franklin.

The one question she figured that she would be asked the most that night once it was revealed that the baby was a girl, was what she planned to name her. Grace had spent some time thinking about that since the ultrasound, but she hadn't been able to settle on anything. It felt wrong to not have someone else's opinion to consider. She and Franklin had never gotten around to discussing what names they'd like if they ever got pregnant.

"So, are you still having problems with morning sickness?" Erin asked as they stood at the island counter in the huge kitchen at the Callaghan home, two cake boxes in front of them.

"Not as much as I was having in my first trimester," Grace told her. "It wasn't much fun for the first three months. I still get occasional bouts, but nothing like what I was having at the beginning. Thankfully." Grace rested her hand on her stomach which was barely showing a bump. "The biggest thing I've struggled with has been the weird changes in what I want to eat. One week I'm all about the sweets, then the next week the very thought of them makes me feel sick."

As others arrived, they congregated in the kitchen, no doubt drawn there by the delicious aromas in the air. Grace knew Makayla had hoped that they could have a barbecue dinner outside, but the day had decided to be very fall-ish. All day there had been a light drizzle falling from dark gray clouds. So now they were eating indoors with fires crackling in the various fireplaces on the main floor of the sprawling home.

They had decided to do a cake reveal and had asked Erin to help them out. But in order to keep it a surprise from even her, they had asked Erin to bake two cakes—one pink and one blue—and then label their boxes so Grace would know which cake to cut open.

She was thankful that the rich aromas in the air didn't upset her stomach. There had been a quick menu change from barbecue to lasagna once the forecast for the day had been for rain. Thankfully, the baby hadn't objected to the change.

"Is everyone here?" Steve Callaghan asked as people began to gather at the large table in their expansive dining room a short time later.

The fire in the large fireplace that was shared with the living room wall created welcoming warmth on this damp evening. The other wall had large windows that looked out on the trees surrounding the home, but at the moment, they were streaked with rain.

"I think we're missing Bennett," Emily said as she came into the dining room with a basket of garlic bread in her hands. She turned to look at Makayla. "He was planning to be here, wasn't he?"

Makayla shrugged. "I assumed he would be, but to be honest, he didn't say one way or the other for sure."

"Maybe he's on a date," Mitch volunteered. "I saw him talking to one of the single women at church on Sunday. It was the same woman who asked me if he happened to be dating anyone at the moment. Felt like I was back in high school. Maybe she decided to make a move."

Grace gripped the back of the chair she stood behind. The thought that Bennett might be out on a date didn't sit well with her. And the fact that it didn't sit well with her didn't sit well with her either. It was none of her business if Bennett chose to date. In fact, she should be happy for him. But for some reason, being happy that he was dating was a feeling she could not muster up right then.

"Well, since everyone else is here, why don't we just go ahead and give thanks for the food," Steve suggested. He held out his hand to Emily, and everyone around the table followed suit, taking the hand of the person next to them.

Grace took Makayla's hand on one side, and Tami's on the other and bowed her head as Steve prayed. Once the prayer had been said, conversation picked up around the table as people begin to pass the food and fill their plates.

Grace was frustrated that the news that Bennett was on a date had tarnished the evening for her. The man had every right to do what he wanted with his time, and it shouldn't matter to her. What also frustrated her was that at a time when she should be feeling Franklin's absence, she was more bothered by Bennett's non-appearance.

That just wasn't right.

BENNETT LEFT THE RESTAURANT and jogged across the parking lot towards his truck. The rain hadn't let up all day, and there was a chill in the air that, if it were just a little bit later in the year, would have made him think snow was coming. Once inside the cab of the truck, he started it and cranked up the heat.

He knew he was late for the dinner out at his folks' place, but he still planned to head out there. When he had agreed to meet a couple from the church about a possible real estate transaction, Bennett hadn't realized that the meeting would drag on for so long. But the opportunity to meet with them had come out of the blue, and Bennett had decided to hear them out. Now he hoped that his dad might have a little time tonight after the dinner was over to discuss an idea Bennett had.

The drive out to his parents' place took a little bit longer than usual since the streets were slick, and everyone was driving with caution. Well, most everyone.

Bennett scowled as a large SUV cut in front of him then accelerated and swerved back into the other lane in front of another car. The driver was obviously in a hurry to get somewhere, but at the rate he was going, the only thing he was going to get was a ticket or a smashed-up vehicle.

When Bennett finally pulled up in front of the house that had been his home throughout his teenage years, he was surprised at the number of vehicles there. Makayla had said something to him about them having a family dinner that night, but apparently it had morphed into something more since he recognized James's SUV among the vehicles there.

He took a moment to look at the house and the warm light spilling from the windows. Bennett had no doubt that his dad had lit fires in the fireplaces. It was that kind of evening.

After shutting off the truck, Bennett climbed out and headed for the front door. He let himself in without ringing the bell or knocking on the door. As soon as he stepped into the foyer, he was greeted with warmth and the sound of happy conversation coming from the dining room.

He shrugged out of his coat and hung it in the closet near the door. As he made his way toward the dining room, there was a sudden burst of laughter, and without even being in the room or part of the conversation, Bennett found himself smiling.

When he stepped into the room, he found himself searching out Grace automatically. His gaze landed on her where she sat between Makayla and Tami. Though conversation appeared to be going on around her, her attention was on the plate in front of her.

"Bennett!" his mother said as she got up from her seat and came around to give him a hug. "We weren't sure if you were going to make it tonight."

"Yeah, sorry I'm late," Bennett said and bent to press a kiss to her cheek. "I ended up having a meeting that ran longer than anticipated."

"That's okay, sweetheart." She reached up and patted his cheek. "We're just glad you're here now."

Bennett found an empty seat between Mitch and Tristan which just happened to be across the table from Grace.

"I thought you were out on a date," Mitch said as he handed Bennett a big pan still half full of lasagna.

Bennett frowned at his brother before turning his attention to dishing up a serving of the lasagna onto his plate. "Why would you think that?"

"Well, I saw you talking with Susan at church on Sunday." Mitch elbowed him and gave him a smirk. "And that was after she had asked me if you were dating anyone."

"I wasn't on a date," Bennett said, declining to give information about either the conversation he'd had with Susan Enns or his meeting earlier.

"Are you going to be going on one in the future?" Mitch asked, apparently unwilling to let the subject drop.

When Bennett happened to glance across the table, he found that Makayla, Tami, and Grace were all watching him. He looked back at Mitch and said, "That's none of your business."

"Maybe we should talk about Sammi's dates instead," Dalton volunteered helpfully.

Bennett had been lifting his glass to take a drink but lowered it as he looked down the table to where his younger sister sat. Her cheeks were bright red in the glimpse he got before she ducked her head. "Do you have a boyfriend, Sammi?"

Even though Steve had been their father for more years of their lives than John McFadden had been, Bennett still found himself falling into that role for his three biological siblings. He always had been the "man of the house" when his father had been deployed, and over the years, he'd never completely shaken that sense of responsibility when it came to Makayla, Ryan, and Sammi. Though he felt protective of all his siblings, those three brought it out more strongly in him.

Sammi lifted one shoulder in a half-hearted shrug. She looked over at him, a small smile on her face. "We've gone out a…few times. He's really nice."

Bennett wanted to drill her about the guy to make sure he really was good enough for his little sister, but he decided to hold off until there weren't so many people around.

"I hope you'll invite him to one of our family dinners," his mom said. "You know we'd love to meet him."

Bennett wanted to laugh at his mom's comment. He had a feeling that Sammi would find many reasons to keep from bringing her boyfriend around too soon. He wouldn't be the first person scared off by their large, loud family. But if the guy could handle all of them, he was definitely a keeper.

"Can you at least tell us his name?" Dalton asked.

Sammi scowled at their younger brother. "As if you don't know."

Bennett turned to look at Dalton. "How would you know what Sammi's boyfriend's name is?"

Dalton met Bennett's gaze, his eyes wide. "I...uh...may have heard her talking to him."

"Yeah. After I had already told you to give me some privacy for my phone call."

Dalton flopped back in his seat, crossing his arms over his chest. "How else am I supposed to find out what's going on around here? Nobody tells me anything."

"Google it," Makayla offered helpfully.

It was apparent fairly quickly that Dalton didn't find the comment as funny as the rest of the people at the table.

"Or you could just do what I do," Tami suggested. "Hang around with Makayla. Sooner or later, you'll hear about everything."

"Oh, hey now," Makayla protested. "I'll have you know that I've kept some very important secrets."

"I can vouch for that," Grace said.

Bennett kept quiet about the fact that he, too, had kept at least one very important secret. He cherished that knowledge. In the days since the ultrasound, his reaction to the news had been both a source of joy and worry. Without meaning to, he'd become attached to the little girl Grace carried. At the oddest moments, he found himself thinking about the role he'd play in her life.

It had taken him a day or so to acknowledge the role that he *wanted* to play in her life. Unfortunately, he was pretty sure that wouldn't be what Grace would allow. In fact, it could be that some other man would step into her life and be father to Grace's little girl, and Bennett would be relegated to *uncle*.

He rubbed a hand against his chest. The very thought actually caused his heart to ache. What was he supposed to do about that? He loved the little girl that Grace carried. Almost as much as he loved Grace.

Around the time he'd accepted how he felt about the baby, he'd forced himself to accept how he felt about Grace. The problem was that he was pretty sure that Grace didn't feel the same way. She'd rejected him as a teenager, but was it possible that once she'd healed from the loss of Franklin—as much as anyone ever truly healed from such a loss—that she might give him another chance? Bennett knew that he had to at least try. If he didn't, he would have failed already. If he tried and she rejected him, then he would know.

So, while he wasn't thrilled that he needed to wait to declare his love for her, Bennett knew that if he wanted to have a chance, he had to let her grieve Franklin first. However long that would take.

"Is everyone ready for dessert?"

His mom's words drew Bennett back to the present, and he glanced across the table in time to see Makayla and Grace exchange a look.

"I'll help you, Mom," Makayla said as she got to her feet.

"Thanks, sweetheart. Bennett, why don't you and Mitch stack the plates so Sammi and Dalton can bring them into the kitchen. Danica, you and Sierra can help me put away the food, and Tristan, you can load the dishwasher."

His mom had always been super organized with them. From the moment she'd started watching Steve's boys, she'd kept them all on a schedule and had given them all chores. There were no mutterings at the commands she'd given, everyone just got to their feet to do their part. Except for the guests, of course, although he did notice Erin scoot into the kitchen with Makayla and Grace.

Within fifteen minutes, they were all gathered back around the table. Grace sat with a round cake frosted with a fluffy white icing in front of her. Bennett knew it wasn't her birthday so wondered what the special occasion was.

"As some of you know," Makayla said as she put down a large stack of dessert plates. "Grace had an ultrasound done this week. As part of the scan, they were able to tell her the sex of her baby."

Bennett sat back in his chair as a cheer went up around the table, exchanging a smile with Grace.

"We thought it would be fun to do a gender reveal tonight with the help of a cake from Erin." Makayla gave Erin a quick wave. "We had Erin bake two cakes that are identical on the outside, so even she doesn't know the gender. So now, we'll have Grace cut the cake and show us whether we're going to be welcoming a little girl or a little boy into the family."

"How about we do a poll before the reveal?" Steve suggested.

Everyone quickly jumped on board with that idea and starting with Tami, they went around the table, each giving their vote. It was no surprise that Tami, Sammi, Danica, and Sierra went with girl, and Dalton, Mitch, and Tristan all said boy. Bennett passed since he didn't want to give anything away. Several people knew he'd gone with Grace to the ultrasound. Makayla also refused to vote. In the end, *girl* got the most votes.

"Now, let's see who was right," his mom said, a broad grin on her face. He supposed that even though Grace was not related by birth or marriage, his mom was looking at her baby as a grandchild. And no doubt she planned to spoil it like one.

Grace got to her feet and picked up the large knife that lay next to the cake. She carefully made first one cut, then another, before using the pie server to pull the piece out.

There were cheers and groans as she pulled it out far enough for people to get a glimpse of pink. Grace's smile at the reveal was the biggest Bennett had seen on her face since Franklin's death. It certainly was a sight better than her reaction at the ultrasound. He'd wondered why she hadn't been happier or more excited, but perhaps she had just needed time for it all to sink in. It couldn't be easy to lose a husband and then gain a child while still grieving.

Whatever her feelings, he was just glad to see that at that moment, she seemed happy.

Chapter Twenty

G RACE HADN'T BEEN SURE how the evening would go. Just by the very nature of what the dinner had been planned for, the spotlight would be on her—at least at the end. She hadn't been sure she was ready for that, but then she'd remembered that each person there had been a part of her life for awhile and supported her unconditionally. They wouldn't judge her if she started crying or if she laughed and smiled. This was her place of safety.

As they all settled down to eat their piece of cake, Grace fielded the question she had anticipated.

"So what're you gonna name the baby, Gracie?" Dalton asked before he'd even taken a single bite of cake.

"I'm not sure yet," Grace admitted. "I'm still getting used to the idea of having a daughter."

"Now this might be a good use of Google," Dalton remarked as he pointed his fork at her. "Names for baby girls. You'd have a ton to choose from, and then you could Google for the meaning of any name you're considering. You wouldn't want a name that meant *breath of onions* or *face of an ox*."

"Oh my goodness, Dalton," Emily exclaimed. "Where do you come up with this stuff?"

Dalton shrugged. "Who knows. It usually just pops into my head."

"You mean it just pops out of your mouth," Bennett said. "I'm not sure it's lingering long enough in your brain for you to consider whether or not you should actually say it."

"Hey. I'm bringing up a valid use for Google. After all, maybe if Mom and Dad had used it before choosing *Dalton*, I might not have ended up with a name that means *valley town* or *the settlement in the valley*. I mean *seriously*! Would it have killed you to look up the meaning before saddling me with this name?"

As snickers sounded around the table, people began to pull out their phones even though—for the most part—mealtime was phone-free at the Callaghan-McFadden house. Makayla was the first to share the meaning of her name.

"Well, it's derived from Michael which means *who is like God.*" Makayla glanced over at Grace. "What does your name mean?"

Grace stared at her phone for a moment before answering. "Apparently, it means *God's favor.*"

As Bennett watched her frown, he figured that she was trying to work out how her name might reflect on her life. With so many losses, she probably didn't feel like she had God's favor.

Bennett was surprised to see that his own name meant *blessed*, and he decided that he liked that meaning because it truly reflected how he felt most of the time.

As more meanings were shared, the consensus was that Tami had been gypped like Dalton since her full name—Tamara—meant *palm tree.* Mitch felt that his name's meaning—*gift from God*—truly reflected how he'd always felt people should view him. That brought on more laughter, but it was Tristan's name that they all agreed was the least accurate in its meaning.

"*Tumult. Outcry. Noise,*" Tristan responded when asked his name's meaning.

Given that he was the quietest member of the family, those words couldn't have been more wrong.

"Nobody tell Kenton that his name means *royal chieftain,*" Dalton suggested. "His ego won't fit through the door."

Soon the discussion turned to possible baby names for Grace's little girl. Grace herself didn't make any suggestions although as the name ideas veered into the bizarre—such as Dalton's suggestion that she combine various family members' names—she finally started to exercise her power of veto.

"Thankfully I still have plenty of time to come up with a name," Grace said. "Knowing that I can buy pink stuff is good enough for now. I don't need to have it monogrammed as well."

Though Bennett had already known the gender of the baby, he was glad that he had made it for the reveal. It was fun to see Grace embracing the pregnancy, though he was sure that she still had struggles with it. Seeing her smile made him smile.

When Grace started to yawn a short time later, the evening wound down pretty quickly. Since everyone had pitched in to clean up, there wasn't much to do before people started to leave. Bennett stayed after everyone had left in order to talk to his dad about the meeting that had made him late for dinner.

"I had someone approach me this week about a possible land sale," Bennett said when he and his dad had settled into chairs in his dad's office.

"What type of land?"

C&M Builders didn't usually buy or sell the properties they worked on except for the houses they flipped. Normally, they worked with a developer who had land they wanted to build on. They'd worked on single homes, and they'd worked on subdivisions, but for the most part, they never owned the land.

"It's a chunk of sub-dividable land along Henderson Highway. Sixteen acres."

"So are you wanting to purchase the land? Do you think with what we're taking on because of the Denton Homes scandal that that's a good idea?"

Bennett sat back in his chair. "I was actually thinking more on the personal side rather than business."

His dad's brow furrowed. "You want to buy the land yourself?"

"I'm thinking about it. You know that the apartment building has been good for us so far, but I think that there will come a time when it won't be enough. If Ethan and Makayla have a baby anytime soon, the apartment will almost be too small for them. The apartment isn't terribly conducive to a growing family." Bennett paused. "I was thinking of seeing if any of the other kids would be interested in subdividing the land and building homes."

His dad nodded. "I see. You know, at one time I had been thinking of something similar. It was around the time we were building the apartment building. I knew it wouldn't be a long-term solution for you kids, but it seemed enough at the time, and other stuff came up that needed our attention. I never really got back to it. I'm not surprised that you've been thinking about it."

Bennett wondered what exactly his dad meant by that statement but didn't push for an explanation. Something told him that it was more than he might want to know. "The idea had crossed my mind, but with everything going on at work and the wedding, I hadn't been thinking much about it until this week. A guy from church—his son was part of my Bible study before moving to Vancouver—approached me to see if I'd be interested in buying the land. He had planned to build on it, but his wife wants to move to be closer to their son and grandchildren."

His dad looked thoughtful. "Do you think you guys would all want to live that close together? I know it's working for the apartment building, but do you want that to continue long-term?"

"I think so. I'd talk to the others before buying the land, but I'm pretty sure Makayla would like to be close to family. I mean, having babysitters close would have to be a bonus. And having cousins nearby to play with? Sounds like a good idea to me."

As they continued to discuss the possibilities, Bennett was glad that he'd come to talk to his dad about it. Not that he didn't have confidence in his own ability to make decisions about stuff like that, but it was good to get input from someone he respected and who would understand what he was thinking of doing.

"Would you be building your home right away?" Steve asked once they'd gone online and done a little more research on the land. "I'm assuming you'd be taking one of the sections for yourself."

Bennett nodded. "But I wouldn't build right away. My apartment is fine for now, and I'd rather wait until I married so my wife could give input to building plans. No sense in me making all the decisions and then have her hate the house."

As he spoke, Bennett tried not to think about who he would like to be his house-planning partner. Unfortunately, right then, he couldn't imagine who else he'd ever be interested in making a home with other than Grace. He'd committed to giving Grace time to grieve Franklin, but sometimes it was hard to do that when there was no guarantee that they would end up together.

"Your mother and I will be praying with you about it all."

For the first time, Bennett wondered if his family was more aware of how he felt about Grace than he'd realized. Unfortunately, he couldn't exactly ask without giving it away if, in fact, they weren't aware. So he accepted his father's comment with a nod.

Then, after saying goodnight to his mom, he headed for home. As he drove, he contemplated calling James. Since the two of them had met at church and become friends, Bennett had found himself confiding in the man over the years. He considered him one of his best friends, along with Ethan, but he wanted to ask specifically for prayer regarding Grace, and he didn't think Ethan was the one to ask for that.

"Hey, man," James said by way of greeting, his voice filling the interior of the truck through the Bluetooth. "Didn't get enough of me at dinner?"

Bennett chuckled. "Well, I didn't get much of a chance to talk with you."

"Something come up?" James asked.

"Sort of." Bennett paused. "I won't keep you long. Just wanted to ask you to pray about something."

"Sure thing," James said then there was a muffled conversation before the line became clear again. "Let me just go to my office."

"Sorry to interrupt your evening." Bennett turned the truck out onto the highway.

"It's not a problem," James assured him. "Erin's just headed to bed. Early morning for her tomorrow."

"Thank you, guys, for coming to the dinner tonight. That cake was so delicious. I'm not sure how you're not twice the size you are."

James chuckled. "Well, I never have been a big one for sweets— much to Erin's dismay when we first met—so she knows to only tempt me with the baking when it's certain things."

"I have no willpower when it comes to cake and ice cream."

"So I've seen." James laughed then said, "So what's on your mind?"

Bennett let out a long breath. "That would be Grace."

"Ahhh. And what about Grace in particular? I assume you're not just wanting me to pray for her in general."

"No, I guess I should say that I would like prayer for *me* in regards to Grace." Over the next few minutes, Bennett gave James the condensed version of their history and what he'd been struggling with more recently.

"I'll certainly pray about that," James said. "I can see how that might be a difficult situation for you to be in. You might be in a different place now, but that might not always be the case. Regardless, I'll pray that God will work it out and that you will be at peace about it all."

Bennett thanked him, feeling a lot more at peace now that he'd found someone that he could talk freely with. The call ended just as Bennett neared the apartment building. As he walked toward the door, he glanced up at the second-floor apartment where Grace lived. There was a faint glow from around the edges of the curtain that covered the bedroom window.

She'd appeared tired at the end of the evening, so he assumed she'd be going to bed soon. Bennett had a few things to do before he headed there himself, one of which was to do something that he hoped would make Grace smile in the morning.

BENNETT: *ASTRID: DIVINELY BEAUTIFUL*

Grace stared at the text that had just come through from Bennett, interrupting her social media browsing as she'd laid in bed. Since it was Saturday, there was no rush to get up. The only plan she had was to go out to the mall a little later with Makayla to buy some maternity clothes.

Her hand curved over the slight swelling of her belly. It was only since finding out the gender of the baby and seeing the physical manifestation in her body that she'd really grasped that the pregnancy was real. There were no moments of denial about it anymore. It just could not be ignored.

And now she was expected to find a name for this baby. But it wasn't going to be Astrid.

Love the meaning, but the name...not sure about that.

She thought he would reply right away, but when he didn't, she continued to read through her Facebook timeline. It was only in the last week or so that she could read other people's happy statuses and see their pictures without having a negative reaction. Whether it was sadness, anger or jealousy, those were the emotions that had seemed front and center whenever she'd had glimpses of other people's happy lives.

It was almost four months since Franklin's death, and life was moving forward. She was settled into the apartment. Most of Franklin's things were in storage now, but she did have a few things set out around the apartment. It felt like home. It felt right.

Bennett: *Are you sure? Astrid Moore has a nice ring to it.*

Oh, I'm sure. That name is going on the "not a chance" list.

Bennett: *Does the list have a lot of names on it already?*

Nope. Astrid is the first. Maybe I'll just add names in alphabetical order.

Bennett: *Cool. I'll be on the search for a B name.*

Grace laughed. She could only imagine what names he was going to find for her. She knew she needed to take the name thing seriously, but since the baby wasn't due for another five months, she figured she had some time. And it was a decision she'd have to make on her own since she and Franklin hadn't discussed names.

Though she hadn't wanted a lot of random input on the baby's name, she found that she didn't mind Bennett's playful attempts to help her out. She considered that as she slid out of bed and headed for the shower. She'd always known that Bennett would make a great father. The way he cared for his younger siblings showed that, so it was no surprise that he was taking an interest in her baby. She just had to make sure that she viewed him as an uncle for her little girl and nothing more.

MAKAYLA HELD UP A PAIR OF PANTS. "I think these are nice. And they've got the panel so they should fit you right up until delivery."

Grace stared at the pants for a moment before returning her gaze to the blouse she held. It seemed ridiculous to spend so much money on clothes she was only going to wear for one pregnancy. If she and Makayla were the same size, she might not mind so much because at least then she could pass them on.

"I can't believe how cute some of this stuff is," Makayla said as she held up a dress. "This is nice, but kind of summery. I guess that's why it's on sale. You're going to need warmer stuff to last through the winter."

Grace realized that she needed to figure out the basics of what she needed. "Yeah. I guess I need a couple pairs of pants along with three or four blouses or shirts. Maybe a skirt and a dress. I have a few sweaters that are probably bulky enough that I could wear them."

"Don't forget underwear," Makayla said. "How are your bras fitting?"

With a chuckle, Grace gave Makayla an eye roll. "I think I'm going to get one pair of pants today and a couple shirts. One package of underwear and a couple bras. That's a good start."

Makayla looked slightly disappointed when it appeared she wasn't going to get a big shopping trip out of the day. "Okay. Are you going to try stuff on here?"

Grace nodded even though she suddenly felt more tired than when she'd walked into the store. She knew that Makayla wanted to do some shopping for baby stuff that day as well, but it was too much for her. Maternity clothes were going to be her limit for the day. And food. Yes, food was definitely going to be up next on their agenda.

"Here." Makayla shoved some clothes into her arms. "Try these on."

Grace trusted Makayla's taste, so she headed for the dressing rooms. The woman showed her to a room, and she began the process of trying on the stuff Makayla had chosen for her. The clothes felt kind of weird. She wasn't used to a loose, stretchy fit around her waist and then feeling the tighter fit starting lower on her hips. However, it was kind of nice to not feel the constriction on her swelling belly.

As she stared at herself in the mirror when she'd put the first outfit on, she knew that the outfits would definitely leave no question to anyone who might be wondering if she was or wasn't pregnant. She smoothed a hand over the loose shirt and the belly beneath.

It was time to embrace it fully.

Chapter Twenty-One

*I*N THE END, GRACE LEFT THE STORE with two pairs of pants, three shirts, and a dress. She would take some time to sort through the clothes she already had to set aside the ones that would still work for a little while longer.

"Ready to go get something to eat?" Makayla asked as they walked out into the mall. "What's the baby wanting today?"

Grace took a second to think about it. "Pasta?"

"Sounds excellent to me."

It wasn't long until they were seated at a booth in the Olive Garden restaurant across the street from the mall. Grace was quick to eat a bread stick as soon as the waitress brought them, after Makayla said a prayer for the food.

"I think I need to have a baby soon," Makayla said as they waited for their soup to arrive.

"Really?" Grace looked at her friend, surprised and yet…not. "That would be kind of fun. For us to have kids close in age."

"I know, right? Now that I'm married, I'm anxious for those around me to get married and have kids. I want us all to be in the same season of life." Makayla smiled. "All of us having kids, so they grow up together. Best buddies from day one. Or two."

Grace smiled. "That would be super fun for them."

"Guess I'm going to have to try to find Bennett and Mitch some girlfriends. Tristan can wait a couple of years."

Grace didn't try to analyze why her stomach clenched when she thought about Bennett having a girlfriend. "Did you know about Sammi's boyfriend?"

Makayla shook her head. "I get the feeling it's a new relationship, so she's being smart and keeping him away from the family for a little while."

"Yeah. You guys can be overwhelming," Grace said with a smile. "But whoever your siblings date, they have to mesh with the family."

"Ellie didn't mesh at all. I can't say I shed any tears when I heard that she and Bennett had broken up. Now I just need to find him a girlfriend that *does* mesh with us."

Grace didn't really want another discussion about a girlfriend for Bennett. "Mitch seems to be friendly with Maya."

Makayla sat back in the booth, a thoughtful look on her face. "She is a sweet girl, that's for sure. And so respectful of everyone. She might be a good option for a girlfriend for one of them. After all, we have no issues with workplace romances."

"Not all will work out as well as you and Ethan have," Grace pointed out.

The waitress returned with their bowls of soup and grabbed the now empty bread basket. The smell of the soup made Grace's stomach rumble, and she eagerly dipped her spoon into the bowl.

"What about you?" Makayla asked.

Grace paused in lifting the spoon then lowered it back into the bowl. "What about me?"

"Would you consider dating and remarrying?"

"No." The answer was automatic, and yet, it didn't sit completely right as she said it. "I think it's too soon, and right now, I just can't...I don't know."

Makayla tore a breadstick in half. "You know, at one time I thought that maybe there might be something between you and Bennett."

Grace's breath caught as her chest tightened. "Really?"

"Yeah, but then you married Franklin, so I guess I was wrong."

Grace didn't know what to say to that. "Bennett needs someone better than me."

"Better than you? There's no one better than you." Makayla sounded so certain of that fact that Grace wanted to laugh.

"I'm sure that there are women better suited to him than me. Especially given that I'm not in a place to be anything but a friend to him."

Makayla nodded as if she understood, but her expression said otherwise. "What do you think about Tami and Keenan?"

As they worked through two bowls of soup and countless breadsticks, they talked more about their friends and their relationship statuses. Grace tried not to think about how that topic of conversation wouldn't apply to her again. Unfortunately, at some point, she'd still have to listen to Makayla talk about how Bennett and some woman—who wasn't her—were together.

Once they finished eating, Makayla broached the idea of going to Babies R Us, but Grace managed to put her off. For some reason, she seemed to be operating on an "as needed" basis when it came to buying stuff for the pregnancy and the baby. She'd needed the maternity clothes, so she bought them, but baby furniture and baby clothes and other stuff...that could still wait for a bit. Makayla looked disappointed, but Grace wouldn't be swayed. There was still lots of time to buy what else she would need.

SUNDAY NIGHT, AS THE WEEKEND drew to an end, Grace went into the kitchen and opened the freezer. She grabbed the lone container of ice cream, frowning at how light it felt. When she saw how little ice cream was left, she let out a sigh. Why hadn't she just finished it off the last time she ate some? The one spoonful left was not enough to satisfy her current craving.

She left the container on the counter and walked out the door. After climbing the stairs, she knocked on Makayla's door. There was no answer which only served to increase her craving. It seemed like the more she was denied what she wanted, the more she wanted it.

Frustrated, she went back down to her floor and was heading for her apartment when she realized that there was probably someone else who had ice cream. She knew that Bennett always had ice cream. Her hesitation was only momentary before she marched over to Bennett's door and knocked on it.

It didn't take long for Bennett to open the door. His eyes widened when he saw her there. "Hey, Grace. What's up?"

Grace sighed. "Baby wants ice cream, and I don't have any."

Bennett smiled, the skin at his eyes crinkling as his smile lines deepened. "Really? Baby wants ice cream, eh?"

Grace rested her hands on her stomach. "Yeah. Could've used a head's up so I could have bought some more."

"So you think I have some?"

She laughed. "Uh yeah. If anyone is guaranteed to have ice cream, it would be you."

Bennett stepped back to let her into his apartment. "Is Baby asking for any flavor in particular?"

"Nope. She's willing to take anything you have."

"Hey, Grace." Tristan greeted her as she walked into the kitchen. He was seated at the island, a bowl in front of him.

"Do you have ice cream?" Grace said as she rounded the counter so she could give the man a hug. "Good to see you."

Tristan returned her hug, a small smile on his usually serious face. "I *do* have ice cream."

"I hope you left some for me because Baby is craving it badly."

Bennett joined them with three tubs of ice cream. "I think you'll find something to help with that here." He set the containers in front of her then opened a cupboard and got a bowl. "Here you go." After he handed her the bowl, he opened a drawer to get her a scoop and a spoon. "Help yourself."

Grace looked at the contents of each tub before deciding to just have a scoop of each. Baby was feeling adventurous. When she was done, Bennett put the ice cream back in the freezer.

"Feel free to join us," he said as he returned to his stool across from Tristan.

"I don't want to interrupt." She picked up the bowl and spoon.

"You're not interrupting," Bennett said. "Tristan came for supper, so we've been talking for a while now."

"Okay." Grace settled onto a stool next to Tristan. "I went to Makayla's for ice cream, but no one was home."

"I think they took Sierra and Danica out to a concert or something," Tristan said. "Dani's been talking about it non-stop for the last few days."

Grace took a bite of the ice cream, savoring its coolness on her tongue. "Thank you, Bennett. This really hits the spot."

"I'm going to have to make sure that I always keep ice cream on hand."

Tristan chuckled. "Like you don't already."

"Oh, but now I have a reason to keep even more on hand." Bennett grinned.

Grace listened as Tristan and Bennett discussed some work-related stuff. Though she wasn't really participating in the conversation, it felt nice to not be alone. She could have taken the ice cream back to her apartment and eaten it while watching something on TV, but this felt better. It was good that Tristan was there because she wasn't sure she would have been comfortable staying there with just Bennett. Too much of Makayla's conversation still played in her head.

"I forgot to send you a name this morning," Bennett said as he picked up his phone.

"You're planning to send me a name every day?" Grace asked.

"Yep. Just presenting you with some options," Bennett murmured as he bent over his phone.

When Grace's phone chirped a short time later, she pulled her phone out of her pocket and looked at the screen.

Bennett: *Briella: God is my strength*

Grace looked up at Bennett. "That's actually kind of pretty."

"It's shortened from Gabriella."

"Well, Astrid went on the *definitely not* list, but this one…well, I think I'll put it on the maybe list."

"Really?" Bennett sounded surprised and pleased.

"I never thought much about the responsibility of naming a child," Tristan commented. He set his spoon in his empty bowl and pushed it away. "I must say, I have wondered about the names of a few people I've come across. Like, what their parents were thinking?"

"Yeah," Grace agreed. "Maybe I'll have to set up a Twitter poll or something. Give my top five and let people vote."

"So you don't have any strong feelings about a name yet?" Bennett asked.

Grace shrugged. "Not really."

"Would you want to have Franklin's name as part of it? I've heard of girls named Frankie."

"I've thought about it, but I'm not sure." The thought had briefly crossed her mind, but she hadn't let herself think about it too much. "Part of me just thinks I won't know the name for sure until I look at her face."

"I suppose you don't really need to have a name until after the baby is born," Bennett agreed. "Some people choose the name sooner as a way to connect with the baby, but I doubt you'd be the first person who waited until the baby arrived to settle on a name."

Grace wondered if maybe her reluctance to pick a name had to do with that connection Bennett had mentioned. It seemed her desire to remain detached ran so deep she wasn't even aware of it sometimes. Maybe that was why she was so resistant to doing anything in advance of the baby's birth. If she had it her way, she wouldn't even set up the nursery until she knew for sure that the baby had been born healthy.

She lived in fear of the worst happening. Was that really a surprise, though? After all, the worst *had* happened to her…several times.

Grace looked at Bennett, taking in the way his eyes sparkled when he laughed at some of the names Tristan had heard when he was in university. There was so much good in the man. Oh, he had his not-so-good attributes as well. His protectiveness could be overwhelming and annoying at times. She knew that his younger siblings chafed at that a lot. She'd heard more than one of them talk about how they felt like they had two dads.

He'd been responsible as a teenager, ready to step into adulthood when so many guys had just been counting the days until they were legal and could party. At eighteen, Bennett had already been working with Steve and going to university full-time. He took his responsibilities very seriously. Too seriously sometimes. Grace knew that if she ever needed help from someone, Bennett would be there for her as surely as Makayla would be.

They were her safety net, and maybe that was why she didn't want to take a risk with Bennett. She couldn't imagine her life without him. And she would take his presence in the only way she could get it. As a friend.

"Tristy," Bennett said.

"Trixie?" Grace asked, tuning back into the conversation.

"No. Tristy. Short from Tristan."

"Oh my goodness," Grace said with a snort. "And for Bennett? Benny?"

"No. No, no, no," Bennett said with a vicious shake of his head. "Please no for a girl."

"How about Bennetta?" Tristan suggested.

"And once again, I say no." Bennett gave Tristan a horrified look. "How about we just say that all versions of your and my name are off limits?"

"I can agree to that," Tristan said.

The three of them laughed again.

"I think I'm just gonna call her Baby. This picking a name is too hard."

"Well, you might change your mind about that the first time you hear a teenage boy call her *Baaaaby*," Tristan said, sounding amazingly like a teenage boy though it had been a good six years since he'd been one.

Grace turned to stare at Tristan before she burst out laughing. She'd laughed at times over the past few months but for some reason, Tristan's comment and the way he'd said it struck her as hilarious. No matter how she tried to stop, every time she looked at Tristan who was regarding her with a lifted brow, she started laughing again.

Before long, the guys were laughing with her. Tears pricked her eyes, but this time they were brought on by laughter instead of grief. She pressed a hand to her side as she took a deep breath and tried to stop once again.

"Really, Gracie, it wasn't that funny," Tristan said when he finally stopped laughing. "Why are we laughing so hard?"

Grace took a deep breath and let it out with a huff, wiping at her eyes. "Well, maybe it was just how you said it. Which was hilarious."

"It was rather funny, Tris," Bennett said. "Especially when you're the serious one. I do have to say, however, that your observation is worth taking into consideration."

"I agree. *Baby* is on the *not a chance* list," Grace said then sighed. "And now I'm back to square one."

"Don't worry. You're not alone on your quest," Bennett assured her. "There's a whole lot of us happy to help you out."

Grace let out another sigh, suddenly feeling exhausted by the fit of laughter. "That is a battle for another day. I am beat."

"Are you feeling okay?" Bennett asked, his brow furrowed.

She gave him a smile. "I'm fine. Just tired. The ice cream hit the spot, and the laugh…well, that was needed too. Thanks, Tris."

She got to her feet and took her empty bowl to the sink.

"Just leave that, Grace," Bennett said from behind her. "I'll put it into the dishwasher with the rest from dinner."

Grace turned from the counter. "Thanks for the ice cream rescue."

"Anytime." Bennett smiled. "You know I always have it on hand." He walked with her to the door and then stood there as she walked to her apartment. "Sleep well, Grace. See you tomorrow."

Chapter Twenty-Two

*B*ennett closed the door and went back to where Tristan sat at the counter, his head bent over his phone. "So, what are you up to this week?"

When Tristan had called to see if he could hang out with him, Bennett hadn't hesitated to say yes. Tristan did that every couple of months. Bennett was never sure what prompted it, but he always had a good time with the guy.

Ever since their families had met, Tristan had been the one that sort of faded into the background. With strong personalities like Gabe, Kenton, and Makayla in the family, it wasn't a surprise that a few of the other kids would be overshadowed. Tristan had been more than over-shadowed. He was like the short kid in the back row that no one could see because everyone in front of him was taller. But…Tristan had embraced the role. Every once in awhile, though, he liked to have some one-on-one time with his siblings, and that's when Bennett would get a call.

"I'm working on designs with Everett for the new subdivision." Tristan set his phone down and leaned back in his bar stool.

"How's it been, working with him? I've heard he's really hands on."

Tristan sighed. "Yeah. He has had a lot of input. I have a feeling he'll be in the office several days this week. He likes to see designs in the beginning stages and give suggestions early on. It does help me to be able to incorporate the things he wants." He shrugged. "Better than going to him with designs and then needing to make changes. I don't mind working with him."

They talked a bit more about the project then Tristan paused and looked at him. "Do you think Grace is doing okay?"

Bennett knew that as a quiet person, Tristan tended to observe more than others might…when he wasn't wrapped up in a project. "Considering it's only been four months since Franklin died, I think she's doing as well as could be expected. Especially when you add in the fact that she's pregnant. I honestly don't know if the pregnancy has helped or hindered her grieving."

Tristan nodded. "I was glad to see her laughing tonight. She always makes me laugh."

"Me, too," Bennett said as he recalled the warmth that had flooded him when Grace had started to laugh. It had been ages since he'd seen her laugh like that. To know that she could still find humor in life was a relief to him.

"We need to try and make her laugh more," Tristan stated as if it was that easy.

"Yep. We can certainly try."

THE NEXT DAY, Grace was late getting into the office. She'd had a doctor's appointment so Maya, their new receptionist, was manning the front desk. Bennett greeted her when he went to get a cup of coffee.

"Good morning, Maya," he said. "How are you today?"

"I'm fine. How are you?" She looked at him with wide brown eyes and a small smile. Even though she'd been with them for almost a month, she still seemed a little reserved at times.

"I'm fine as well," he said, giving her what he hoped she interpreted as a friendly smile. "When Grace comes in, could you come to my office, please?"

Her brows rose slightly, and her smile disappeared altogether. "Sure."

"It's nothing to be concerned about. I just have a project that I'd like you to take on. Since Grace has her own work, I thought maybe you could help with this one. And it will help you to understand better what we do here."

Relief relaxed her face, and she smiled again. "Okay. That sounds like fun."

"I hope so," Bennett said. "If it's not fun, at least I hope it will be interesting."

Back in his office, Bennett began to put together the notes he had on the project he wanted to involve Maya in. He wanted the young woman to feel like she was important to the company. To have her feel as if she had an important role. Though she was there to help Grace and to cover for her when the baby was born, he hoped that she would continue to work for the company in years to come. They were growing and expanding and needed someone like Maya who could help out where needed and be there to work alongside Grace.

Around ten-thirty, Maya appeared in his doorway. "Is it convenient now?"

Bennett nodded and moved the file he was working on to the side and then got to his feet. "C'mon in. Have a seat." Once she had settled into the chair across the desk from him, Bennett sat back down. "First of all, would you be interested in visiting a work site?"

"A work site?" Maya's brows drew together.

"Yes. We have several sites with different types of work. Mitch has at least one renovation on the go and several new building sites. Visiting a site or two might give you a better idea of what we do. It will help you understand terms that are tossed around as well as give you the opportunity to meet more of the employees."

"Yes, I'd like to do that," Maya said with a nod. "I would like to know a bit more about that side of the company."

"Great. I'll talk to Mitch to set it up." Bennett jotted a note on the writing pad in front of him. "Now, onto the project."

GRACE KEPT GLANCING toward the hallway. She wasn't jealous, just curious. Definitely just curious. When Maya had said that Bennett wanted her to come to his office for information on a project he wanted her to do, Grace had felt…anxious. And then, the longer Maya was gone, the more the anxiety morphed into something else. Something Grace didn't want to feel, let alone admit to. It would be wrong to feel that when she was still grieving.

"Hey, sweetie," Makayla said as she appeared beside Grace's desk. "How did the appointment go this morning?"

With effort, Grace kept herself from glancing down the hallway towards Bennett's office. "It went well. So far everything looks good. Blood pressure was normal. I'm only up a couple of pounds since the last visit, which is surprising considering the way I've been eating."

"Yeah, well, there are those other times you've been throwing up what you ate, so I guess it all balances out," Makayla remarked.

"I'm not throwing up nearly as much as I did during the first trimester. While I'm glad for that, I have a feeling that it will mean a slightly higher weight gain next month."

"I don't think you need to worry too much about that. Eat healthily and don't worry about the weight."

"Easy for you to say," Grace told her. "You aren't the one who will have to lose it all afterward."

"Oh, but I'll be there to feed you diet food."

Grace rolled her eyes. "Lovely. Just lovely."

Makayla gave her a grin before looking around. "I thought Maya was in today."

"She is," Grace said, hoping her tone stayed neutral. "I guess Bennett had asked her to come to his office when I got in to discuss a project of some nature."

"A project?" Makayla frowned. "I don't remember him talking about anything like that in our meeting last week. He's supposed to tell me before he takes you or Maya for additional work."

Grace shrugged. "That's just what Maya said."

"Okay, well, I'll have a chat with him to remind him that we need to be kept in the loop. Is it a problem if she has something else to work on?"

"No, it's not a problem," Grace said, because it wasn't…on the work side of things. In fact, there were days she struggled to find work for both her and Maya, so a project would help with that.

"Sounds good, but I still want Bennett to get in the habit of asking first. Once you're on maternity leave, he won't be able to just take her for his own projects whenever he wants."

Grace nodded and tried not to think about a time when she wouldn't be coming into work each day. Her job was a huge part of her life. She absolutely loved working for C&M Builders and had figured she'd be doing that for years to come. Now she was having to hand off parts of her job to someone else, and her future held a time when she might be out of the office for almost a year. Her stomach knotted at the idea.

Maya came back a short time later, a notepad clutched in her hand. She sat down on the chair in front of the computer that had been set up for her on the semi-circular desk.

"How did it go?" Grace asked.

"It was good. Bennett thinks I should go out and visit some of the work sites to get a better understanding of the company."

"Yes, that would definitely help. When does he plan to take you to the sites?" Grace posed the question as if it were a scheduling concern because that's all she wanted it to be—despite what her heart may be trying to tell her.

It was too soon for anything else.

"Oh, I don't think Bennett plans to take me. He said something about checking with Mitch."

Grace hated herself for feeling relieved about that. How could she possibly be feeling this way when she'd managed not to for so many years? She needed to still be mourning the loss of her husband.

And she was.

There wasn't a day that went by that something didn't remind her of the fact that Franklin was no longer in her life. Some days the grief was more intense than others. The sea of grief didn't hold her as deeply as it had two or three months ago, but she certainly wasn't free of it, by any shot. Which left her feeling all kinds of confused about Bennett.

How could she be feeling anything at all for another man when her husband hadn't been dead even four months? People would say it was wrong. But was there a right and wrong when it came to grief and love? Would loving another mean she loved Franklin any less? Was what she felt for Bennett even love? Or was it just a connection—a sense of gratitude—because he showed her each day that she was special. He took care of her. Whether it was carrying her garbage down to the bins or carrying groceries up to her apartment, he showed her in a million small ways that he cared.

And her heart was thirsty for that right then.

Makayla had Ethan to focus on, and between her job and Keenan, Tami had more than enough demands on her time. Grace knew both would be there in an instant if she needed them, but she hesitated to pull them out of their lives to deal with her grief and loneliness. At times, it felt like they were moving forward while she had fallen behind. So, if she took Bennett up on his offer to help sometimes, who could blame her? Right?

Except at times, it felt like more than just a friendship.

And it was too soon for that.

Chapter Twenty-Three

Early December

G RACE HAD HOPED THAT by this point—a few weeks into the third trimester—she'd be used to the aches and pains, but no...every day it seemed there was something more that hurt or itched. Yeah, the way her skin itched sometimes drove her nuts. She rubbed a hand over the stretched skin on her belly. It felt harder than usual, tight, as if the baby was pressing her back out against Grace's hand.

She was thankful it was Saturday because she really didn't feel like getting out of bed. For the last couple of days, she'd been feeling...different. She hadn't said anything to anyone—especially Makayla since she could be as over-protective as Bennett. Between the two of them, Grace's every need was taken care of. Well, most every need. She still didn't have someone to rub her aching back or throbbing feet, though that was probably because she hadn't asked. And she never would.

Though she still felt Franklin's absence in her life every day, the baby was a reminder that life moved forward. She knew that Franklin would want her to embrace life, to not raise their child in an environment cloaked in grief and sadness. She wasn't quite to that point yet, so she was thankful she still had almost three months to go before the baby arrived.

Grace sat up and swung her feet over the side of the bed. Moving slowly, she rubbed her belly as she walked to the bathroom. She glanced out the window, groaning when she saw that they'd had another dump of snow overnight. At least she didn't have to go out in it.

Back in her bed once she was done in the bathroom, she sat for a moment to take a drink from the water bottle she kept close at hand. She contemplated eating one of the granola bars she kept beside the bed. There was no way she was up to making breakfast. In the end, she decided she wasn't hungry enough to eat and would have something more substantial for lunch. She slid under the blanket and pulled it up to her chin, grateful for the warmth and comfort of her bed. In spite of the nagging ache in her back, she was able to fall back to sleep.

A bolt of pain and a tightening of her stomach jerked her awake a short time later. Her hand reached to press against her belly as she tried to catch her breath. Was that just a particularly intense Braxton Hicks or something more? When the pain returned, stronger than before, real fear gripped Grace. The next pain took her breath away, and, in a panic, she reached for her phone. The first name she saw on her contact screen was Bennett's, and just the thought of having him help her eased the panic back just a bit.

Just as he answered, another pain struck, robbing her of breath and words.

"Grace?" He paused. "Grace? Is something wrong?"

"I need…help."

She could hear him talking, but the pain eclipsed his words. Thankfully, he had keys to all the apartments in the building, so he'd be able to get into hers.

"Gracie?" This time her name was accompanied by a gentle touch on her face. "What's happening?"

"I need to go to the hospital. It hurts…" Another pain hit. They were coming too quickly.

"I'm calling 911," Bennett said as he crouched down next to the bed and grabbed her hand.

She could hear him talking on the phone, but she focused on trying to breathe through the pains. This was why she hadn't focused on the baby. Or names. And she hadn't bought anything for the nursery yet either. She hadn't allowed herself to become attached to the baby.

Because of this.

She hadn't been able to convince herself that she was going to have a healthy baby.

Grace shut everything else down but her ability to fight through the pain. It was too soon. Even though she had done what she could to stay healthy for this baby, it hadn't been enough. It seemed as if she was destined to lose everything. What had she done to deserve having everything stripped away like this?

"Stay with me, Gracie." Bennett's voice reached her, and she tightened her grip on his hand. "They're going to be here right away. I'm going to buzz them in."

Grace didn't want him to go, reached out for him when he moved away, but then another pain tightened around her stomach, radiating to her back. It kept robbing her of breath, and she felt panic rising as she tried to fill her lungs with air.

After what felt like an eternity, she heard Bennett's voice again. "She's right through here."

"How far along?" a man's voice asked as hands touched her.

"Twenty-nine weeks," Bennett said.

"Ben?" Grace reached out her hand as she looked for him.

He came back to her side and took her hand as he looked down at her. Brushing the hair back from her face, he said, "It'll be okay, Gracie."

She looked into his eyes and saw the determination there, and Grace understood that if he could make everything okay, he would. But she knew—she just knew—that there was nothing he could do. Still, for now, she was going to cling to him and the conviction of his words.

She closed her eyes as another pain overtook her, and then they were moving her. Lifting her onto the gurney. She lost her grip on Bennett's hand and opened her eyes to look for him again.

"They're gonna take you to the hospital, sweetheart," Bennett said as he bent over her. "I'll be there as soon as I can. I'm going to let Mom and Dad and Makayla know what's happening."

"Please be there," Grace said, well aware that she was pleading, but she didn't want to be alone. Makayla was supposed to have been in the delivery room with her, but she, Ethan, and the girls had gone to Minneapolis to visit Ryan and do some Christmas shopping at the Mall of America.

"I'll be there," he assured her as they pushed the gurney out of her bedroom.

But then she became aware of a dampness between her legs and knew that there would be no stopping anything.

BENNETT PUSHED OUT the back door of the building and headed for his truck at a jog, his breath coming in white puffs in the cold air. He had to make sure he arrived at the hospital as soon after Grace as possible. There was a sick sense of dread in the pit of his stomach. He just couldn't believe that this was happening.

"Please, Lord, protect Grace and the baby," Bennett prayed aloud as he backed his truck out. He pulled his phone out and set it in the cup holder then instructed it to call his mom.

"Hello, sweetheart," his mom said when she answered. "How are you doing?"

"I'm on the way to the hospital. I think Grace has gone into labor."

His mom gasped before saying, "Is she okay?"

Bennett thought of the pain he'd seen on Grace's face and how pale she'd been. "I'm not sure, Mom. She seemed to be in a lot of pain."

He was glad that the traffic was light as he drove to the Women's Hospital which was where the ambulance attendants had said they were taking her. But even without the traffic, it was slower going than usual because of the snowfall they'd had overnight. He wasn't going to be reckless driving because his goal was to reach Grace's side, not end up in the hospital himself. Thankfully, his truck could make it through drifts on the road that a car might not have been able to.

"Do you want us to come?" she asked.

"Maybe wait until I get there and find out what's going on. But could you phone Makayla and let her know? Tami's at work so we might see her there."

"Do you think they'll let you be with her?"

Bennett hoped they would. "I guess it depends on what they're going to do and if she agrees to have me in there with her. I know Makayla was supposed to be her support person."

"Okay, sweetie," his mom said. "I'll make the calls. Let me know as soon as you know anything."

After the call had ended, Bennett continued to pray as he drove through traffic, trying not to get upset when he hit a red light or ended up behind a vehicle that couldn't drive on the roads as easily as he could. When he finally pulled into the parkade next to the Women's Hospital, Bennett felt a little calmer, but it didn't stop him from jogging across the street to the entrance of the building.

Unfortunately, it seemed to take an eternity for him to get directions to the right place. By the time he reached the information desk on the floor where they'd taken Grace, his worries had escalated as he'd played over and over in his mind everything that might be going wrong.

"Are you Bennett?" the nurse said when he approached the desk.

"Yes, I am. I'm here for Grace Moore."

The woman nodded and got up from her chair. "Come with me."

Bennett followed the woman down the wide hallway. He was glad that there was no issue with him being there with Grace. He hadn't wanted to have to lie about being her significant other and the father of the baby, but he would have done it if it meant Grace wouldn't have been alone. Thankfully, Grace had apparently told them to let him in, so any questions about his presence there were silenced.

The nurse turned into an open doorway and pushed aside a curtain to reveal Grace lying on a bed, blankets covering her. Another nurse stood beside the bed, attaching monitors to her. A female doctor was beside the nurse, looking over a chart. Grace had been watching them, but at Bennett and the nurse's arrival in the room, she looked over at the door, and relief flooded her face.

"Bennett," she said as she held out her hand to him.

He moved to her side, mindful of the other people in the room, and took her hand once again. Warning signals were firing in his brain. It was one thing to help Grace out because she was pregnant, but this was something more. This was something that was going to cement things within him. Within his heart. Even though he'd finally acknowledged his feelings for her, he'd tried not to think of her as anything more than a friend who needed help.

But this...this was way more than friendship for him.

"So far, the baby doesn't appear to be in any distress," the doctor said to Grace, drawing Bennett from his thoughts. "We will keep monitoring her, but at this point, I'm not sure we'll be able to stop labor. We're going to give you a steroid shot in hopes of strengthening the baby's lungs, and try to do what we can to slow the labor."

"What are...what are her chances?" Grace asked, her grip on Bennett's hand tightening.

The doctor met Grace's gaze straight on. "We will do everything we can for her. There will be a team on hand when you deliver to take care of her right away. At twenty-nine weeks, she has a pretty good chance, but I'm afraid I can't offer any guarantees beyond the fact that we will do everything in our power for her."

"But there's a chance she could live?"

"Yes, a good chance. We're going to be fighting for her. We need you to do that too."

Bennett saw it then, the way Grace was pulling into herself. She was bracing for the worst-case scenario. Tristan had mentioned that he thought Grace wasn't connecting with the pregnancy or the baby, and Bennett could see it now too. He'd thought it was just the grief...the thought of going through it all without Franklin...but now he could see it was something more. She had been afraid of losing the baby.

And it seemed that her worst fears—and his too—were being realized.

Chapter Twenty-Four

*I*T SEEMED THAT SINCE DELIVERY was imminent, they felt it was okay to give her an epidural since it would help to keep her from pushing too soon. Plus, if she needed to have an emergency C-section, her pain control would already be in place. Given that she'd never experienced pain like that in her life, Grace was grateful for the epidural.

Once the pain had eased, Grace found herself drifting in and out of sleep. They had brought Bennett a chair, and he stayed by the bed with her. She'd seen him on his phone and assumed that he was letting his mom and others know what was going on.

Part of her felt that she should tell Bennett that he could go. There was no reason for him to hang around. This wasn't his baby, he didn't have to stay there with her. But the bigger part—the more selfish side—wanted him to stay. Needed him to stay. She couldn't do this alone, and he'd been there for her ever since Franklin's death. She hoped that he would stay with her through this as well.

She let out a long breath. On the one hand, she wanted it all to just be over. If the baby was going to come regardless, she just wanted it to be done. Pain—not physical this time—gripped her heart. She was certain that she was going to lose this baby, just like she'd lost Franklin. Why she had thought God would let her have this, she didn't know. Did He think she was strong enough to endure yet another loss in her life?

"It's okay, Grace." Bennett's voice was low, and she felt a light touch on her cheek.

It wasn't until she opened her eyes and looked at him through tears that Grace realized she'd been crying. Again. "I'm not sure that it will be."

Not wanting to see the expression on Bennett's face, Grace squeezed her eyes shut. She knew it wouldn't change anything by burying her head in the sand, but right then, it was the only way to get through this process when her body was letting her down. Failing her.

The next few hours passed in a blur of beeps, nurses checking on her, and the doctor talking to her about the situation. She was grateful that they were trying to present a best-case scenario even though she knew that the odds were not completely in their favor. Slowly, she found herself disconnecting from it all. There was nothing she could do. Nothing she could change. The course had already been set before her, and there was nothing she could do but follow it. They weren't presenting her with options anymore. Now they were just telling her what was going to happen.

Through it all, Bennett was by her side. Occasionally, he would leave, and Grace assumed it was to make phone calls or to get something to eat or drink. A couple of times she woke up and he wasn't there, but the nurse was quick to assure her that he was coming back. She knew she should tell him to leave. This wasn't his responsibility. He didn't need to be spending his Saturday waiting for the worst to happen, watching as she slowly fell apart.

But she wasn't strong enough to tell him to go.

BENNETT WENT BACK into Grace's room after phoning his mom to give her the latest update. Not that much had changed. They were trying to slow the labor to give the steroid shot a chance to work on the baby's lungs, but from what the doctor said, there was no way to stop it completely. Apparently, she was also on antibiotics because of her water having broken already. All of this was new territory, and a lot of the terms they were using were foreign to him.

All he could do was pray that the baby would still survive. On one of his trips out of the room, he'd done what he probably shouldn't have and Googled the viability of a baby born at twenty-nine weeks. The good news was that the neonatal care available to the baby at this hospital was excellent.

The truth was that he was more concerned for Grace than the baby. He could see the resignation in her eyes. She was expecting the worst to happen and preparing herself for it. Bennett wanted to tell her to be strong, but that just seemed wrong in the circumstances. She'd been strong through so many other times in her life, but this might be the last straw for her. If the baby didn't survive, Bennett didn't know what Grace would do. But he planned to be there with her right through it all.

He couldn't find it in his heart to leave her alone.

"She was eight centimeters on the last check," the nurse told the doctor when she came in to check up on them.

Grace's eyes were open, and she seemed to be watching the nurse and doctor as they talked together. He couldn't tell if she was taking in what they were saying or if she'd retreated to some place in her mind.

Without thinking, he reached out and took her hand. Her fingers flexed against his, but she didn't let go.

"Okay, Dad, when she's fully dilated, she might feel the urge to start pushing. Once the baby is born, they're going to be working on her a bit here and then will take her to the NICU. Most likely you won't be able to see her for any length of time here in the room, but just know that they are doing everything they can for her when they take her away."

Grace's hand tightened on his, and he looked down. She laid a hand on her stomach and curled forward slightly. "I'm feeling pressure."

"Let me see what's happening," the doctor said, and once again they put her in the position to check her.

Bennett chose to focus on Grace's face, reaching out to brush a strand of hair from her face. She glanced up at him but then turned to watch the monitor that showed the baby's heart rate. He was grateful that the baby seemed to be doing well so far. Obviously, that could change at a moment's notice, but Bennett was grateful for any extra time the baby could have in Grace's womb.

"I think you're ready to push," the doctor said as she came around to Grace's side. She took the time to look down at Grace. "I want you to bear down and help your body to do what it needs to do. I know you're worried, but she'll be in great hands when she gets here. Once she's been stabilized in the NICU, you'll be able to go and see her."

Grace nodded, but she remained quiet. Bennett kept hold of her hand as the next contraction hit her. As they continued to come, his respect for Grace grew. They had let the epidural begin to wear off some so she could feel to push, and in doing so, the pain had returned. Though Grace hadn't said anything about it, her grip on his hand had tightened, and her lips had flattened.

The nurse on Grace's other side gave her continual encouragement and direction on how to push and would count through each contraction. It seemed to go on forever, but Bennett knew from looking at the clock that it had only been about fifteen minutes when the doctor said that the baby's head was crowning. It was possible that the baby being smaller was contributing to the quickness of this part of the delivery.

It was then that reality seemed to clear away everything else in Bennett's mind. Grace was having her baby, and he was there for it. If he thought he'd felt a connection with the baby after the ultrasound, he knew it was going to be nothing compared to what he was going to feel after this.

There was movement in the room, and he glanced over to see that more people had joined them in the room. Their presence reinforced the seriousness of the situation. He looked down at Grace to see if she'd noticed them, but her eyes were closed as she bore down for another contraction, her grip on his hand almost painful.

"I can see the top of her head," the doctor said. "We're almost there."

Bennett had appreciated the calm presence of the doctor and how she'd made it all feel like a team effort, which it truly was. Though clearly, Grace was carrying the team.

"You can do this, sweetheart," Bennett said as he bent his head close to Grace's.

She opened her eyes, and for a moment their gazes met and held. Hers held so much sadness and resignation that Bennett's heart ached. He pressed a kiss to her forehead, unable to look at her.

He felt her tense again as the next contraction seized her body. The nurse counted out loud as Grace squeezed his hand painfully. Bennett found himself holding his breath along with Grace as she pushed.

It took three more contractions before the doctor announced that the baby had arrived. Immediately, people were at the doctor's side to take the baby. Bennett's gaze followed them as they took her to a small bed with lights over it and began to work on her.

"Dad, if you want to take some pictures, you can do that now. We'll be taking her to the NICU in a couple of minutes."

Grace immediately let go of his hand, and Bennett moved away from the bed, pulling out his phone as he walked to where they were working on the baby. As soon as he looked at the little girl lying on her back, a slightly bluish tint to her skin, Bennett lost his heart to her as surely as he had lost it to her mother. He used his phone to take a few pictures of her while he heard the doctor telling Grace to push again.

The baby had a shock of dark hair, not too surprising since Franklin had had dark hair. It lay in damp curls on her head. They were rubbing her with a blanket while someone was suctioning her. He heard her make a few little noises as they worked, but soon they were rolling her out of the room. Bennett watched them go, wishing he could go with her, but he knew that for now, he needed to be there for Grace.

GRACE FELT ALONE THE MOMENT she let go of Bennett's hand. She could hear the conversations going on in the room, but she blocked them out. It was over. She'd done her part—poorly as it had been—now it was up to the doctors to save the baby. It was out of her control.

Now she just wanted to sleep.

But then she felt a familiar hand grip hers. "Gracie? Have a look at your little girl."

She opened her eyes and saw Bennett standing beside her, a hopeful expression on his face.

"She's beautiful, sweetheart."

Grace didn't want to look. Didn't want to see the child that might not live. But she lowered her gaze long enough to see the picture on Bennett's phone. Of her baby. She was so tiny. So very tiny. Grace felt something clench in her chest, and she looked away.

"Did you have a name for her?" the nurse asked as she unhooked a couple of the monitors they'd been using.

When Grace didn't respond, Bennett said, "Not yet. Grace wanted to wait until she saw the baby to choose the name."

The nurse smiled. "Yeah, some people like to do that. I've had a few people tell me that they've actually changed the name once they met their baby."

Bennett stayed by Grace's side while he sent a quick message to his mom and Makayla with a picture of the baby attached. When they had finished cleaning everything up, they took Grace to another room, since the one she'd been in had been set up for an emergency delivery.

"You should be able to go see the baby in an hour or so," the nurse said once they were settled in the room.

Bennett looked around, a bit surprised that it was such a nice-looking room. It didn't seem like a normal hospital room.

"How long will I be in here?" Grace asked, drawing Bennett from his perusal of the room.

"If you're doing okay, they will probably let you go home tomorrow," the nurse told her. She hooked Grace up to a machine and began to check her blood pressure. "Something you'll want to look into is getting a breast pump so that you can begin pumping and then you can bring the milk into the NICU, and they'll use that to feed the baby. You can also pump while you're in the NICU visiting the baby."

"Can you let us know as soon as we can see her?" Bennett asked.

The nurse nodded. "For sure. If she's stable, it shouldn't be too long."

Bennett wondered how much, if anything, Grace was taking in. When the nurse had left, and it was just the two of them, Grace turned to look at him.

"You can go now, Bennett," she said. Her gaze moved toward the window. "Thank you so much for helping me. I don't think you know how much it meant to me."

"I was glad to be here for you," Bennett assured her. "I'd like to stay until we get an update on the baby."

Grace nodded but didn't say anything further. When her eyelids slid shut, he figured she was going to take a well-deserved nap. He settled into a chair in the corner of the room, hoping that someone would come to tell them they could see the baby. A quick check of his phone showed that both his mom and Makayla had replied to his message earlier.

Mom: *She looks so tiny but beautiful! Will be praying for her and the doctors and, of course, Grace.*

Makayla: *Ooooh! I'm in love! I can't wait to get back so we can see her. Take more pictures if you get the chance.*

Bennett: *I will see if I can get more pics. Grace has been moved to another room. She's sleeping now. I'm hanging around here until we get an update then I'll head for home.*

Makayla: *How is Gracie doing?*

Bennett scrubbed a hand over his face and let out a quick breath.

Bennett: *She's…okay. Physically she's fine. Physically the birth went fine for her. I think emotionally, she's shut down. The only thing she's asked was when she could go home.*

Mom: *We will continue to pray. I'm sure this is rough on her.*

Makayla: *Thank you for stepping in for me, Ben. I know this can't have been easy for you either. But I also know you're the best person to be with her right now.*

Bennett: *I'm happy to help her out. I'll send you an update when I have one.*

Bennett rested his head back against the chair and closed his eyes. He must have fallen asleep as well, but he woke to a hand giving his shoulder a gentle shake. Opening his eyes, he saw the nurse standing next to him. He straightened, fighting against the exhaustion that seemed even worse now that he'd had a little rest.

The nurse gave a tilt of her head toward the door. Bennett felt a surge of alarm as he followed her from the room. Once in the hallway, she turned to him and gave him a reassuring smile.

"I didn't want to wake Grace just yet, but I know you wanted an update as soon as possible. Your little girl is doing just fine. She weighed in at just over sixteen hundred grams." At his no doubt puzzled look, she quickly added, "Right around three and a half pounds."

"That's…small," Bennett said with a frown.

"Yes, it is small, but for her being just twenty-nine weeks, that's a good weight. She's on CPAP to help her a little, but she is breathing on her own. Another good sign. You can probably go see her in about an hour."

Bennett nodded then, after a quick debate with himself, said, "I need to explain a little about Grace. She might appear a little distant."

"Yes, I had noticed that, but thought maybe it was just the shock of the early birth."

"I'm sure that's part of it, but mainly, it's because of some extenuating circumstances. I'm not actually the baby's father. Grace's husband—the baby's father—died unexpectedly before Grace even knew she was pregnant. Before that, she'd lost her grandmother and her parents. Right now, I think she is scared of having one more loss in her life. So I'm not sure if she'll be able to see the baby right away. I'll go see the baby before I leave today and hope to reassure Grace on how she's doing."

The nurse glanced to the open doorway. "I'm so sorry to hear that, and it explains a lot. We will keep that in mind."

"Thank you. She isn't without support, my whole family is here for her, but when push comes to shove, she's the one who's having to deal with all the emotions on a scale that none of the rest of us do."

"For sure," the nurse said with a nod. "I'll let you know as soon as you can head to the nursery to see the baby."

"Thank you," Bennett said with a quick smile.

Grace was still sleeping when he returned to the dimly lit room. The day seemed to have stretched on forever, and yet it was only seven-thirty in the evening. He took the time to send the update to his mom and Makayla before leaning forward in his chair, elbows resting on his thighs as his hands gripped his phone. He bent his head and spent some time praying.

"Bennett?"

Lifting his head, he saw Tami coming towards him. He got to his feet and gave her a hug. "Hey, Tami."

"How's she doing?" Tami glanced over at the bed where Grace was still sleeping. Tami wore scrubs, so Bennett assumed that she was just coming off her shift. "Actually, you can tell me as we walk."

"Walk?" Bennett asked, keeping his voice low.

"To the NICU. Let's go see the baby." Tami linked her arm through his. "She's doing really well."

As they walked, Bennett shared about the labor and delivery, being very honest with his thoughts about how Grace had been. "I hope the fact that the baby is doing so well will help her state of mind."

"I hope so, but to be honest, I'm not sure it will matter," Tami said. "One of us is going to have to do some tough love with that girl. I'm not minimizing what she's been through, but there's someone who needs her right now. Someone who's totally dependent on her. She needs to find a way to balance her grief and fear with joy over the birth."

Bennett couldn't agree more, but he really didn't want to be the one who told her that. It might be better coming from Makayla or Tami. At least from his perspective. He really didn't want to jeopardize the fragile relationship they'd developed over the past few months.

"I'm just glad that I was able to get a position in the NICU earlier this year. Never imagined I'd be taking care of Grace's baby when I ended up here."

Tami showed him how to get into the NICU and where to wash his hands, giving him a warning that he needed to do it each time he came into the nursery. At some point during the day, someone had put a bracelet on him that identified him as being…well, they had assumed he was the baby's father. Tami reviewed some other rules for the NICU, stopping to chat with a nurse or two as they made their way through the nursery.

As they approached an enclosed isolette, Bennett felt his heart thudding. He took in the sight of the little girl, laying so still, attached to monitors. "Is she okay?"

Chapter Twenty-Five

*S*URE THING, HUN," Tami said. She explained what the monitors each did and used medical terms that Bennett didn't understand.

Bennett just nodded, having heard all he really cared about already. The baby was okay.

"You want to touch her?" Tami asked as she opened the isolette.

Bennett felt his heart literally flip in his chest. "Yes."

Tami guided him through the process, talking about how soon they might be able to hold her. All Bennett cared about at that moment was physically connecting with the baby his heart had already connected to so many weeks ago. As he stroked his finger across her hand, it flexed, her tiny fingers widening then curling into a fist.

"She's beautiful," Bennett said softly, a bit surprised he could talk at all.

"Yes, she's a wonderful combination of Grace and Franklin," Tami agreed.

At one time, the reminder that the baby really wasn't his might have hurt, but right then, he could only agree with Tami. "I hope that Grace will agree to see her. I think it would make all the difference in the world."

Tami slipped an arm around his waist and gave him a squeeze. "If it takes her a few days to come around, it will be okay. You'll be able to come visit, and I'll keep an eye on her, too. What Grace won't have a lot of time to do is to make a decision on the baby's name."

Bennett hoped that Grace would be up to that because it really was something no one else could do.

He didn't stay much longer at the hospital after that. Tami said she'd go back and check on Grace, so Bennett felt okay leaving. As he stepped out into the cold night, he was surprised at how little had changed while he'd been in the hospital even though it felt like everything was different now.

There was a little girl in the world who would be loved and cherished by so many people, even though her father wasn't going to be there for her.

GRACE LISTENED AS BENNETT and Tami left the room. She kept her eyes closed, wishing she could just fall back to sleep. Being asleep meant she didn't have to deal with people asking her how she was. Or encouraging her to go see the baby. She didn't want to deal with either of those things. Not yet. Because she honestly didn't know how she was feeling. It wasn't a cop-out. She really didn't know.

It was as if all her emotions had been dropped like different types of fruit into a food processer that was then set on puree. How did someone separate the fruits out afterward? They didn't. And she couldn't either. It was a mishmash of all the emotions she'd been feeling since Franklin's death.

Grief.

Loneliness.

Fear.

Anxiety.

Worry.

Guilt.

Rinse and repeat.

She might have flitted from one emotion to another quite quickly, but most the time, there had usually been one or maybe two identifiable ones. Since the minute she'd realized she was going into labor, it felt like every emotion was present at every second. It left Grace exhausted…too exhausted to try and figure it all out. But with people continually asking her how she felt, she was forced to. Which was why she would much rather be sleeping.

Grace shifted onto her side, wincing a bit at the pain as she turned her back to the door. She closed her eyes, only to have the image she'd seen on Bennett's phone come to mind. Her eyes popped open, and she stared at the window and the darkness beyond. She knew what she was supposed to be feeling right then—all the feelings she already had—but she should also be happy that her daughter had been born safely. And that, from the sounds of things, she was doing well. From what the doctor had said, the baby had a good chance of making it.

But there were no guarantees, and that right there was enough to rob her of any happiness.

She heard movement behind her and quickly closed her eyes. Had Bennett returned from visiting the baby already? She could hear the person moving around and determined pretty quickly it was the nurse.

"You awake, sweetie?" the nurse asked as her fingertips settled against Grace's wrist.

Grace debated if she could fake it, but in the end, she slowly opened her eyes and looked up at the nurse.

"How is your pain level?" the woman asked as she gave her a smile. "I can get you some more meds if you need them."

"I think I'm okay," Grace told her after taking a moment to consider her body.

"Can I help you to the bathroom? You need to be able to pee, or we might have to catheterize you."

Grace didn't want that. She let the woman help her sit up and then get to her feet. The floor didn't seem all too steady beneath her feet, so she had to brace a hand on the mattress while the nurse took her other hand.

"Just give yourself a minute. You wouldn't think it would be an issue, but sometimes finding your balance can take a while."

Grace stood there, hoping that Bennett didn't return. "I think I'm okay."

The nurse still didn't release her but kept a hand on her elbow as they moved toward the small bathroom in a corner of the room. She was surprised how much effort it took, but in the end, she was successful, and the threat of a catheter was gone. She was beginning to regret that she hadn't read up more on what was going to happen after the birth.

She'd thought she'd have time yet to do that. The plan had been for Makayla to go with her to the birthing classes that were supposed to start when she was thirty weeks. Which would have been next week. She hadn't been reading any pregnancy and birthing books either, and now her ignorance was coming back to bite her.

Grace was surprised that through all the checking the nurse did, she didn't once mention the baby, nor did she suggest that Grace go see her. Once she was settled back in the bed, the nurse smiled at her again.

"If you need anything, use the buzzer to give us a call," the nurse said. "And if you're up to seeing the baby, let us know."

That was it. Just the offer to take her to see the baby. No pressure. No look of judgment.

Grace was grateful. "Thanks. I'll see how I feel."

Left alone in the room once again, Grace let out a long breath and closed her eyes. She had no idea if Bennett planned to come back. On the one hand, she hoped that he would, but she knew that he had no obligation. She'd made sure he'd known that. So, if he didn't come back, she would only have herself to blame.

"Hey, sweetie." This voice was familiar, but it wasn't Bennett's. Grace opened her eyes to see Tami at her bedside, a large smile on her face.

"Hey, Tami."

"Looks like you're doing okay," Tami said, her gaze flitting from the IV stand to the monitors. "How are you feeling?"

"A little sore, but I suppose it could have been worse. I didn't tear, apparently."

"That's great. The only possible upside to a premature birth is that the delivery is usually a little easier on the moms because the babies are smaller." Tami settled a hip against the bed. "You'll probably get to leave tomorrow."

"I hope you're right. I'm ready to go home."

"Just an FYI, in case you didn't know it yet, you have five days to come up with a name for the baby," Tami said. "Hopefully, it won't take you that long. We like to have names to call the babies we work with in the NICU. Do you have any ideas?"

Grace stared at Tami for a moment before shaking her head. She knew her friend wasn't going to cut her any slack when it came to the baby. "I hadn't settled on anything. I thought I'd have a few more months."

Tami nodded, an understanding expression on her face. "Unfortunately, you don't have that time now, so you need to come up with a name soon."

Though Grace wanted to protest the urgency of Tami's words, she knew that in this particular case, Tami, no doubt, had the law on her side. "I'll come up with something soon."

"Maybe seeing the baby will help," Tami said.

Grace had known that her friend would bring it up. For some reason, the nurse had cut her some slack on going to see the baby, but it didn't appear that Tami was going to. "Maybe tomorrow. I'm tired right now."

Tami took her hand. "I know this is hard for you, sweetie, but the baby is doing well. She's breathing on her own and is a good weight. I know you're worried that you're going to lose her too, but the majority of babies born at this week in the pregnancy and at this weight, survive. Most with minimal issues. The odds are on your little girl's side."

"There are no guarantees," Grace said, trying to ignore the tightness in her chest as she heard Tami talk about the—her—baby.

"You're right, there aren't, but you can't live in fear. Your baby deserves more. She deserves to have her mother there with her." Tami pushed away from the bed and retrieved something from the doorway. "For now, you need to pump. The baby needs it."

Grace eyed the rolling cart as Tami pushed it closer. "Wouldn't it be better to give her formula?"

"Nope. I mean, if you aren't able to produce milk, or the baby's not gaining weight, then formula is an excellent option. But if you're able to pump, it would be good for her."

"I don't know about this," she said.

"Lucky for you, I do know about this." Tami approached the bed with a contraption that Grace wasn't entirely sure about.

The next several minutes were a cross between a comedy of errors and emotional trauma. Finally, Tami had everything hooked up correctly and then told her to relax. That it would help with something called *letdown.*

Relax? Is she kidding?

Grace tried to take a deep breath but didn't want to dislodge the stuff that they'd finally gotten into place. She leaned her head back and closed her eyes. Tami continued to chat about random stuff. Christmas. Keenan. Her grandmother. Keenan. Christmas shopping. Keenan.

Thankfully, it seemed as if she didn't expect any responses, and Grace found that she was, in fact, able to relax. Though it was all a rather awkward situation, she was kind of glad it was Tami who had helped her rather than a stranger.

"You might not get a lot right now, but it's the good stuff, and your milk will come in soon," Tami informed her as she began to disconnect her from the contraption. "You'll need to get one of these for home too. You can pump in the nursery, and we'll help you to breastfeed once the baby's ready for that."

Grace felt a weird sensation go through her at the thought. That seemed to demand a closeness Grace wasn't sure she could handle, but she would cross that bridge when she got to it.

"You'll need to pump again in a few hours," Tami said as she finished putting everything away. "If you have trouble, the nurse can help you."

"Thank you," Grace said because even though she still wasn't sure about the situation with the baby, she was grateful for Tami's help.

Tami approached the bed and bent to take Grace's face in her hands. "You're welcome. But you need to see your little girl. She deserves to have her wonderful mama by her side." She pressed a kiss to Grace's forehead then straightened. "See you tomorrow."

Left alone once again, Grace stared at the breast pump. How was she going to do this? The emotional tumult hadn't calmed at all within her. It was quite possible that after talking to Tami, it was even worse. She knew that wasn't Tami's intention, but regardless, it was the result.

Right then, she wanted to sleep and claim the bliss of oblivion for just a little while.

BENNETT SAT BESIDE TRISTAN the next morning in church, but his thoughts were on the little girl and her mom in a hospital a few miles away. He planned to head over there as soon as he was done at church. His folks had asked about visiting, but Bennett knew that they wouldn't let them into the nursery, and if Grace was going to be coming home that day anyway, they might as well just wait.

He had no idea what he was going to say to Grace, but he knew that he somehow needed to convince her to see the baby. It no longer mattered how he felt about her. It didn't matter how she felt about him. All that mattered was that she come to understand how important it was that she step up and be what her daughter needed her to be. She could grieve for Franklin and still be the mother her daughter needed. He knew she could do it. She just needed to believe that too.

Though he'd gone home the night before, he hadn't slept particularly well, so he was still tired. As he listened to the sermon, he tried to follow along, but it was difficult. For the most part, he felt that he was calm in the face of most stressful situations. He and Ryan both tended to be that way. However, he felt anything but calm when he thought of the situation with Grace and her baby.

"Did you need someone to go with you?" Tristan asked as they stood outside the sanctuary once the service was over.

Bennett shouldn't have been surprised that Tristan had picked up on his anxiety. "I think I'll be okay, but thank you." He slipped an arm around Tristan's shoulders and gave him a quick squeeze.

"I'll be praying for you."

Bennett appreciated his words more than ever because of the tension and unease he felt. As he drove away from the church a short time later, he felt the urge to turn around and go home. He had no idea what kind of reception he'd receive from Grace, but if she wasn't able to be there for her baby, then he was going to be.

He'd prayed through the night that Grace would have gone to see the baby, maybe even given her a name. The nurse had assured him that they would take her to the NICU if she expressed an interest, so he hoped that had happened. That would definitely be the best-case scenario.

When he arrived at the nursery, he found Tami was working. Unfortunately, she gave him a rueful shake of her head when he asked if Grace had been there.

"I stopped to see her last night before going home, but she was still not willing to accept that her little girl was a strong fighter. On the positive side, though, she hasn't resisted pumping milk for the baby and continued to do it through the night. I would count that as a step in the right direction."

After he had washed up, Tami brought him over to the isolette where the baby was. As he gazed down at her, clad only in a diaper and a cap on her head with wires attached to various parts of her body, Bennett hoped that Grace at least named her soon. She might just end up with a daughter whose nickname was Baby since that's what they were having to think of her as.

"So, she's still doing okay?" Bennett asked.

"Better than okay. She's tolerated the milk that Grace pumped, and her weight is stable. She's still breathing on her own, and we should be able to step her down from the CPAP to oxygen in the isolette soon."

Bennett knew that Tami would give it to him straight, so he was happy to hear positive things from her. "How long until she's able to come home?"

"I can't give you a definite date. For babies born really premature, it can take until their due date or later for them to be able to go home. Other babies who aren't quite so premature can be strong enough to go home a bit before then. I would say that she'll be here—depending on her weight and ability to continue to breathe on her own, among other things—a minimum of seven to eight weeks."

Bennett let out a quick breath. That seemed like an eternity, but perhaps it was an eternity they needed in order for Grace to come around. Distancing herself from the baby while she was in the nursery was one thing, but it wasn't something that could continue once she got home. The baby would need Grace more than ever then.

Chapter Twenty-Six

After spending a bit more time with the baby, Bennett made his way to Grace's room. When he got there, he found the nurse from the day before was on shift again and was talking to Grace.

"Are they releasing you?" he asked as he came to a stop next to the bed.

Grace was dressed and seated on the edge of the bed. She looked up at him and nodded. "Yes. I've passed all the tests necessary for me to leave the hospital."

"I'll be right back with a few last-minute instructions for you," the nurse said then slipped out of the room.

"Do you want to go by the nursery before we go?" Bennett didn't want to pressure her right then, but he wanted to give her the chance.

Her gaze dropped to the floor, and she shook her head. "I want to go home."

Having already prepared himself for that answer, Bennett didn't argue. There would come a time for that in the near future, but the hospital wasn't the best place for that discussion. "Do you have everything you need?"

"The nurse is bringing me some information then we can go," Grace said as she slid to her feet. "Thank you for giving me a ride home."

"You're welcome. I was already here, so it worked out."

She glanced at him as the meaning of his words seemed to dawn on her. Before she said anything, the nurse returned with a packet that she gave to Grace. "Just remember that you have four days left to name your little girl."

Grace nodded and added the envelope to her bag which Tami must have brought in for her since Bennett knew she'd come into hospital with nothing. He waited while they finished talking and then the nurse pushed a wheelchair close to where Grace stood.

Though Grace gave it a bit of a look, she got into it without question. Bennett took her bag from her and walked beside the wheelchair to the elevator and then to the entrance.

"Do you want to just wait here while I get the truck?" he asked.

Grace shook her head. "I don't mind walking. Just have to go a little slow right now."

They walked in silence as they left the hospital and headed down the sidewalk and across the street to the parking structure. Once there, Bennett paid for his parking then they took the elevator to the floor where he'd parked. He helped her up into the truck, realizing then that it might not have been the most comfortable vehicle to bring.

Bennett started up the truck but didn't pull out of the parking spot. "Everything okay?"

"Yep."

He let the worship music he'd been listening to on the way to the hospital fill the cab of the truck. This version of Grace was even more subdued than usual. It hurt his heart to see her like that, especially when he knew that there was something in her life that could bring her so much joy, but she didn't want to embrace it. Thankfully, the baby was too young to understand that of all the gentle hands touching her, none were her mother's.

That needed to change. And unfortunately, he was the one who was going to have to try to make her change.

Bennett had a sick feeling in his stomach, knowing that of all the people in Grace's life, he was the most expendable. He was going to have to be the one to risk—and likely lose—his friendship with her in hopes of getting her to accept her daughter. That thought hurt, but accepting that ahead of time would hopefully make it bearable.

Once they got to the apartment building, Bennett carried her bag up to her apartment. After Grace had opened the door, Bennett followed her in and set her bag down.

"Tami gave me information on where to go to rent a breast pump for you. I'm going to take care of that now."

"You don't need to do that," Grace protested as she lifted a hand to brush a strand of hair off her face. "I can take care of it later."

"I think it would be better if I just picked it up for you now. It will save you from having to go out." Bennett moved toward the doorway. "I'll be back in a bit."

Grace frowned but nodded. "Thank you."

"Did you need anything else?"

"No. I think I have what I need."

Bennett left the apartment and jogged back down the stairs to his truck. He reviewed the instructions that Tami had given him. She'd phoned around and found a place that had a pump available to rent. She said she'd talked with Grace about how to use it and how to handle what she pumped, so all Bennett had to do was go and pick up the pump.

He was happy to do this for Grace. Bennett had a feeling that it might be the last thing he was going to be able to do for her. When he got back to the apartment, he was going to have a talk with her. He knew it wasn't the greatest timing, but she needed to face this situation. She needed to step up and embrace her role as mommy. And if she was going to be mad at anyone for being blunt about things, better it be him rather than Makayla or Tami. She needed their support right then.

The process to rent the machine was fairly smooth, and it wasn't long before he was on his way back to the apartment and Grace.

Grace wandered around the apartment. Things still looked the same as they had twenty-four hours ago and yet, once again, everything had changed. She lifted a hand to her heart, clutching at the fabric of the T-shirt she wore.

She wanted to retreat to her room and crawl into bed, pretend that nothing had happened. That the life she had carried within her didn't hang in the balance. Her hand slid to her stomach. She still had a bit of a bulge, but the firmness was gone, and her heart clenched at the loss.

With a shaky sigh, she walked toward the bedroom, pausing as she passed the room that was going to be the baby's nursery. It was still empty. She had never put anything into the room. When she'd moved in, she could have put some of the boxes there to store them, but she'd somehow just not felt right doing that. She hadn't been ready to set it up as a nursery, but she couldn't deny what the room was intended for. Grief and fear filled her heart.

What if she never had the chance to use it for its intended purpose?

She turned away from the empty nursery and headed for her bedroom. Moving slowly, she stripped the sheets off the bed and replaced them with clean ones. After she had shoved the dirty sheets into the washer, she replaced the towels in the bathroom. Even though she was moving slowly, at least she felt like she was getting something done.

All the while, she had an uneasy feeling about being alone. She'd been alone since Franklin's death, but after she'd found out she was pregnant, she'd once again had someone with her. Whether she'd been happy about it or not.

A knock on the door jerked her from her thoughts. Bracing herself for another interaction with Bennett, Grace opened the door. He stepped into the apartment carrying a couple of bags. She closed the door as he walked over to the table and put the bags down.

"Here are the instructions that came with the machine, and you need to have your own collection kit." He pulled something out of the plastic bag and put it on the table. "Tami said she'll pick up what you pump and take it in on her shift."

"Okay. Thank you." She watched him place his hand on the back of one of the dining room chairs. He had on a pair of black slacks and a dark blue turtleneck under his leather jacket which he'd likely worn to church. He looked tired, and his lips were pulled tight.

"The thing is, you need to be the one taking the milk to the baby, Grace." His voice didn't waver even though he sounded tired.

She didn't want to hear what he was saying. "Maybe in a few days."

Bennett leaned toward her a bit. "No, you need to do it today. You need to go back there this afternoon. You need to see her. Touch her. She's your daughter, Grace. She needs you."

Grace automatically shook her head. "I can't do that, Bennett. I can't get attached to someone else who could die on me."

"She could *live*," Bennett said with determination. "She's going to live."

"You can't guarantee that," Grace said, anger beginning to course through her. "You can't guarantee that everything is going to be okay."

"No, I can't, but that little girl needs you. It doesn't matter if she lives past your own death or if she dies in three days. You are her mother. You need to be there."

Grace's hands tightened into fists. "This doesn't concern you, Bennett. It's not like you're her father. You have no right to tell me what to do."

Bennett's expression tightened. Something that looked an awful lot like hurt flashed across his features, but it was gone so quickly, she wasn't sure.

"It does concern me, Grace. More than you know." Bennett paused, his brow furrowing. "I love you. And I love that little girl."

Grace felt her heart stop for a beat then begin to pound again at an alarming rate. He loved her? Like really loved her? She'd suspected that he had feelings for her a long time ago, but she hadn't thought that was still the case after she'd married Franklin, and Bennett had gone on to date other women.

"I can't...I won't love you, Bennett. That's never going to happen." Grace watched his face for any reaction, but he remained stoic. Her heart hurt from the words she'd said to him. "It can't."

Bennett straightened. "You're living your life in fear, Grace. You need to let that go."

Grace needed the conversation to end. She needed for him to leave her alone. Her heart was hurting, and she just wanted to be alone with her pain. "Isn't it rather selfish of you to tell me that? I mean, it's not like you don't have an ulterior motive. But my husband hasn't even been gone a year. Why do you think I'd be even remotely interested in another relationship so soon?"

"All I want is for you to be happy, Grace." Bennett's shoulders slumped as his head bent forward a bit. "I have already accepted that I'm not going to be the person who makes you happy. Right now, I want the baby to be that person." He straightened his back then shoved his hands into the pockets of his jacket. "Give her a name and love her, Grace. That's all I'm asking of you."

Without waiting for her to reply, Bennett turned and headed for the door. Grace crossed her arms tightly over her chest. Pain leaked out of her heart, slowly filling every part of her body as Bennett walked out of her apartment. She bent her head as tears pricked at her eyes and then spilled over. Putting one heavy foot in front of the other, she made her way to the bedroom and crawled under the covers.

Finally, she let the emotions of the past day spill out, sobbing with the grief and fear of it all. Why was she here again? Alone. Hurting. Afraid. Wasn't it enough that she'd lost Franklin?

She thought of the picture Bennett had shown her of the baby. She'd had dark hair like Franklin. He would have fallen in love with her at first sight. He would have visited the nursery as often as he could have. He would have given her a name right away.

He would have been so disappointed in Grace.

Grace turned onto her back and stared at the ceiling for a moment before closing her eyes.

Please, Lord, let her live. Let her be healthy. And please take away my fear of losing her so that I can love her fully. And help Bennett.

Because while she was willing to take the chance of loving her daughter, she just couldn't do it with Bennett. It wasn't as if she didn't love them both, but she wasn't going to open herself to the possibility of losing them both. It was enough that she was doing it with her baby. Her daughter.

Grace felt the tug of her exhaustion and drifted off to sleep, knowing that the alarm on her clock would wake her up when it was time to pump again.

The alarm went an hour later, dragging her from a deep sleep.

Time to pump for Olivia.

Grace's eyes popped open. *Olivia?* She lay there for a moment, testing out the name. *Olivia. Olivia...Joy.* The name lingered in her mind for a moment before settling into her heart. She swung her feet over the side of the bed, wincing a bit with the pain of sitting, before she got to her feet.

She made her way to the kitchen, stopping to pull the packet of information from the bag she'd brought home from the hospital. After getting a glass of milk from the fridge, she went to the table and set up the pump like the directions told her. Once it was all set up, she settled back with her milk, and as the pump worked, she started to fill out the form to register Olivia's birth.

A couple of hours later, Grace had taken a shower and found a small cooler and some ice packs to use to take the milk to Olivia. She packaged it all up along with the packet of information she'd filled out and headed down to her car. As she drove to the hospital, she felt a quiver of excitement at the thought of seeing her daughter. There was still fear lingering in her heart. She knew that something could still happen to Olivia, but she was trying not to dwell on that.

The only way she was going to be able to do this was to not think about it. Not dwell on the fact that her daughter could be there one day and gone the next.

No, definitely do not think about that...

Grace pressed a hand to her stomach as it clenched in fear at the thought. She was almost tempted to turn around and let Tami pick up the milk later.

But then Bennett's words came to mind. She had to keep them in mind. Olivia deserved that.

It was six o'clock by the time she showed up at the NICU. Tami was shocked to see her but quickly walked her through what she needed to do before she could go to Olivia's isolette. As the first sight of her daughter, Grace pressed her hands to the transparent cover, tears filling her eyes.

She looked so tiny. But oh, so beautiful. Her head was covered by a pink cap, and Grace wondered how her dark hair looked. Her baby's small chest moved with steady breaths. She was alive.

Tami slipped her arm around Grace's shoulder and gave her a hug. "I'm so happy to see you, Mama."

"She's perfect."

"Yes, she is." Grace gazed down at her. "Olivia Joy is perfect."

"Oh, sweetie. That's the perfect name for her. Olivia Joy Moore."

"Welcome to the world, my little love," Grace whispered. "Your daddy would have loved you."

Chapter Twenty-Seven

January

S O. ARE YOU READY FOR OLIVIA to come home?" Tami sat on the floor of the nursery, a pile of plastic bags beside her. She'd been tasked with unpacking the diapers Grace had bought and putting them on the change table. She'd also put the wipes into the warming container.

Grace rocked slowly in the comfortable rocker-recliner that Makayla and Ethan had given her. She had no doubt she'd be spending a lot of time in it. The day after meeting Olivia for the first time, Grace had begun to prepare the nursery. She'd started by painting it a soft rose pink—cliché, but she'd loved the shade of pink she'd found. Next, she'd gone on the hunt for the perfect bedding. Emily, Makayla, and the other girls had joined in, sending her links to various options they'd found. Then there had been the baby shower a couple of weeks ago, which had provided her with enough baby clothes to last Olivia a long time.

Ethan and Mitch had managed to wrangle together the crib and the change table. They were white in color and added to the soft beauty of the room, perfectly complementing the gray and pink chevron-patterned bedding. The skirt of the crib was pink with lots of ruffles. It seemed perfectly suited to a little girl named Olivia Joy. Her name also hung on the wall in puffed letters of gray and pink that Emily had made.

As she gazed around the room, her fingers stroked the soft baby blanket that Emily had also made. Grace was supposed to be folding it to go into the bag of things she was taking to the hospital to bring Olivia home. The car seat was already at the hospital since they had needed to do the car seat test with Olivia in it before they'd agreed to let her come home.

Finally, Grace's thoughts circled back to Tami's question. "Some days I think I am, but at other times I'm not sure I'm going to be able to handle this on my own."

"See, that's where you're wrong," Tami said, a hard edge to her voice. "Where you've always been wrong."

The tone of her friend's voice had Grace looking at her in surprise. "What do you mean? It's not like I have a husband to help me with this."

Tami leaned back against the wall as she shook her head. "No, you don't have a husband, but right above you, you have Ethan, Makayla, and Sierra. Below, you have me, and you have Mitch. Emily and Steve are just a phone call away. You. Are. Not. Alone."

Grace stared down at the carpeted floor. She knew that Tami was right. Sort of. But when Olivia woke in the middle of the night, Grace was the one who would have to get up with her whether she'd had enough sleep or not. And it didn't escape her notice that Tami didn't mention anything about Bennett.

"I don't really understand why you haven't ever truly accepted the people in your life. You are so focused on what you've lost that you don't see that you've also gained." Tami shifted, drawing her legs in to sit with them crossed. "You lost your parents, but you still had your grandmother. And when she passed away, you had Steve and Emily—who view you as one of their own, by the way. And on top of that, you have a boatload of siblings you'd never had before. And two best friends who would stick by you through thick or thin." Tami hesitated. "And I know it was horrible to lose Franklin, but you've got a daughter to love. And you might have had the chance at another love."

Might have had. Grace's stomach clenched.

"God has known what you've needed, and for every loss you've had, He has been there for you, Grace. For your daughter's sake, you need to understand that you have many caring people in your life—people God has brought to you—and accept their help. And their love."

"I can't do that," Grace said as her hands grasped the blanket in her lap. "Everyone I love dies."

"Everyone, Grace?" Tami asked. "Everyone? Is this your way of letting me know that you don't love Makayla and me? That we aren't important to you?"

"What?" Grace gave Tami a startled look. "Of course, you're important to me. Why would you say that?"

"Because you say that everyone you love dies, and yet Makayla and I are still fine. Steve and Emily are fine. Not everyone you love dies." Tami reached over to lay a hand on hers, her dark eyes serious. "I'm not in any way dismissing the losses you've had. In fact, I struggle to understand why you have had so many. But as someone who loves you, I hate to see you missing out on so much because you're living in fear."

"I'm not living in fear. I mean, I did go to the nursery to be with Olivia."

Tami nodded, her hand slipping off Grace's. "Yes, you did, and I'm so happy that you did that. But you need to treasure all the relationships in your life. Cherish them. Don't hold yourself back out of fear because of the thought that you might lose them. Open your heart to truly love, sweetie. Show your daughter what it's like to live and love without fear. That's something Keenan has taught me."

Grace brushed away the tears that had begun to fall. "I don't like being scared, but I hate losing people I love even more. So it's just been easier to not allow myself to love people in the same way I did my parents."

"I know it's not easy, sweetie, but here's a verse for you that Keenan shared with me. He says it's one of his life verses. After he shared it with me, I memorized it for myself, and it says, *There is no fear in love; but perfect love casts out fear, because fear involves torment. But he who fears has not been made perfect in love.* It's from 1st John 4:18 if you want to look it up. But I think you need to memorize it, then embrace it and believe that if loss is still to come, God—along with all of the rest of us—will be there for you." Tami got to her feet and bent over to give her a tight hug. "Think about it. See you tomorrow for release day."

Grace smiled at the thought. "Yes. Release day." She hesitated then added, "I love you, TamTam. I really do."

"I love you, too." Tami gave a quick wave then left the nursery.

Grace let her head drop back against the recliner. Tami's words had had claws, and they were now sunk deep into her heart. She couldn't deny anything of what Tami had said, but it was terrifying to consider opening herself up to truly loving people. It had been difficult to open up her heart to Olivia, but over the past two months, she'd fallen more deeply in love with her little girl on a daily basis.

And she wouldn't give that up for anything. If something did happen to Olivia, at least she'd have the wonderful memories of this time together. Well, not all the memories had been wonderful, but the few scary ones they'd had, paled in comparison to the progress she'd made. In time, Grace hoped that the most vivid memories of all of this would be the positive ones. The next day would be the best memory to date, and Grace realized that she needed to accept the help of those around her to give her and Olivia even more positive memories.

GRACE PULLED THE CAR into a spot in front of C&M Builders and put the car in park. She didn't turn it off, though, because while it was a warmer than usual January morning, it was still chilly, and she wasn't entirely sure she was going into the building.

It had been a week since Olivia Joy had come home, and after panicking the first night, she'd called Tami for help. Her friend had ended up spending the first three nights with her as she'd gotten used to having a baby who needed her, without having monitors and nurses to help her. But for the past four nights, she'd been able to handle the baby by herself.

This trip to the office was the first time she'd ventured out with the baby. Over the past week, she'd had a steady stream of visitors. Some from church, but mainly it had been Tami's and Makayla's families. Everyone had been to visit except Bennett. Since the day he'd confronted her about going to the NICU for Olivia, he'd totally pulled back, and to her knowledge, he'd never returned to see the baby.

As she thought about everything Tami had said, she realized she had gained a new perspective on Bennett as well. Following her conversation with Tami, Grace had read through blogs and websites and books, trying to figure out if it was right for her to be having feelings for a man when her husband hadn't even been gone a year. Sadly, none of them had been able to give her a definite answer. The underlying message she seemed to pick up on was that everyone's journey of grief was their own. What might feel right for one person, might feel wrong for another.

Because it was Bennett she had feelings for, her situation was a bit different since she'd known him forever. And, quite possibly, she'd loved him for that long too. She had just been unwilling to accept how she felt. It wasn't that she had loved Franklin less because of her feelings for Bennett, but it seemed there was room in her heart for both. Loving Bennett wouldn't diminish what she'd had with Franklin, she knew that now.

Finally, as she'd laid in bed the night before, she'd prayed and asked God for peace and direction. When Olivia's cries had woken her a few hours later, Grace had gotten out of bed with the surety of mind that Franklin would not want her to live her life tied up in grief over him. Whether it was with Bennett or someone else, Grace knew that Franklin would have wanted her to love again, if the opportunity came her way.

Letting out a shaky breath, Grace turned off the car and got out. She opened the back door and leaned in to lift the car seat off its base. The car seat cover blocked the wind and the cold as she hurried toward the front door of the office. It was her first time back since having Olivia. She'd been on maternity leave since Olivia's birth, with Maya stepping up to handle all the responsibilities that had once been hers. Surprisingly, she hadn't felt the loss of the job the way she'd thought she would. Instead, it had been a relief to not have to worry about anything but her daughter.

She opened the door to the entryway and then the one leading into the foyer. Maya looked up and smiled when she spotted Grace.

"Hi, Grace!" Maya stood up as Grace set the car seat on the desk. "Ooooh. Can I see her?"

Grace lifted the cover, and, after a quick check on the baby, she turned the seat around for Maya to see.

"Oh my word, look at that hair." Maya looked up at Grace. "She's just beautiful."

"Thank you. I was surprised at how much hair she had. Some has fallen out, but she's kept quite a bit. Definitely got that from her daddy."

"Did I hear the voice of my favorite baby's mommy?" Makayla asked as she appeared from her office. "I didn't know you were coming in today."

"I was going to run to the store for a couple of things and decided to drop by."

Makayla bent over the car seat. "Oh, she's sleeping." The disappointment in her voice was clear. "That's not acceptable."

Grace laughed. "It's not just acceptable, it's preferable when I'm out and about."

"Still," Makayla huffed.

"I can't wait until you have a baby of your own and then I can pester you about waking it up."

Before Makayla could reply, the door to the foyer opened. Grace lifted the car seat to move it off to the side so Maya could deal with whoever had walked in.

"Hey, guys," Makayla called out. "Look who's here for a visit."

Grace turned slightly, freezing for a moment as Bennett came into her line of sight. Their gazes met for an instant before Bennett looked down at the car seat she held. Grace looked past Bennett, expecting to see Mitch or Tristan. Instead, her gaze landed on a tiny woman with a big smile.

She moved past Bennett, her eyes focused on the car seat. "Is that a baby?"

"It certainly is," Makayla said. "The cutest baby on the planet. So brace yourself."

The woman approached as quickly as her high heeled boots would let her. She bent forward to peek inside, her long curls sliding off her shoulder. "Oh my goodness, Makayla. You are so right." The woman then straightened and aimed her bright smile at Grace. "You must be

Grace. I'm Emma Holt. I've heard so much about you. It's great to finally meet you."

Grace glanced from Makayla to Bennett and then back to Emma. "It's nice to meet you too."

Who exactly was this woman? Makayla hadn't mentioned anything about her. Why was that?"

Since the car seat was getting a little heavy, Grace moved forward to put it back on the desk.

"I can't get over how beautiful she is. Her cheeks are so chubby. And that hair!" Emma was once again peering into the car seat. "Her name is Olivia, right?"

Grace nodded, wondering how this person could know so much about Grace while she knew nothing about Emma Holt. For the first time since she had gone on maternity leave, Grace found herself missing the job and the office because she felt out of the loop.

Bennett had moved to stand beside the desk and was talking with Maya. The front door opened again, and this time it was Tristan who walked in. He smiled at Grace and came over to give her a hug.

"Oh no," Emma said. "The boss has arrived."

"I'm not your boss," Tristan said with a slight smile and a shake of his head. "That would still be Bennett. He's the boss of all of us."

"And don't you forget it," Bennett said before looking at Grace. "Nice to see you, Grace." Then he turned back to Maya. "I'll be in my office if anyone needs me."

And then he was gone.

Grace felt the sudden prick of tears and was grateful when she heard a small squeak from the car seat. Blinking rapidly, she bent to move the handle out of the way so she could release the straps and lift Olivia out. Cradling her close, Grace watched as her little girl blinked a couple of times before opening her light blue eyes and looking right at her.

"Hi, sweetie," Grace said as she bent to press a quick kiss to her nose.

"By the way, Emma is an interior designer, and she's been consulting with Tristan on some new projects that Ethan and Bennett have taken on," Makayla explained as she slipped a hand over Olivia's hair.

Grace was glad to be brought up to date on what was happening with the company, but the way Bennett had acted hurt her. Since the night he'd made her face her new reality, he'd kinda disappeared from her life. Between his hours at work and the time she'd spent at the hospital, they never seemed to run into each other at the apartment building. She'd even spent Christmas and New Year's Eve at the hospital with Olivia instead of going to the Callaghan-McFadden celebrations. On top of that, Steve and Emily had gone to Mexico for three weeks to help out at a mission school, so there hadn't been family dinners for the whole month of January.

As for their friends, it seemed they had all been caught up in their own lives following the holidays, so there hadn't even been any social gatherings. Well, unless she just hadn't been included. She hadn't been sure if it was circumstance or on purpose that she and Bennett hadn't seen much of each other. Given his reaction just minutes ago, clearly it had been on purpose. Bennett's purpose.

Had he changed his mind? Decided that she wasn't worth the effort?

She couldn't blame him for that. It had taken her far too long to accept her feelings for him. She'd pushed aside what she'd felt as a young adult, figuring it would wither and die over time. Instead, it had just stayed beneath the surface for years, waiting for her to come to her senses. If she'd been strong enough, with the love Bennett felt for her and what she felt for him, they might have been in a very different place by now. If she hadn't let fear take hold of her when her grandmother died.

Instead...

Grace looked down at Olivia who had managed to find her mouth with her fist. How could she regret how things turned out when she had this little girl in her life now? Wishing things had been different would have meant wishing away her time with Franklin and Olivia. She couldn't do that.

So now what was she going to do?

It had been just over eight months since Franklin had died. The grief had eased some, helped by the little girl who needed her to be present and emotionally available. Not that there hadn't still been times where she felt a deep loss, but she'd discovered that finally acknowledging her love for Bennett hadn't lessened what she'd had with Franklin and her love for him.

Would people think it was too soon? Maybe.

Did she think it was? Not anymore.

At this point, the bigger question was how Bennett felt.

"I need to talk with Bennett," Grace said as she glanced over at Makayla.

"Let me take Olivia for you," she offered.

Grace looked down at the baby. They were a package deal. If she was going to approach Bennett, she wanted to do it with her daughter. "I think I'd like Bennett to see her."

Makayla's brows drew together for a moment, then her face relaxed as she smiled. "Come see me afterward."

"I will."

Shifting Olivia up to cuddle on her shoulder, Grace plucked a blanket from the car seat and laid it across the baby. Then, saying a prayer for strength, Grace headed down the hallway that would take her to Bennett's office.

Chapter Twenty-Eight

*B*ennett forced himself to focus on the email that he'd opened on his monitor. He wasn't going to think about Grace. And he most certainly wasn't going to think about the little baby who'd been bundled up in the car seat sitting on the receptionist desk.

Walking into the office to find Grace there with the baby had been a surprise. He'd known that the baby—Olivia Joy—had come home from the hospital a week ago, but he hadn't seen either of them. It wasn't that he'd gone out of his way to avoid them, but it just seemed that with their schedules and with Grace not being at work, their paths just hadn't crossed.

When she'd told him that she couldn't love him, it had been like a knife to his heart. However, it hadn't been unexpected, which was why he'd been able to walk out of her apartment without begging her to reconsider. There wasn't anything more he could do to convince her that it was worth the risk to love again. And though it had been hard, he'd finally accepted that there would never be anything other than friendship between them. It wasn't like he'd had a choice after she'd so bluntly told him she wasn't interested in his love for her.

The only positive thing out of the whole situation was that Grace had stepped up and become the mom her daughter deserved. He hadn't seen the baby since the day he'd taken Grace home and challenged her to let go of her fears. Walking out of Grace's apartment, he'd known that he would be Uncle Bennett to Grace's little girl. He would just be one uncle among the many she'd have as part of the Callaghan and McFadden clan. And though Bennett had known he'd be okay with that and the place he'd have in Grace's life, he'd needed a little time and space to accept it. Distance to help lessen the bond he felt to the little girl.

"Bennett?"

He turned from his monitor to the door of his office. Grace stood there, her blonde hair laying in soft curls on her shoulders. The baby was propped up on her shoulder, a pink blanket covering her tiny body.

Bennett looked from the small bundle to meet Grace's gaze then pushed back from the desk and got to his feet. "Hi, Grace. How are you doing?"

With a smile, Grace walked into the office and sat down in the chair across the desk from him. Trying not to jump to any conclusions about why she was there to see him, Bennett sank back down into his chair and snagged a pen. He ran his fingers over the smooth surface as he waited for Grace to reveal why she was there.

"I'm doing pretty good. Adjusting to being a twenty-four/seven mommy. It's definitely different than going to the NICU for a few hours every day."

"How is she doing?" Bennett asked as he glanced once again at the baby cuddling against Grace's shoulder.

"So good. She's eating like a champ and sleeping in four-hour chunks at night." Grace lifted a hand to rub the baby's back. "I'm sure you heard she gave us a couple of scares early on."

Bennett nodded. Tami had called him as soon as the breathing episodes had happened. The setbacks had meant that the baby had had to go back on oxygen, but thankfully, it had only happened twice. She'd seemed to turn a corner after that second time and hadn't had any more problems. It had taken everything in Bennett to not rush to the hospital to be with Grace and Olivia, so he'd been relieved to hear from Tami that Grace had managed to keep from falling completely apart. That was definitely an answer to prayer.

"Yes. I heard. I'm glad she was strong enough to pull through them."

There was a moment of silence before Grace said, "How are you doing?"

"Good. We've been super busy which has been surprising since winter is usually our slow time, but we managed to land a few contracts for some commercial interior work. Of course, with Mom and Dad gone for several weeks in January, I've also been out at the house a fair amount to make sure Dalton and Danica were doing okay."

Small talk over, Bennett gripped the pen. When he'd walked into the office and seen her, he hadn't anticipated having any sort of conversation at all beyond a few social niceties.

Grace's brows drew together for a moment, and she kept rubbing the baby's back as she swayed gently. "I should've spoken to you sooner about this." She hesitated. "I'm so thankful for the talk you gave me the day you brought me home from the hospital. It was just what I needed. I appreciate it more than you will ever know."

Bennett swallowed as he had a sudden memory of all the feelings he'd had at that moment. The love. The hurt. The heartache. "I'm glad things worked out. You need each other."

"Yes, we do." The blanket slipped a little to show a tiny back clothed in pink. "Would you like to hold her?"

Bennett's immediate internal response was *Yes!,* but he wasn't sure he was at the point where he could hold her without losing even more of his heart to her. Even having just touched her little hand when she'd been in the isolette had created a bond that Bennett wasn't sure could ever be severed. She might not ever feel it, but it would always be there for him.

"I'm not really a baby-holding type person. Maybe when she's a bit bigger."

Grace regarded him for a moment, her blue gaze serious. "So even though you were there when she was born and you visited her in the NICU, you never planned to hold her? If Tami had offered you the chance to hold her, you wouldn't have agreed?"

"I would have done it if you hadn't been there for her. But now she has you and a lot of other people. She doesn't need me."

"I happen to feel differently," Grace said. She got to her feet, one hand bracing the back of the baby.

Bennett watched as Grace came around the desk. He felt a flutter of nerves that he wasn't totally familiar with. How was it that a tiny bundle of baby made him so nervous?

As she reached his side, she bent forward, one hand cupping the back of the baby's head, the other on her diaper-clad bum. Bennett had no choice but to drop his pen on the desk and reach out to welcome the weight of Grace's daughter into his arms.

"Bennett, meet Olivia Joy." Grace's hands touched his arms briefly before straightening. "She weighs just over five pounds now."

As he looked down into a pair of light blue eyes framed by dark lashes, Bennett felt a mix of love and fear. And suddenly he understood how Grace had felt and the fear she'd lived with. The fear of loving someone because losing them would hurt so much. She might only weigh five pounds, but she felt a lot heavier in Bennett's arms. She had dark curls that Bennett remembered from the brief glimpse he'd had of her in the delivery room.

He ran his fingertips over her hair, marveling at how soft it was. "She's beautiful, Grace, and her name fits her perfectly."

Grace turned to lean back against the desk. "It does, doesn't it? I thought it was going to take me awhile to come up with the right name, but I literally woke up from a nap with her name in my head. Olivia Joy just belonged to her."

As he stared down at the little girl, Bennett felt a wave of sadness. Franklin would never get a chance to love his daughter, and Olivia wouldn't have the opportunity to know her father. Bennett resolved that he would do his best to share the good memories he had of Franklin with Olivia as she got older. She deserved to know that her father had been a good man and that he would have wanted—and loved—her.

Bennett relaxed back into his chair, the baby cradled against his chest. He knew he should be handing Olivia back to Grace and thanking her for coming by. And then he should get back to work. But he just couldn't seem to find it in himself to give her up just yet.

He glanced up to see Grace watching him, an expression on her face that he'd never seen before. She frowned for a moment before letting out a quick breath. "I wanted to talk to you about something else."

"Does it have to do with work?"

Grace waved her hand in the air. "No, I'm not worried about the job. Makayla said that Maya is doing a great job."

"Yes. She's done well." Bennett ran his hand over Olivia's head. "Of course, she's still not you, but she's handling the job fairly well."

"I'm glad. It helps me to know that things aren't falling apart while I'm not here." She hesitated. "But that's not what I wanted to talk to you about."

"Oh?" Bennett really hoped that she didn't want to have a talk about what he'd told her during that last conversation they'd had in her apartment. He really didn't want to revisit that time. It had been one of the more challenging things he'd ever done.

She didn't move away from the desk and made no move to take Olivia from him. "I know that I said some things that day in my apartment that must have hurt you." She hesitated. "I'm so very sorry about that."

"It's okay. I know I dumped a lot on you. The most important thing is that you were able to find the strength to accept your role as mommy."

"Yes. That was important, for sure, but it wasn't the only important thing."

Bennett looked at Grace to find her standing with her arms crossed and head bent. There was a small kernel of hope within him, but he refused to acknowledge it. She'd made it clear that since it hadn't even been a year since Franklin's death, it was too soon to even consider a relationship with someone else.

Now, not even two months later, it would still be too soon.

"Can we go out tonight?"

Bennett froze. "Go out? Tonight?"

"Yes. Tami said she'd watch Olivia."

Bennett looked back down at Olivia. "Uh. Sure, we can do that."

"Great. Will six-thirty work?" Grace asked as she straightened.

After Bennett nodded, Grace bent to take Olivia from him. He got a whiff of a subtle floral scent as her hair slipped over her shoulder. "I'll be ready. Is it casual?"

She held Olivia close to her shoulder. "Jeans would be fine."

After a quick smile, Grace slipped out the door. Bennett leaned forward and picked up his pen again. As he considered what was to come, he found he was still a bit confused.

Was this an apology evening out?

Or something more?

"DO I LOOK OKAY?" Grace asked as she stood with Tami in the kitchen of her apartment.

Tami gave her a quick hug. "You look beautiful. Always."

Grace hadn't been sure what to wear, but in the end, she'd settled for a pair of black jeans. New ones because she didn't quite fit into her old clothes yet. She'd thought she would have an easier time getting back to her original weight because she hadn't gone the full nine months, but it seemed that her body shape had changed. Possibly permanently. Just one more thing to accept in her life. She should be used to embracing change by now.

She tugged at the sleeves of her deep rose-colored sweater then bent over the bouncy seat where Olivia lay watching her. "You be good for Auntie Tami."

"We're going to eat pizza and watch reality TV." Tami ran her fingers through Olivia's curls. "And give each other manis and pedis. Oh, and eat lots of chocolate and ice cream."

Grace laughed. "Well, you two have fun. Hopefully, Bennett enjoys what I have planned. Erin gave me the idea when I was chatting with her yesterday."

"I think it will be fine. It's something fun to do, and conversation friendly. All mixed in with some healthy competition."

Grace hoped she was right. Bowling wasn't the most exciting thing around, but she hadn't wanted to just sit staring at each other across a table at a restaurant. And bowling had been the date they were to have gone on before her grandmother's death had changed everything. Hopefully, this could be the start of what had never gotten off the ground before.

"Have fun and don't worry about Olivia. She's going to be just fine," Tami assured her with another hug.

After giving Olivia a kiss, Grace put on her jacket then grabbed her purse. Picking Bennett up was as easy as walking across the landing between their two apartments. She knocked then stood there nervously waiting for him to answer.

When he did, Grace took in his outfit, seeing he'd taken her jeans comment to heart. He wore a pair of dark blue jeans and a white shirt under his black leather jacket. She could see the reservation on his face as he stepped out of his apartment and closed the door.

"Ready?" Grace asked, hoping he'd relax soon. She hoped she relaxed soon too.

"Yep." They headed down the stairs, side by side. "Are we taking my truck?"

"Nope. My plan. My car."

"I guess I trust your driving," he said, a reluctant tone in his voice.

Grace came to a stop on the second from the bottom step. Bennett continued on but then turned around when he realized she wasn't beside him. He lifted a brow as he waited for her.

"You *guess* you trust my driving?"

"Well, I can't remember the last time I actually rode in a car that you were driving."

Grace felt her heart skip a beat as a slow smile spread across Bennett's face. "I will do my best to get you to our destination in one piece."

"I appreciate that," Bennett said with a tilt of his head.

The butterflies that had taken up residence in her stomach eased at their interaction. She tossed a smile at him over her shoulder as she headed for the door leading to the parking lot. It was a bit funny to see Bennett fold his tall frame into her car, which wasn't really that small but definitely smaller than his truck.

"Where are we going?" Bennett asked as he moved around to get the seatbelt fastened, his shoulder bumping hers.

Grace thought about making him guess, but instead, she said, "Bowling."

"Bowling?" Bennett looked at her, his eyes going wide. "Really?"

She wondered if he remembered.

"That's what we had planned to do," he said, his voice soft. "Before."

"Yes. Before." Grace came to a stop at a red light and glanced over at him. "I thought it might be a good place to start."

There were a couple of beats of silence. "Definitely a good place to start."

GRACE STOOD WITH HER HANDS on her hips, staring at the score-board. "Were you planning to let me win when you asked me to go bowling for that first date?"

"Yeah, I was." Bennett tried not to laugh at her expression as she swung to face him. The lane they had been given was against the far wall, and there were only a couple other lanes occupied, so it almost felt as if they were alone in the place.

Both her eyebrows rose as she said, "So why aren't you doing that now?"

Bennett shrugged. "I don't have to impress you anymore."

Grace's eyebrows rose even further at that comment. "And why not?"

"Well, first of all, you asked me out on this date, so I figure the ball is in your court when it comes to needing to impress," he said, keeping his tone light and teasing. "Second, you know pretty much everything about me. I don't think letting you win at bowling would give you any more insight into me."

"You could still be a gentleman and let me win," Grace pointed out.

Bennett laughed then. "Sweetheart, you make it pretty hard for a guy to let you win. I'd have to aim straight for the gutter every turn in order for that to happen. You've never been the best bowler in the family."

Grace gave him a rueful look. "I had hoped to have a nice fun evening together."

"I *am* having fun," Bennett assured her. "This is the best date I've ever been on."

She gave him a dubious look. Bennett walked to her side and put his arm around her shoulders, planning to give her a quick reassuring hug. But then her arm slid around his waist and held him tight. He looked down at her and let out a quick breath when he found her gazing up at him.

"Your best date? Really?" she asked. "Even though it included hotdogs, greasy fries, and smelly shoes?"

"Those things didn't make it the best date ever." Bennett hesitated but then decided it was time to go all in. He'd done it in her apartment, and the result had been anything but what he'd wanted. This time, how-ever, it was his hope that she'd be more receptive to his letting her know how he felt. "This is the best date because I'm here with you. When you're with the person you love, it really doesn't matter where you are."

Grace smiled at him. "I agree."

For a moment, Bennett wondered if his heart was going to ever start beating again. Was she just agreeing on principle, or was she saying something else? Before Bennett could ask her for clarification, her arm slipped from his waist as she moved to stand in front of him. She put her hands on his waist, clutching at the material of his shirt as she stood barely an arm's length away, her face lifted to his. He rested his hands over hers and waited.

Her brows drew together slightly before she took a quick breath. "You have always been there for me, Ben. I think I've always felt a sense of security knowing that regardless of our relationship, you would be there for me. Whether it was just in the background like these past couple of months or front and center like when I had Olivia, you've been there. And I'm sorry."

"Sorry?" Bennett frowned. "For what?"

"For letting fear dictate so much of my life and how that has impacted you." As she hesitated, the sounds of the bowling alley filtered into their little bubble. The clack of balls as they hit the pins. The mechanical whirl of the pins being reset. "I don't want to do that anymore. Olivia deserves a better life than one filled with fear. And so do I."

"Love should overcome fear. Always." Bennett reached a hand up to run his fingertips across Grace's cheek. "I just want you to be happy and live your life to the fullest."

"I thought that love had finally overcome fear when things changed with Franklin, but my fear hadn't gone away. I hadn't made a conscious decision to choose to love over fear since things had developed so slowly with him. However, I am glad that for whatever reason, the fear faded long enough for us to have something special together."

Bennett nodded. "Franklin loved you, and he was happy—I know he was. And I was glad to see that you were too. You both deserved that."

"I can't wish away these past years," Grace said, her hands tightening even further on his waist. "Because that would mean losing Olivia. But now I want to focus on the future, and I want to do that without allowing the fear of losing the people I love to cripple me." She paused, her gaze leaving his for a moment. When she looked back at him, there was a sheen to her eyes. "I don't want to think of losing you, but I've found that the fear of not having you in my life is greater than my fear of losing you."

Bennett felt his chest tighten as he listened to what Grace was saying. "I'll always be in your life, Grace. I'm not that easy to get rid of."

Grace tilted her head. "No, but you've kind of disappeared from my life the past couple of months, and I didn't like how it felt. I've missed you."

"I've missed you too, but you needed to focus on Olivia."

"Yes, I did. But Olivia is doing great now, and I want to focus on you. On us." Her brow furrowed as she looked up at him. "If that's what you want."

Bennett took her face in both his hands. "Of course, it's what I want. I love you, Grace." Tears spilled over her cheeks, and he used his thumbs to wipe them away. "I know that it hasn't been that long since Franklin passed away, and I'm willing to wait however long you need to grieve for him."

"I think I'll always grieve for Franklin, but he respected you, and I think he'd be okay with this. With us." She reached up to touch his face. "I do love you, Bennett. For the first time, I'm able to say that without fear clouding it."

Bennett wrapped his arms around her and pulled her close. He hadn't anticipated having the most important conversation of his life in a bowling alley. And yet it was perfect. The relief he felt at knowing that she loved him and that, for the first time, they were on the same page was intense.

"I love you, Grace." He tipped her chin up with his fingers, and as Grace slid her hand behind his neck, Bennett bent to press his lips to hers.

"Strike!"

The yell and the cheers that followed ended their kiss as they pulled apart to glance over at the noisy lane. Then they looked back at each other and laughed.

"So are we gonna finish this game?" Grace asked. "I still need to lose."

"We'll find something you excel at for future dates," Bennett said and gave her a quick kiss on the lips before letting her go.

As Grace took up her position to throw the ball, Bennett found himself looking forward to loving Grace and watching her throw gutter balls for the rest of his life.

*B*ennett looked at the family that was gathered around the large table in his parents' home. Thanksgiving had brought most the family home, though there were some noticeable absences. Hockey season was underway which meant Kenton couldn't make it. He was playing a game later on that day so they would have the television on for that. Though it wasn't a holiday weekend in the States, Ryan had taken a couple of vacation days to join the family for their Thanksgiving dinner.

There was a fire in the large fireplace because it was a chilly October day. There was no snow yet, for which Bennett was grateful for. Something else he was grateful for was the family present. It had been several months of ups and downs in the family since that night in the bowling alley with Grace.

He glanced down to his left and the beautiful little girl sitting in a high chair between him and Grace. Now ten months old, she was a lively little girl who loved to pull herself up on any piece of furniture she could crawl to. To date, Olivia had hit all her milestones and didn't seem to be suffering any ill effects from having been born prematurely.

"Da!" she proclaimed loudly as she hit the tray of her high chair with her sippy cup. When she looked up at Bennett, she gave him a broad grin, showing off the two teeth she had already. With her light blue eyes framed by long dark lashes and a head full of dark brown curls, she was a stunning child, and Bennett wasn't just biased. People constantly commented on her appearance when they took her out.

As the meal drew to a close, his dad got to his feet. It was hard to see how the past eight months had taken a toll on his dad.

"When we were together for last Thanksgiving, I never would have imagined the journey some of us would be embarking on. Maybe it's a good thing we didn't know, but I have taken comfort in the knowledge that God did know and has walked with each of us through the darkest times as well as the times of rejoicing." His dad paused, his gaze going to each person seated at the table. "I would love it if each of us could share what we're thankful for. Makayla, sweetie, would you start."

Bennett swallowed hard when his sister nodded. He knew that there would be tears amidst the thankfulness. That proved to be true for more than just Makayla as people continued to share in turn. As it neared him, Bennett felt a flutter of nerves.

"Bennett?" his dad said after Ryan finished.

He glanced over at Grace and met her gaze with a smile before running a hand over Olivia's silky curls. "This time last year, I didn't have any idea of the journey that lay ahead for me. Or that in the midst of sorrow, there would be the hope of love. It feels like I've loved Grace forever, but the love I had for her all those years ago is nothing compared to what I feel for her now. Though it hurts to know that it took Franklin's death to open this door, I'm so grateful that Grace took a chance on our love."

He turned once more to look at Grace and reach across Olivia's tray to take Grace's hand. "Grace, thank you for loving me and for accepting the love I have for you and Olivia. I know it wasn't easy to make that decision so I'm beyond grateful. And now I'd like to ask you to consider taking one more risk with me." Bennett paused and tried to swallow past the sudden tightness in his throat. "Grace, will you marry me?"

Olivia's fingers grabbed at his and Grace's clasped hands. "Da!"

"Well, I think you have Olivia's answer," Grace said with a smile, her eyes bright with unshed tears. "And mine is the same. Yes, I will marry you, Bennett."

Keeping their hands clasped, Bennett drew Grace to her feet. He reached into his pocket and drew out the ring box he'd placed there earlier. He let go of her hand long enough to free the ring from the box and then he slid it onto her finger. She still wore the band Franklin had given her on their wedding day but it was on her right hand, and some day it would be Olivia's.

Once the ring was in place, Bennett pulled Grace into his arms and lowered her head to kiss her. As she returned his kiss, her hands came up to cup his face. There were cheers and clapping around them, and when the kiss ended, and they moved back from each other, Grace smiled up at him.

"I love you, Bennett, and you and Olivia are who I'm most thankful for today. I can't wait to spend all the time God gives us together."

Bennett hoped that God would give them many more years together, but he planned to try to live each day with Grace as it if was his last, and cherish every moment.

ABOUT THE AUTHOR

Kimberly Rae Jordan is a USA Today bestselling author of twenty-plus Christian romances. Many years ago, her love of reading Christian romance morphed into a desire to write stories of love, faith, and family, and thus began a journey that would lead her to places Kimberly never imagined she'd go.

In addition to being a writer, she is also a wife and mother, which means Kimberly spends her days straddling the line between real life in a house on the prairies of Canada and the imaginary world her characters live in. Though caring for her husband and four kids and working on her stories takes up a large portion of her day, Kimberly also enjoys reading and looking at craft ideas that she will likely never make.

As she continues to pen heartwarming stories of love, faith, and family, Kimberly hopes that readers of all ages will enjoy the journeys her characters take in each book. She has no plan to stop writing the stories God places on her heart and looks forward to where her journey will take her in the years to come.

Visit Kimberly Rae Jordan on the web:
    Website: www.KimberlyRaeJordan.com
    Facebook: https://www.facebook.com/AuthorKimberlyRaeJordan
    Twitter: @KimberlyRJordan